I HAD DREAMS

TRACEY L. PERGER

To Judy
TLPerger
Rev 12:11

Xulon PRESS

I HAD DREAMS
by Tracey L. Perger

Printed in the United States of America

ISBN 978-1-60034-983-6
IBSN 1-60034-983-8

Unless otherwise noted, all Scripture quotations are taken from the *Holy Bible*, New King James Version, copyright © 1982. Used by permission of Thomas Nelson, Inc. Nashville, TN. All rights reserved.

Scripture quotations marked KJV or King James Version are taken from the *Holy Bible*, King James Version, copyright © 1984. Used by permission of Holman Bible Publishers, Inc. Nashville, TN. All rights reserved.

Scripture quotations marked NLT are taken from the *Holy Bible*, New Living Translation, copyright © 1996. Used by permission of Tyndale House Publishers, Inc. Wheaton, IL 60189. All rights reserved.

"Fallen." Words by Michael Tait, Chad Chapin, and Wayne Kirkpatrick. Music by Michael Tait and Chad Chapin. © 2003 Out Of Twisted Roots Music (BMI) admin. By EMI CMP/CEC Animal Music (BMI) / Warner-Tamerlane Publishing Corp. (BMI) & Sell The Cow Music (BMI). All rights on behalf of Sell The Cow Music Admin. By Warner-Tamerlane Publishing Corp. (BMI)

Front and back covers created, designed, and formatted by Angela Brumit and Jennifer Neily.

www.xulonpress.com

DISCLAIMER

This book is based on a true story, however, it was intentionally written as a novel. All of the names have been changed and some details have been added, deleted, changed or enhanced for dramatic purposes.

ACKNOWLEDGEMENTS

I would like to thank everyone who helped me write this book. This was a very difficult book to write and I know that it was very difficult for some of the people who helped me with it to talk about the experience. I would like to express my deepest appreciation to Ruth Perger, Michael Perger, Paul B. Perger, Paul M. Perger, Jeremy Perger, and Leon Perger. Thanks, also, to Margaret Orton, Paige Jones, Elizabeth Chadwick, and Buddy Neely for being there through it all; Bob and Sherry Stafford, for giving their lives to Christ and saying what I needed to hear which was not necessarily what I wanted to hear; Sherry Wilson and Wayne Tanksley, for supporting me through the investigation; Shing Sutton, Teresa Fryer, Krys Midgett, and Michelle Wyckoff for spiritual and emotional support during the legal and writing processes; Pastor Maury Davis and my Cornerstone Church family for your spiritual guidance, support and prayers; Dt. Joe Towers, Domestic Violence Division; Dt. Bill Pridemore, Cold Case Homicide; D.A. Mary Houseman; D.A. Tom Thurman; D.A. Katy Miller; and Susan Tucker, Victim Counselor/

Liaison, for a job well done; and those who proof-read, edited, and made suggestions: Paul M. Perger, Michelle Wyckoff, Candice Duvall, Kathy Baker and Amanda Mills. A special thank you goes to Angee Brumit and Jennifer Neily for designing the covers. I appreciate the love and support of these and many others. Thank you all for helping me make my new dreams come true. Saving the most important for last; I thank my Heavenly Father. Thank You, Lord, for taking this horrible experience in my life and turning it into something beautiful for You!

DEDICATIONS

I dedicate this book to the memory of my beautiful children, Hezekiah Myles Crutcher and Jessica Louise Crutcher. They are loved much and missed dearly.

I, also, dedicate this book to my Lord and Savior, Jesus Christ. May this book always glorify You, Lord. Revelation 12:11 "And they overcame him (Satan) by the blood of the Lamb and by the word of their testimony." NKJV

And to the perpetrator of the crime committed... "As far as I'm concerned, God turned into good what you meant for evil. He brought me to the high position I have today so I could save the lives of many people" from eternal damnation in hell. It is my prayer that your life will be one of those saved through all of this. (Quote taken from Genesis 50:20 NLT)

1993

Chapter 1

"Rachel, it's time to get up," Emily said trying to rouse her six-year-old daughter.

"Ugh!" Rachel groaned as she squirmed around in bed, burrowing deeper under the covers.

"C'mon, you gotta get ready for school."

"Oh-kay," Rachel grumbled.

As the sun beat in the window on this late-September morning in a suburb of Nashville, Rachel forced herself to wake up. She ran her hand through her sandy blond hair and rubbed her blue eyes. A few minutes later, she came padding into the kitchen with her three-year-old half-brother, Michael, and two-year-old half-sister, Leslie, not far behind still in their nightclothes. Emily smiled as she set the three cereal bowls on the child-sized picnic table, which served as their kitchen table. It fit the kids just fine, but Emily usually ate standing by the counter or sitting by herself in the living room. There just wasn't much money after the divorce. The child support payments had stopped coming in some time ago. Henry, her ex-husband, had been released from jail five days earlier. He had been locked up for three months for failure to pay his child support. Hopefully, he learned his lesson and some money would start rolling in again.

Emily ruffled Michael's dark brown, slightly wavy hair as she kissed Leslie's soft, black, curly hair. "Good morning."

"Good morning, Mommy," they said in unison.

After breakfast, Rachel dressed herself, brushed her teeth and hair and got her backpack on. Rachel would walk next door to the neighbor's house. Robert would drive his two children and Rachel to school in the morning and then Emily would pick them all up in the afternoon. It worked out quite well because Emily didn't have to rush in the morning and she could drop Robert's kids off on the way to take her kids to her mother's before going to her second shift job.

Emily sent Rachel out the door with a hug. She looked up and saw Robert waiting by the car. "Good morning, Robert!" Emily hollered as she waved.

After Rachel left, Emily pushed the door shut behind her and went back into the kitchen to wrap up breakfast. The living room and kitchen sat back to back along the inside wall of the duplex. The bedrooms sat back to back along the outside wall. The small bathroom was between the master bedroom and the kitchen along the backside of the building. A small hallway connected all of the rooms. It wasn't much, but it was home all the same.

She took Michael and Leslie into their room. "Here, Michael, put this on." Michael took the jeans and t-shirt from his mother and moved over to the bed.

"Here you go, Les." Leslie took the clothes her mother offered and stomped her way to her bed. Everything was a big deal, a big show for Leslie. She gave drama queen a whole new definition!

As Emily left the room, she looked back to see the kids removing their pajamas exposing their light brown skin. She headed back into her room to clothe her five foot, eight inch, medium build body. She had green eyes and light brown, long, straight hair. People often told her how pretty she was, but she just didn't see it. To her, she was just average all the way around. After picking out her clothes for the day, Emily sat on the edge of her bed.

All of a sudden, smoke filled the small two-bedroom duplex. As she looked out her bedroom door, Emily saw dark orange flames in the living room. When she stood up, her head was in the smoke. There was a very definite line of smoke around chest level. She tried to remain calm as she hurried into the hallway headed for the kids' room. She bumped into something. She reached down and felt curly hair identifying the object as Leslie.

She ushered her back into her bedroom. She knelt down below the smoke, finding Michael sitting on his bed crying. Leslie was crying also. She took both children in her arms.

"It's okay," she said in as calm of a voice as she could muster. "You lie down on the floor and Mommy will be right back."

She took a deep breath and stood back up in the smoke feeling her way to the window. She had to keep her eyes closed because the smoke was stinging them. Of course, the smoke was so thick and so black she couldn't see even if she could have kept her eyes open. When she reached the dresser in front of the window, she climbed up on it and raised the window. She couldn't raise the screen, so she butted it with her shoulder hoping it would pop out. It was rock hard. *What on earth?!* she thought. She tried again. The screen wouldn't budge. *Why is it so hard? I need air. One more try.* She hit the screen again with her shoulder. Still nothing budged, still rock hard. *I have to get air and then I will try again.*

As she was climbing off the dresser she heard Robert outside calling her name. She yelled as loud as she could, "We're in the kids' room, Robert! We're in the kids' room!" She took a deep breath and the whole world went black.

Chapter 2

"9-1-1 Emergency. How can I help you?"

"There is a fire!"

"What is your address?"

"I'm at 254 Bailey Street, but the fire is across the street."

"Do you know the address there?"

"It's 255... It's the house with the flames and smoke coming out the windows and roof!"

"All right. Is anyone in the house?"

"I have no idea."

"Is it a house, a trailer, or what?"

"It is a duplex."

"Is it siding or brick?"

"It's brick. It has black smoke pouring out of the roof. You can't miss it!"

"Okay. We'll get a unit right over."

"All right."

~ ~ ~ ~ ~ ~ ~

Robert saw smoke as he turned the corner. *I wonder where the fire is.* As he approached, he realized that it was Emily's house on fire. He threw the car in park and jumped out running toward the house screaming "EMILY! EMILY! SOMEONE CALL 9-1-1!"

The man who lived in the other half of Emily's duplex, Brandon, wandered out of his apartment rubbing his eyes. "What's going on?"

"We have to get them out!" Robert shouted to Brandon as he ran up the front steps.

The flames were loud but he thought he heard a faint voice. He couldn't make out what it was saying. It sounded like it might be Emily. *They are in there!!! I have to try to get them out.*

Then, he heard someone yell, "I called 9-1-1! They are on the way. Don't try to go in there." Robert turned to see Mr. Greenwood standing on the porch of the house across the street. Mr. Greenwood was the maintenance man who took care of all the properties.

"Emily and the kids are in there! We have to get them out!" Robert yelled.

Mr. Greenwood ran across the street and went around to the back of the house.

Robert kicked Emily's front door in. The fire was so hot it singed his hair. He ran around to the side of the house. Mr. Greenwood couldn't get in the back window and had come around the side. He boosted Robert up to the window. Robert pushed the window box air conditioner into the house and raised the window the rest of the way. The smoke was so thick Robert couldn't go in. Just then, they heard fire trucks approaching. Mr. Greenwood lowered him back down and they ran back to the front of the house. Robert looked down the street and saw the fire trucks, as well as the crowd that was quickly gathering.

Robert began frantically waving to the fire trucks and screaming; "There are people in there!"

As the firemen dismounted the truck, Robert shouted again "There are people in there!"

"Do you know how many?"

"Three! A mother and two small children."

"Do you know where they are?"

"I think I heard the mother's voice coming from this bedroom a few minutes ago. I haven't heard anything since." Robert was pointing to the window that Emily had tried to open. "I got the window on the side open," Robert said leading the way to the side of the house as the fireman put his mask on.

"All right. Stand back!" The fireman went in the window.

Robert and Mr. Greenwood stood there watching all of the commotion. Firemen were hooking hoses up to each other stringing them together. There was no water on the water truck, so they had to access a hydrant two blocks away.

News crews began arriving and pulling out cameras, micro-phones, and other equipment. They started asking questions, but everyone ignored them, watching to see if their neighbors were going to make it out alive. The media turned their attention and their cameras onto the burning building.

The fireman passed the little girl out the window. One of the paramedics took her and laid her on the ground. "This one is alive. She has a strong heartbeat, but feeble attempts at breathing. Critical condition. Needs oxygen." He began CPR on the girl and placed an oxygen mask over her face. The hoses were finally long enough and they began spraying the living room, as a little boy was passed out the bedroom window. Another paramedic took him. "He's alive, but barely. Weak heartbeat, no attempts of breath. He is critical!"

The fireman came back out the window. "We can't get the mother out through the window. She is alive, but unconscious," he yelled.

"Bring her through the front door," the fireman with the hose yelled. "I have the fire contained."

Robert watched in horror as the paramedics placed Emily's limp body on the ground. "Strong heartbeat. Strong attempts at breathing. Secure oxygen to stabilize." Robert looked again at the children both with oxygen masks on their faces. They were moving them onto stretchers. They placed an oxygen mask over Emily's nose and mouth and moved her onto a stretcher.

An ambulance pulled away with its siren wailing. Robert thought both of the children were in it, but then he saw one of the kids being loaded into another ambulance. He couldn't tell which child it was. Then they loaded Emily into the same ambulance and the second one drove away, its siren merging with the fading sound of the other one.

"I don't think the kids are going to make it," the paramedic who worked on Michael said to another.

"Oh, I hope they do, but I have to agree with you. The little girl is in pretty bad shape."

Robert felt an arm around his shoulder and he turned to find his wife standing next to him with tears in her eyes. She turned him and guided him back to their house. "There was nothing you could do. They are in good hands, honey."

"I know, but I couldn't even get in the house to save them."

"But at least you tried. Let's sit here on the steps so you can tell the police what you saw and what you did to help."

Chapter 3

"**M**s. Payne?"

"Yes?" Emily's mother said, obviously confused.

"This is Officer Summers with the Metro Police Department. Do you have a daughter named Emily who resides at 255 Bailey Street?"

"Yes..."

"Ma'am, your daughter and two small children were in a fire and have been taken to Donelson Hospital."

"Oh, my god," she sighed, sinking into the nearest chair. "How are they?"

"I am not sure, Ma'am. You'll want to get to the hospital as soon as possible."

Oh, my god. A fire. Where are my shoes? I can't believe this. It must be bad. Emily would have called me if she could have.

The phone rang again. "Hello!"

"Hi, Terri. I was calling to see if Emily is ready to go yet."

"Oh, Abby!!! Thank God you called. I need you to take me to the hospital. My car is in the shop and the police just called and said that there was a fire at Emily's house. She and the babies were there and I need to get to the hospital."

"Oh, my god! I'll be right there." Abby just lived around the block from Emily's parents. She and Emily had been friends since Emily was pregnant with Rachel. They did everything together, and today, Abby was going to go to the doctor with Emily to see about getting a tubal ligation. Emily was a wreck about it and had asked Abby to go with her to help her through it. She was supposed to drop the kids at Terri's at 9:30.

Terri ran around the house frantically looking for shoes, keys, and anything else she might need. When she saw a car pull in the driveway, she ran out the door before Abby even stopped. Abby drove to the hospital as fast as traffic would allow. She didn't even bother to try to find a parking spot but pulled up to the emergency room doors.

"Hello. I'm Terri Payne," Terri said running up to the receptionist's desk. "My daughter and grandchildren were brought here in an ambulance a little while ago?"

The receptionist looked over her shoulder and shouted, "The grandmother is here."

Terri was all abruptly shuffled into a small, white room with bright lights. "Yes, right this way."

Not knowing what was happening, Terri stammered, "How are they? Where are they? How did this happen?"

"Ms. Payne, I'm Sarah, the nurse who has been caring for your grandchildren. Your daughter and granddaughter have been transported by Life Flight to Vanderbilt and we are preparing your grandson for transport next."

"Oh, my god. Are they going to make it?"

"It is really too soon to say. We've done all we can here to stabilize them. Vanderbilt is much better equipped to handle this. That's why we're transporting them. Would you like to drive to Vanderbilt or do you need a ride?"

"I'll let you know." Terri told Abby, who had come in while she was talking to the nurse, all that she knew. They decided it would be best if Abby went home and contacted the rest of Emily's family and friends, and Terri got a ride to Vanderbilt. She would call Abby when Emily regained consciousness. Looking back at Sarah, Terri said, "I'll need a ride."

"Officer Summers here will take you."

"Can I see my grandson?" Terri needed some reassurance that they were alive. She needed to see them, to hold them, something.

"No, ma'am. I'm sorry, but we're getting him ready to go in the helicopter."

"Let's go. I'll get you there as quickly as possible." Officer Summers said leading Terri to the police cruiser out front.

"You're the one who called me?" Terri asked recognizing the officer's voice.

23

"Yes, Ma'am." They got in the car and Officer Summers sped out of the hospital parking lot. "Someone said that Emily has another child? Where is she?"

"Oh, Rachel! I forgot all about her. She is at school." Terri had to shout to be heard over the chopper overhead. She watched it land on the roof of the hospital.

"I think that it would be best if we went and got her first," Officer Summers replied.

"Oh, ok. Yeah, she wouldn't have anywhere to go after school if they admit Emily," Terri said, thinking out loud, refusing to take her eyes off the helicopter until it was completely out of sight. "She is at Lincoln Elementary."

On the way to the school, Terri asked, "Were you at the house? What happened? How bad is it?"

"Yes, I was there. The cause of the fire hasn't been determined yet, but the fire investigators are there doing a complete evaluation. The house is still standing but the roof is pretty much gone. I'm sorry, but that's all I know. I didn't go inside so I don't really know how bad it is."

"I meant how bad are my daughter and grandchildren's injuries?"

"I don't know, Ma'am. I'm sorry. We'll have to wait and see what the doctors at Vanderbilt say. I can say that Vanderbilt is a wonderful hospital and they are in the best possible hands."

Terri was trying to wipe the signs of crying off of her face when they arrived at the school. They walked into the school office as the secretary looked up. "May I help you?"

"I need to see my granddaughter, Rachel Payne. It is an emergency."

"Do you know who her teacher is?"

"No. She's in first grade. Please hurry."

The secretary looked up Rachel Payne in the student list as Terri began filling out the sign out sheet on the desk. "She will be here in just a minute. Would you like to have a seat?" she asked, indicating a bench along the wall.

Rachel walked into the office and saw her grandma sitting with a police officer. She could tell her grandmother had been crying. She ran to her, "What's wrong, Grandma?"

"Rachel, your house caught on fire. They have taken your mom, Michael and Leslie to the hospital. I came to get you, so you could come to the hospital with me."

Rachel threw her arms around her grandmother and began to cry.

"Let's go!" Officer Summers said.

As they walked to the police car, Terri was holding Rachel tightly as tears streamed down both of their faces. When they got in the car, she held Rachel to her bosom. Rachel had a number of questions, but was unable to ask them. She could tell her grandmother was too upset to talk about it. She cried and prayed silently. *Dear Jesus, don't let my mommy die. I don't want Michael or Leslie to die either. Please help them, Jesus. Please help them.*

The ten-minute ride seemed to last ten hours as Terri's mind ran wild with all the possible scenarios. Terri prayed and cried all the way to Vanderbilt University Medical Center.

Chapter 4

Emily woke up to the feeling of someone trying to remove her high school class ring. She jerked her hand back. *Where am I?* Then it all came flooding back to her. "Where are my children?" she demanded.

"Hello, Ms. Payne. How are you feeling?"

"Where are my children?" she asked again.

"No need to worry about the children. How are you feeling?"

The tube in her nose hurt and she tried to pull it out. The nurse grabbed her hand. "Emily, you have to leave that there for a bit."

"It hurts and I want to see my kids!"

"I know it is uncomfortable, but it is necessary for your breathing."

"It's not uncomfortable, IT HURTS and I want it out!" She pulled on it again and again the nurse grabbed her hand.

"Now, Ms. Payne, you have to leave it alone or I will have to restrain you. I'll go get the doctor and ask him if it can be removed, but you have to promise me you will leave it alone until I get back."

"Fine. Tell him I want to see my kids." The nurse walked out of the room without saying a word.

Emily looked around the cold emergency room. She knew she was in a hospital, but didn't know which one or how long she had been unconscious. The lights were so bright she had to squint at first. As her eyes adjusted to the light, she saw machines everywhere. She looked down and saw EKG terminals stuck to her chest. She also noticed an IV in her right arm and an oxygen detector on her left forefinger. Then she saw "Vanderbilt University Medical Center" stamped on the sheet that covered her to just above her breasts. She saw a clock on the wall. She squinted harder to read it. It was blurry, but it looked like it was around 12:00. She began to cry. *I want to see my kids. Why won't they tell me how they are? Why won't they let me see them? No need to worry about them!? She obviously isn't a mother. No mother would tell another mother not to worry about her children. That is what motherhood is all about, isn't it? Where is that doctor? This tube hurts like crazy.* Just then a tall man in his early forties entered the room. He had salt and pepper hair and green eyes.

"Hi, Emily. I'm Dr. Stevenson. How are you feeling?"

"I'm fine, but this tube hurts and I want to see my kids."

He looked at the oxygen count read out. "I'll order the tube removed, but you can't see the kids just yet. The doctors are still with them and we have to make sure you are stable. Nurse, get her an oxygen tank and mask. Emily, if you have a hard time breathing

28

just place the mask over your nose and mouth and breathe deeply through your nose."

"Can you at least tell me how they are?"

"I'm sorry, Emily. I really don't know. The pediatrician will come see you later and tell you how they are. I am going to look you over and then tell you what is in store for you."

When he finished his examination, the doctor said, "You still have a lot of soot in your lungs from inhaling all that smoke. We are going to take you to another room where the technician will put you in a big tube called a hyperbolic chamber. The air pressure will increase causing you to cough up all the soot in your lungs. It is kind of like being in a submarine. It won't be pleasant, but it is necessary. We have to clear your lungs out. While you are in there, I will check on your children and tell the pediatrician that I recommend allowing you to see them after you are done in the chamber."

"The chamber" sounds like prison!

They removed the tube from Emily's nose, the EKG terminals on her chest, her oxygen sensor and disconnected the IV tube without removing the needle, then moved her to a wheelchair. As soon as she was in the wheelchair she put the oxygen mask on. It surprised her how weak she was. They wheeled her through the maze of the hospital and into a small room with a big tube. The tube was about four feet in diameter and seven feet long, taking up most of the room. There was a bed in the tube, which was now sticking out the end. A technician was waiting patiently for her.

"Ms. Payne, my name is Jamie. I will be with you throughout your stay here in the hyperbolic chamber. I need you to lie here on this bed and we'll slide you in. Once you are in there and settled, I will seal the tube and increase the air pressure. It will feel like you are in a vacuum. The increased pressure will make it harder for you to breathe and you will in turn breathe more deeply causing the soot in your lungs to break up and come out. You will be able to talk to me. Just speak and I will be able to hear you. I will also be able to talk to you."

"How long will this take?"

"That depends on how much soot you have in your lungs and how long it takes you to expel it. After reading your chart, my guess is about two and a half hours."

Emily slowly got up and moved onto the bed. She was so weak, it took all of her energy just to get up. The orderly that had brought her here was on her right and Jamie was on her left. The bed was so narrow she felt like she was falling off the sides. She laid there for a few minutes. The orderly left.

"Ready?"

Emily nodded. Jamie removed the oxygen mask then walked around to the end of the bed. She gently slid the bed into the tube. The bed finally stopped moving. Emily looked around her. She could see most of the room through the Plexiglas tube.

"I'm going to close it now." Emily twisted her head around and watched as the large round door closed off the tube. *I feel like I am in one of those tubes you put the money in at the bank. What a ridicu-*

lous thought! As soon as I am done with this I get to see my kids. It was that thought that gave her strength.

"I am going to increase the pressure now. If you start feeling like you are going to pass out, tell me and I'll lower the pressure a little."

Emily felt the pressure increase. It really wasn't all that bad. *Just relax and get some rest. If I sleep, maybe the time will go by faster.*

Sleep was out of the question. Emily began coughing. It was dry coughing at first, but before long, she was producing a lot of mucus. She looked around, but didn't see Jamie anywhere. Lying flat on her back was very uncomfortable. "Can I roll over?"

Jamie came to the side of the tube. "Yes, you can move around if you'd like. Get comfortable."

Emily twisted and turned. There was very little room in the tube, but she finally got onto her side. As she was turning, she noticed a clock on the wall. It was only 1:07. She had only been in the tube for about 25 minutes. *Two hours to go. Where are Michael and Leslie? How are they doing? 1:11, will I make it two hours? I can't watch the clock. I'll drive myself crazy. I wonder if I have enough energy to roll onto my left side. I have to get that clock out of my sight.*

It took nearly five minutes for Emily to turn completely over, but she finally did it. Totally exhausted, she tried her best to relax, both physically and mentally, as she continued to cough all kinds of gross things out of her lungs. She couldn't totally relax, but she did succeed in resting a bit.

Chapter 5

*T*his *bed feels like it is getting harder and the tube seems smaller. What time is it? It seems like I have been in here forever!* Emily twisted and turned again. She finally got turned enough to see the clock. 3:23. Jamie heard her moving around and came to the side of the tube.

"How are we doing?" she asked.

Emily tried to speak, but was very hoarse. "I'm very thirsty and my throat hurts. Is it time?"

"Not just yet. You are still coughing a lot."

"I have been in here almost three hours!" Emily exclaimed.

"I know and you are doing very well."

"I want to see my kids now," Emily looked at Jaime with a pleading look in her eyes.

"Not just yet. It won't be much longer," Jaime said trying to calm her down.

"Can you at least tell me how they are doing?"

"I don't know."

"Well, can you find out?" Emily asked desperately.

"I'll see what I can do."

Emily heard Jamie on the phone. "This is Jamie Smith down in the hyperbolic chamber. I am calling to check on the status of Michael and Leslie Payne."

"Carter, their last name is Carter." Emily said.

"I'm sorry, yes, Carter. All right... Okay... Uh-huh... All right... Well, thank you." Jaime hung up the phone and looked down at her clipboard.

"Well?" Emily demanded.

"Leslie is in the PICU."

"Where is Michael?"

"Don't worry about Michael. He is being taken care of."

"What is the PICU?"

"Pediatric Intensive Care Unit."

Emily laid there for a second as this sunk in. *"Leslie is in the Pediatric Intensive Care Unit. Don't worry about Michael. He is being taken care of." What does that mean? How can I not worry about my son? Wait. She didn't hesitate to tell me that Leslie is in PICU, but she won't tell me where Michael is? PICU is the worst place you can be in a hospital. OH MY GOD, Michael must be in the morgue!!! Michael must be dead!* Then she began to cry and thrash around. "Let me out of here."

"I'm sorry, Emily. You can't come out yet."

"My kids need me!" she screamed.

"I'm sorry, Emily. It won't be much longer now," Jaime said in a soothing tone.

Mom! She will tell me the truth no matter how bad it is. "Is my mother here?" Emily practically yelled.

"Yes. She is in PICU with Leslie."

"Get my mother down here, please."

She heard Jamie on the phone again. "Would you please send Mrs. Payne down here. Her daughter is asking for her... I understand that, but Ms. Payne won't calm down until she sees her mother and the treatment won't work while she is this upset... All right, I'll tell her." Jamie hung up the phone and picked it back up again. "I need Dr. Stevenson paged pleased... Yes, have him call extension 4531... Yes, 4531... thank you." Jamie hung up the phone again and returned to the side of the tube. "Your mother is on her way down."

Emily couldn't stop crying as she heard the page for Dr. Stevenson. A few minutes later, she heard a phone ringing.

"Hyperbolic? Yes, Dr. Stevenson... she has pretty much stopped coughing... she is asking about her kids... she is just crying now... All right... I just asked them to send her mother down. Hopefully Mrs. Payne will calm her down... Okay, fifteen minutes?... All right, thank you."

Fifteen minutes 'til I get out of here. I can make it.

Just then there was a rap on the door. Jamie opened the door and Emily saw an orderly standing there. He turned to look at someone beyond Emily's range of vision. "Mrs. Payne."

Terri came around the wall and through the doorway. She walked over to the tube as Jamie closed the door. "Can she hear me?" Terri asked Jaime.

"MOM!" Emily yelled.

"Yes, just talk and she can hear you."

Terri turned and looked at her daughter through the glass. "Emily! How are you?"

"I'm fine, Mom. She won't tell me anything about the kids. All she said was 'Leslie is in the PICU. Don't worry about Michael. He is being taken care of.' What does that mean? Is Michael dead? You gotta tell me if he is dead!!!"

"No, Emily, Michael is not dead." Terri shot Jamie a contemptuous glare. "He is in PICU, too. In fact they are in beds side by side."

"How are they, Mom?"

"They are not doing well. They are both on life support. Leslie is trying to take a breath on her own every once in a while, but Michael isn't even trying."

"Oh, my god." Emily began to cry again. "Well, at least he isn't dead. What have the doctors said?"

"Not much, Honey. They want to keep them on life support and monitor them. They just don't know anything yet. They are hoping that they will respond when they hear your voice."

"Jamie, it has been more than fifteen minutes. You gotta get me out of here. My kids need me."

"I am waiting for Dr. Stevenson to call back. He said he would call in fifteen minutes."

"Well, page him again. My kids need me," Emily insisted.

Just then the phone rang. "Hyperbolic? Yes, Dr. Stevenson... her mother is here now... she is begging to go to her kids... All right. Thank you."

"Emily, Dr. Stevenson said I can take you out of there now. He will be up to see you later. They have a room ready for you on the fifth floor."

"I want to see my kids first."

Jamie adjusted the air pressure and Emily immediately began to feel the difference. She had gotten used to it and began to cough again. Once the pressure was back to normal, Jamie opened the door and slid the bed out. She handed Emily the oxygen mask, which Emily quickly placed over her face and took a deep breath. The urge to cough began to subside. She moved back into the wheelchair.

Jamie handed her a small bottle and then began to rub something cold onto Emily's head. "This is waterless shampoo. We will use it to wash the junk out of your hair."

"I don't care about my hair. I want to see my kids," Emily demanded again, getting very frustrated.

"Don't you want to look pretty when you see them?"

"They are my children and they NEED me! They don't care what I look like!" She shot a please-help-me look at her mother.

"Is this really necessary? I can wash her hair later."

"Well, I suppose, but I have to finish what I already started."

After almost four hours in the hyperbolic chamber room, Terri pushed Emily's wheelchair towards the Pediatric Intensive Care Unit.

Chapter 6

From the elevator, all the way to the Pediatric Intensive Care Unit entrance, the walls were hand-painted with a child-like jungle scene, using the boldest colors possible. *Wow, what an artistic wall! I'll bet the children LOVE it!* Emily thought as her mother wheeled her slowly past it. Then Emily realized her mother was talking to her. "Mom, could you say that again?"

Whispering loudly, Terri said, "I don't want to talk so loud that everyone can hear me. I said I want to warn you that the kids don't look good. It is actually scary to see them like that—with all the tubes and monitors and stuff. They are also rather pale. Just be prepared."

"I'll be fine as soon as I see my kids." Then, something dawned on her that she hadn't thought about. "Mom, how bad were they burnt?"

"Oh, Emily, I didn't tell you, did I? Oh, baby, I'm sorry. They are in here because of smoke inhalation. Leslie has a little burn on the back of her right shoulder and that is it. Michael wasn't burnt at all."

"Oh, good. That is a relief."

They had stopped at the door to the PICU. "Are you ready?" Terri asked.

"I don't think a mother is ever ready for this, but yet I couldn't be more ready. Does that make sense?"

"Yes, it does."

As her mother pushed her wheel chair into the PICU, Emily noticed the difference between the beautiful, bold colors of the hallway and the stark, bright white of the PICU. The floor, the walls, and the ceiling were white. The sheets, the blankets, and the drapes were white. To her left was the nurses' station and to her right were other beds separated by white curtains. The beds formed a semi-circle around the nurses' station. In the first bed, there was a small girl, probably six or seven years old. Her mother was sitting in a chair reading a book to her. The child looked as if she was sleeping, but the mother read on, stopping only to look up and watch as Emily was wheeled past. She had a look of compassion on her face. Then there were two empty beds. Directly across from the door there were two beds, about four feet apart with a curtain pulled around them. Emily's wheelchair stopped just before the curtain. Terri came around the wheelchair, kissed Emily on the forehead and pulled back the curtain.

"Which one do you want to go to first?"

"Leslie."

Terri pushed Emily in between the beds and up against the side of the bed on Emily's left. She used the guardrail on the bed to support her as pulled herself up to a standing position. She laid her head on Leslie's belly, put her thumb in Leslie's little fist and began to cry.

"I'm here, sweetheart. Mommy is here. I'm here, baby girl. I'm here."

Every two or three minutes Leslie would make gasping sounds and movements. The first time she did it Emily was afraid, thinking that Leslie was not getting enough oxygen. Emily looked up at her mother. Terri saw the fear on Emily's face and explained, "The nurse said that when Leslie does that, she is trying to breathe on her own. The rest of the time the machine is breathing for her."

Emily stood bent over the bed with her head on Leslie's belly for about twenty minutes, just saying over and over again, "I'm here, sweetheart. Mommy is here. I'm here, baby girl. I'm here."

Then, when she couldn't handle it anymore, Emily slowly moved back to the wheelchair. Terri jumped up to help her. Emily's back hurt from staying in that bent over position for so long and she was beginning to have a hard time breathing. Terri got the oxygen mask and handed it to her. Emily put it over her nose and mouth. She tried to breathe the oxygen deeply, but she couldn't stop crying long enough to get a deep breath.

After a few minutes, the tears began to subside. She sat, breathing the oxygen, and looking around. There were machines all around her. Some had numbers on them that kept changing; others had numbers that stayed steady. Some were beeping and others were silent. She couldn't tell what all the machines were, but she knew they were attached to her children. Tubes and wires were stuck to or in their little bodies everywhere—a tube in their mouths, one in their noses, IVs in their arms, and EKG electrodes stuck all over their chests and backs. She heard the curtain move. She looked back and saw her father standing there. Just seeing him made Emily begin to sob again.

"Dad!" She cried as her father put his hand on her shoulder. He bent down to give her a hug.

"It'll be all right." He stood there holding her for a few minutes.

Then as he moved over to Leslie's bedside, Terri asked Emily, "Are you ready to love on Michael for a few minutes?"

"Yeah."

As Terri was pushing the wheelchair over beside Michael's bed she said, "When you are done loving on Michael, will you go to your room so that you can get some rest?"

Emily couldn't argue with the fact that she needed rest. All she really wanted to do was sleep, but she didn't want one of her children to die while she was sleeping. As if reading her mind, Terri said, "Emily, you have to take care of yourself so that you will be strong enough to take care of the kids. They will be fine while you are getting rest. I'll be right here with them and Dad will be with you. If nothing else, the machines will keep them alive. If anything changes, we will wake you up right away. Okay?"

Emily didn't answer. She stood up next to her only son's hospital bed and kissed him on the cheek. She began to weep for her little angel. She tried to scoop him up into her arms, but all the tubes got in her way. She managed to get her arm under his shoulders and she laid her head on his chest. She just stood there weeping and speechless. Unlike Leslie, he didn't even try to breathe and she knew in her heart that he was no longer in that body.

"Marvin, why don't you take Emily now? I don't think she can take this much longer."

Marvin lifted his spent daughter and gently sat her back in the wheelchair. Emily wanted to stay, but she didn't have the strength to speak, let alone argue about it. He handed her the oxygen mask and wheeled her out of the PICU.

Chapter 7

When they reached the elevator, Emily finally found her voice. "Dad, where is Rachel?"

"I don't know. I went straight to the PICU when I got here. We'll find her. I know she is in the hospital somewhere. Your mother told me that the police drove her to the school to pick her up on the way here. I also know that Grace Elgin picked Larry up and brought him down here."

Larry was Emily's youngest brother. At eleven years old, he and Rachel were more like brother and sister than uncle and niece. Knowing that Rachel was playing with Larry and under the care of Larry's Sunday school teacher, Grace, Emily felt more relaxed. *Well, at least I know that one of my kids is all right.*

The elevator took them up two more floors. When the doors opened, Marvin followed the arrows on the sign to find room 532. Once in the room, Marvin helped Emily up onto her bed. When she was settled in and breathing easily with the oxygen mask, her father called the nurses station.

"This is Marvin Payne, Emily Payne's father in room 532. I was calling to see if you know where Emily's daughter, Rachel, and brother, Larry, have gone... yes, ma'am... that would be great. Thank you." He cradled the phone and whispered, "Grace is watching them down in the playroom. The nurse is going to call down there and have them sent up."

It wasn't long before the room was full of well-meaning friends and acquaintances. Sheila, the children's godmother, had arrived first. Shortly after that Judy (the pastor's wife), Sherry, Jessica, and Paul from church arrived.

Rachel had to fight through a crowd when she came in the door. "Mommy, how are you?" she cried as she climbed up onto her mother's hospital bed.

"I'm fine, Sweetheart." Emily embraced her healthy child firmly.

"What's this?" she asked pointing to her oxygen mask, which was currently hung around Emily's neck.

"That helps me breathe. Sometimes it is hard to for me to breathe because I breathed in a lot of smoke at the house." Rachel laid her head down on her mother's shoulder.

"Emily, I was wondering if you would mind if I set up a fund in which people can donate money to help you get back on your feet. The house is pretty much gone and you are going to need some things."

"Yeah, Sheila, that's a great idea. It would be a great big help."

"Well, I am the godmother to these children, so I figured this is one way I can help you take care of them." She put her hand on Rachel's shoulder. Emily laughed.

After a short while Marvin shooed everyone out of the room. "She really needs to get some rest. Terri is downstairs with the kids if you want to stop by there. Feel free to call and check up on them later if you'd like. We'll call you if anything changes."

Everyone said their goodbyes. Grace took Rachel and Larry home with her. Emily melted into the pillow as exhaustion began to set in. Marvin clicked on the TV. Emily was beginning to relax when the six o'clock news started. Her fire was the top story. She bolted up in the bed and listened carefully.

"At around nine o'clock this morning a duplex in Hermitage caught on fire. The occupants of the home were Emily Payne, age 24, and her two children, Michael, age 3, and Leslie, age 2. Payne and the two children were taken to Vanderbilt Medical Center by Life Flight. Payne is listed in stable condition and the children are in critical condition. A third child was at school at the time. According to fire investigators, the fire began because a couch was placed too close to a baseboard heater. It is not unusual to see fires this time of year when people start to use their heaters. More from Jay Smith on that part of the story..."

"Please turn it off, Dad." Emily was crying.

"What's wrong, honey?"

"They are saying this is my fault. I put that couch there. My children are in PICU because of me?"

"Oh, honey. You didn't know it was too close. Besides, why don't we wait and see what the police tell you, Okay? You know you can't always trust the media."

The subject was changed abruptly when Jason, Emily's younger brother, walked in the door.

"Perfect timing," Marvin said as he rose to greet his son. As he hugged Jason he whispered, "Don't talk about the fire. She is very upset and she needs to calm down."

"Hey, Sis. How are you feeling?"

"I'm alive, but I am really tired."

"Well, why don't you get some rest and I'll talk to you later. I'm going to talk to Dad for a while. I'll be here when you wake up," Jason said lowering himself into the chair opposite the one his father had been sitting in.

"Okay."

Emily dozed off while Jason and Marvin talked quietly. Once they were sure Emily was asleep the conversation took a twist.

"We should call Scott," Jason said.

"I don't see the point in calling him until we know what is going on with Michael and Leslie. We know Emily is going to be all right, but we don't know about the kids yet." Marvin didn't see the point in bothering his oldest son with the news until they had a prognosis. Scott would want to come down and there was no point in him leaving his family in Ohio to come down here and see Emily in a hospital bed and his niece and nephew on life support.

"We should at least tell him that the fire happened and that we don't know if the kids are going to survive or not. He is their uncle. He should be informed anyway and then the decision should be his about when and if he is going to come down."

"Will you stay here with Emily? I am going to run down and see the kids. I'll, also, ask Mom what she thinks about calling Scott. Maybe we can corner one of the nurses into telling us something more."

"Yeah, I'll stay with her. Oh, and good luck getting anything out of a nurse," Jason said with a chuckle.

Chapter 8

"**D**id she wake up?" Marvin asked Jason when he came back in the room.

"Nope. Not a peep."

"Well, your mom said that the kids are still in the same condition. Nothing has changed. The nurse said that they are going to do some tests in the morning to determine if there is any brain activity and, if so, how much. We will have to wait until they do that test before we will know anything about their prognosis and chances of survival." Marvin sunk back into his chair.

"What did she say about calling Scott?" Jason asked.

"She said we probably should. She won't let go of hope, but Michael isn't even trying to breathe on his own. Like I said, we won't know for sure until morning, but she agreed that we should call him and tell him everything we know."

Jason sat listening as Marvin called his oldest son two states away.

"I have some bad news, Scott... Emily's house caught on fire this morning... No, they are not all right. Emily is in stable condition and Michael and Leslie are both in critical condition... No, Rachel is fine. She was at school already... Well, it doesn't look good. They are going to do some tests in the morning to check the level of brain wave activity and then they will be able to give us a full prognosis... Okay. The number here is (615) 555-9532... No, that is a direct line to Emily's room. Jason and I are here with her, Mom is with the kids in PICU, and Grace Elgin has Rachel and Larry."

When the phone rang an hour later, Emily began stirring around.

"Okay, I'll tell everyone... Have a safe trip... Okay, we'll see you tomorrow... Love you, too."

"Who was that?" Emily inquired.

"That was Scott. He is coming down. He won't be able to be here until late tomorrow afternoon, but he is coming."

"Why did you call Scott? Do you know something I don't know?" Emily knew her family wouldn't be calling people out of state unless they knew something.

"No, well, yes, but it has nothing to do with my calling Scott. I called Scott because we thought he had a right to know what is going on."

"I agree he has a right to know what is going on, but he is coming down? What do you know that I don't, Dad?"

"I went downstairs to see the kids and I talked to one of the nurses. She said that they are going to do some tests at ten o'clock tomorrow morning, which will measure the brainwave activity. With those test results they will be able to give us a more accurate prognosis."

"So, what time is it now?"

"It is 9:15. You try to get a good night's sleep and then it won't be long until we know something," Marvin said trying to comfort his daughter.

"I want to see the kids again and then I would like to see the news again at ten," Emily stated.

"Are you sure you want to watch the news?" Marvin was concerned about Emily getting upset again. He thought it best that they concentrate on the truth, not what the media was saying.

"Yeah, I can handle it. The thing about the couch just caught me off guard. Like you said, we'll talk to the police and find out exactly what they think happened before I jump the gun."

"All right then, we'll watch the news."

"Well, Em, I'm sorry I didn't get to spend much time with you, but I am going to head on home after we see the kids so I can get some rest too," Jason said. "You might need me tomorrow, and I should be well rested. I am also going to get the spare room at Mom and Dad's ready for Scott."

Marvin and Jason helped Emily into the wheelchair and gave her the oxygen mask just in case she needed it. Emily started getting nervous when the elevator doors opened on the third floor.

"Are you sure you are up to this?" Marvin asked.

"Yeah, I have to see them before I go to bed or I won't be able to sleep. I don't know how long we will stay, but it probably won't be long," Emily was more exhausted than she had realized.

When they entered the PICU, Terri was sitting on the chair between the kids holding Leslie's hand. "Oh, hi!" she said as they all three pushed into the curtained off area. She jumped up and hugged Jason.

"How are you, Mom?"

"I'm holding up under the circumstances. There has been no change. Leslie still tries to breathe on her own occasionally. I won't give up hope." Terri fought the tears.

"Well, we aren't either."

"Jason, is this the first time you have seen them?" Emily asked.

"Yeah, I came straight up to your room when I got here and I never left your side."

They took turns talking to, hugging and kissing the kids. After about a half an hour, Emily couldn't handle it anymore. She fell into her wheelchair and placed the oxygen mask over her nose and mouth again. She looked up at her father and without saying a word he wheeled her out of the PICU.

Marvin pushed the up button on the elevator and Jason pushed the down button. Jason bent down and hugged Emily. "I'll be here around 8:30 in the morning. If you need anything, call me."

"Okay. Night, Jay." Emily managed in just over a whisper.

Back in her hospital bed, Marvin and Emily watched the last few minutes of a show before the news came on. The fire was still the top story. They repeated exactly what was said on the six o'clock broadcast. After they did the piece on fire safety, the reporter said, "If you are interested in helping financially, a fund has been set up for the family entitled the Michael and Leslie Carter Memorial Fund at any First Financial Bank."

As they cut to the next story, again, Emily was in tears. "Memorial Fund? The kids aren't dead! They are going to be fine. Right, Dad?"

"They are alive, Em. We have hope. We'll just have to wait until morning to know what to expect next, but they ARE alive."

Emily cried herself to sleep as Marvin fumed at the audacity of the wording of the fund title. *Why would Sheila title it the Memorial Fund? What on earth was she thinking?*

Chapter 9

Emily awoke to the sound of someone entering her room. "Good morning, Ms. Payne," the phlebotomist said as she looked at her chart. "I'm here to draw your blood."

Emily offered her right arm and looked away to the left. Her father began to stir in the recliner where he had spent the night. Remembering where he was and why, Marvin awoke quickly. He saw the phlebotomist and asked, "How did you sleep last night, Emily?"

She hadn't sleep well at all – tossed and turned all night long. *How are the kids? Why is Scott coming down? Is there more to it than what she was told?*

"Not well, but that doesn't surprise me."

The phlebotomist finished drawing her blood just as breakfast arrived.

"I want to go see the kids as soon as I am done with breakfast, Dad, so if you want to get something to eat, why don't you go now?"

"Are you sure?"

"Yeah, I'm fine."

Marvin left to go to the cafeteria, leaving Emily alone for the first time since the fire started almost twenty-four hours ago. Emily picked at her food and prayed to a god she wasn't sure even existed. "God, if you're up there somewhere, please save my kids. Don't let them die this way. They're too young to die. If someone has to die, God, let that be me. Leave the kids here, please. I'll do anything you want me to do. I promise." With tears streaming down her face, Emily forced herself to eat at least half of her breakfast so she would have the strength to endure the unknown that this day would hold for her. She couldn't explain it, but she just had a feeling it wasn't going to be a good day.

~ ~ ~ ~ ~ ~ ~

Marvin returned carrying a cup of coffee in each hand. He handed one cup to Emily. He could tell she had been crying, but decided to leave it alone. They sipped their coffee in silence.

There was a rap at the door and then it opened slowly to reveal the timid face of a man in a doctor's coat, but it wasn't Emily's doctor. "Ms. Payne?"

"Yes?" Emily asked curiously.

"Hi," he said as he pushed his way into the room. "My name is Dr. Johannesburg. I am from the psychology department. Dr. Stevenson asked me to come up and do a psychological evaluation on you to see if there is any brain damage due to the lack of oxygen that you endured."

"Whatever," Emily said full of attitude.

Dr. Johannesburg began asking Emily a lot of stupid questions. Eventually, she got so tired of them she said, "You know what? This is ridiculous. If I have brain damage it is because my children may be dying. I have better things to worry about at this time than what shape this is!" she said as she pointed to the card that the doctor had just showed her. "Now, if you don't mind, would you please leave?"

Dr. Johannesburg glanced over at Marvin who just shrugged his shoulders with a knowing look on his face.

"All right then. I think we are done here. I don't think that there is any lasting damage to your brain, but I will give Dr. Stevenson a complete report. I am sincerely sorry to hear about your children."

"Thank you, Doctor." Emily said without looking at him. "What time is it, Dad?"

"It is 8:30. Jason should be here any minute."

"Well, as soon as he gets here I would like to go down and see the kids before they take them for the tests. Do you think we could?"

"Sure." Just as Marvin was getting up to help Emily move into the wheelchair, Dr. Stevenson walked in. Marvin lowered himself back into his chair.

"Good morning. I just spoke with Dr. Johannesburg in the hallway and he tells me you should be fine psychologically. I know this is a rough time for you, and if you ever need anyone to talk to, the staff in the psychology department is wonderful." Jason slipped quietly into the room. Dr. Stevenson paused.

"He's my brother. Please, continue," Emily said.

"Based on Dr. Johannesburg's report, combined with my own findings, Ms. Payne, I have come to the conclusion that you are healthy enough to be released from the hospital at this time. I think as long as you continue to do the deep breathing exercises that the nurse showed you last night, you shouldn't have any light-headed-ness, or any other problems. The nurse will be in shortly with your discharge papers."

That is good news, so why do I want to cry. Emily wondered.

Chapter 10

Marvin helped Emily get moved over to a wheelchair. He placed the oxygen tank on the back of the wheelchair as she put the mask around her neck. On the way downstairs, they stopped at the nurses' desk to let them know where they were going.

"I am almost done with your discharge papers if you'd like to wait."

"No, I want to see the kids. They are taking them for the test in less than an hour and I want to see them before they go. We can complete my paperwork later."

"All right. Well, just let me know when you get back," the nurse said.

As soon as Marvin opened the door to the Pediatric Intensive Care Unit, Terri stopped them.

"They want us in here," she said pointing to a small room on the left behind the nurses' station. Marvin wheeled Emily into the tiny room. There was a small round table and four chairs. There was barely enough room for the wheelchair. Everything was white – the walls, floor, ceiling, table and chairs. Only the legs of the table and chairs were black. There were no pictures on the walls. It was just a drab, white, boring room. Once Emily was situated in the corner out of the way, her parents and Jason took seats around the table, leaving one empty chair.

"Where are the kids, Mom?" Emily asked.

"They took them for the tests a little early. They had an opening in the schedule so they fit them in. They said they should be done by ten o'clock."

Tears welled up in Emily's eyes again. "I was hoping to see them before the test." Emily took a deep breath and tried to relax. Terri laid her hand on Emily's shoulder as they waited in silence.

It seemed like a day and a half passed by before there was a light rapping on the door.

"Come in," Marvin said. Two young men and one middle-aged man squeezed into the room. They were all wearing doctors' coats over buttoned- down shirts with ties.

"Ms. Payne," the older one spoke offering his right hand. "I'm Dr. White and these are two of my residents, Dr. Tremont and Dr. Elmington." Emily accepted his hand and the hands of Dr. Tremont and Dr. Elmington in cordial handshakes. "Dr. Elmington is going to tell you the results of the tests."

Dr. Elmington took a seat in the only empty chair. "Ms. Payne, as you know we ran the Electroencephalogram, EEG, this morning. Michael's test was conducted first. There are four categories of brainwaves, ranging from the most active to the least active. The most active state is beta. A person actively involved in something or concentrating would be in beta. The frequency of beta waves ranges from 15 to 40 cycles a second. The next state in order of brain-wave frequency is alpha. A person taking a rest is often in an alpha state. The frequency of alpha waves ranges from 9 to 14 cycles per second. The next state in order of brainwave frequency is theta. This state occurs during total relaxation, but while conscious, such as while daydreaming or doing mundane activities in which the mind wanders. This frequency range is normally between 5 and 8 cycles a second. The final brainwave state is delta. Here the brainwaves are of slowest frequency, and usually occurs when one is sleeping. They typically center about a range of 1.5 to 4 cycles per second. Our machine doesn't register anything less than a .5 because anything lower than that means the patient is brain dead. Michael's brainwave activity didn't register."

Totally confused, Emily asked, "Can you, please, speak English?"

"I'm sorry, Ms. Payne. Let me put it this way. There is very little, if any, activity going on in Michael's brain. The chances of him waking up are very slim and if he did, he would be in a vegeta-tive state for the rest of his life. His chances of ever surviving off of the life support are about a billion to one. Technically speaking, Michael is brain dead. I'm so sorry."

Emily wailed loudly – a deep guttural wail that reverberated throughout the third floor of the hospital, like that of a heifer whose calf had been taken away. Terri collapsed onto Marvin's shoulder and began to weep. Marvin tried to remain strong for everyone while Jason sat in shock. Eventually, the wail subsided into weeping and then into sobbing. Finally, Emily managed to say, "And Leslie?"

Short and to the point, Dr. Elmington replied, "the same."

Emily wailed again. She slumped in the wheelchair as the wail faded into a quiet weeping. Her whole body convulsed as she wept. Marvin let go of his crying wife and reached over to put the oxygen mask back on his daughter's face. "Take a deep breath, Honey." She did and began to relax. She took another deep breath and relaxed a little more.

When she had completely regained her composure, Dr. Elmington said, "I hate to burden you with this now, but you need to think about what you want to do next. You can leave them on life support as long as you want to, or we can turn it off. I don't need an answer now, but think about it."

"You said that if they, uh, ever regain consciousness, uh, they will probably, uh, be, uh, vegetables, right?" Emily stuttered.

"Yes, that is correct. They will probably be in a vegetative state for the remainder of their lives."

"Then I want the machines turned off, but I want to wait until my brother gets here from Ohio. He should be here at about five o'clock this afternoon."

"That won't be a problem, but I want you to think about it more between now and then and discuss it with the rest of your family. If you change your mind, let me know."

Dr. Elmington, Dr. Tremont, and Dr. White all offered their condolences and quietly left the room.

No one spoke for a few minutes. Then Terri said, "Are you absolutely sure that you want to turn off the life support?"

"Yes, I am sure."

"You can't change your mind once it is done."

"What are you saying, Mom? You think I should leave them on it?" Emily didn't mean to yell at her mother.

"I didn't say that. I just want you to make sure this is what you really want because you can't change your mind. If you leave them on it, you can change your mind later on."

"Why leave them on it? What would be the point? I can't go through this the rest of my life, holding on to a hope that the doctor said isn't there. I can't put Rachel through this, or you. And, how is it fair to them to make them live on machines for the rest of their lives? No. I have to do this. It is what is best for everyone involved. Painful, yes, but best nonetheless."

"Well, if you're that sure, I'll go ahead and call the family."

"I'm that sure. Now, I want to go see my children."

Chapter 11

Emily sat in a rocking chair, which had been placed between the two children's beds. She was looking down into Michael's delicate, innocent face as she cradled his head in the crux of her left elbow. With tears welled up in her eyes she whispered, "I love you, sweetheart."

She looked up as the nurse approached with Leslie in her arms. She placed Leslie's head in the crux of Emily's right elbow and laid her legs across her brother's legs. A tear escaped as Emily whispered, "I love you, precious."

Terri stood behind Emily's right shoulder and laid her hand on Leslie's forehead while Marvin held the same position on the other side. Emily looked at her mother first and slowly scanned the room.

Scott stood next to Terri. He had arrived safely less than an hour ago. His wife, Tammy, was driving down and would be arriving tomorrow.

Henry and his mother were there as well as Cathy, Emily's divorce attorney. Cathy was there as a friend, but also to make sure that there were no problems with Henry or his family. Terri's brother, Joe, sister-in-law, Rhonda, and parents had arrived that afternoon. Her other brother, Jack, and Marvin's parents were due in tomorrow. A few of Emily's friends, Katherine, Marsha, Abby, and others were standing behind her extended family. Jason was standing next to Marvin with his hand on Michael's arm. Larry and Rachel were too young to enter the PICU so Grace was still caring for them.

Emily thought, *Well, the gang's all here. The stage is set.*

"I guess it's time to say goodbye," she whispered. She kissed Leslie on the cheek and then kissed Michael on the cheek. She allowed the tears to flow freely for a few minutes as a deafening silence filled the room. Then she signaled to the nurse.

The nurse silently flipped both life support systems off simultaneously. The rhythmic heaving of the children's chests stopped, but other than that there was no change.

"Time of death 6:05 pm, Friday, October 1, 1993". The other nurse wrote down the time on both charts.

The sound of sniffles and sobs harmonized the silence. No one moved as the nurses detached the wires from the children. A rush of air could be heard as the tubes were removed from their mouths.

"I'll leave you now. If you need anything..." Terri and Marvin both nodded. The nurses quietly slipped out of the room.

Emily looked back and forth between her children with tears freely flowing for the longest time. Unbeknownst to Emily, the crowd slowly and quietly dispersed leaving only her parents and brothers.

Still no one spoke. There were no words.

The nurse brought in a chair and Terri sat down. The men sat on the beds.

"Emily, would you like..." Terri was pointing to Leslie. Emily nodded. Marvin took Leslie's body and handed her to Terri.

The men eventually slipped out as well, leaving Emily and Terri, mother and grandmother, the two people who loved these children more than anyone else holding their lifeless bodies.

Neither spoke as they both cried—hearts utterly broken with no end in sight. The future had come crashing down around them in a split second. With the flip of a switch, all their dreams had vanished. Their hearts had been ripped violently out of their chests, as all they could do was hold the limp bodies of these beloved children for the last time.

After a few hours, Emily mustered a small, quiet, "Mom?'

"Yes, Dear?"

"Are you ready?" she whispered.

"I'll never be ready, but, yes, it's time."

Terri pulled the curtain back signaling to the nurse.

"Are you ready?" the nurse asked as she entered the curtained off section of the Pediatric Intensive Care Unit where, as far as Emily was concerned, her life had come to an end.

Emily and Terri just nodded.

The nurse gently removed Leslie's body from her grandmother's arms as Terri stole one more kiss. She laid her on the bed. Then she came and pried Michael out of Emily's arms. Terri put her arm around her daughter and helped her walk out of the PICU for the last time.

Marvin, Scott, Jason, and Abby were waiting on a bench in the hallway. Emily slumped down onto the nearest bench. Scott, her older brother by two years, put his arm around her and pulled her head onto his shoulder. There were no tears left in her. She sat there sullenly only half listening as her parents talked quietly about what was to happen next.

"I called the funeral home while you and Emily were with the kids. They'll leave them here over night and then transport them to the funeral home tomorrow. We need to get them some clothes to be buried in and bring them to the funeral home at two o'clock. Emily will have to pick out caskets and all that stuff then, too."

"All right. Well, I can't worry about tomorrow right now. First, I have to make it through the night," Terri said, running her hands through her hair.

All of a sudden, Emily stood up and started to walk back towards the PICU. Marvin tried to stop her. Emily gently pulled away from her father's grasp, "I'll be okay."

Marvin reluctantly let go and watched his daughter go back into the PICU alone. Emily walked up to the nurses' station and spoke to the only nurse sitting there. "I need their armbands."

"Oh, okay. You stay right here and I will get them for you."

Emily wanted to see the kids one last time, so she crept over and peeked behind the curtain just as the nurse pulled the body bag away from Michael's face. Emily bolted out of the PICU, white as a ghost.

"What's wrong?"

"What happened?"

Her family could not figure out what had made Emily flip out like this. Emily sat on the bench silently as the color slowly returned to her face.

The nurse came out and handed the armbands to Terri. "Emily asked for these."

"What happened in there?" Terri demanded.

Utterly confused, the nurse said, "Nothing. Why?"

Terri explained how Emily had bolted through the doors, looking scared to death and wouldn't say a word.

"I don't know. She asked me for the armbands. I told her to wait by the desk and when I came back she was gone."

Emily couldn't verbalize the image that was now in the forefront of her mind. *If only I had listened to the nurse.*

Chapter 12

“We'll meet you at your house,” Emily said to her parents as they walked out the hospital doors into the parking garage. “I'm going to ride with Abby.” She and Abby walked in silence toward her car.

Once settled in the passenger seat, she said, “I could really use a smoke.”

Abby lit a cigarette and handed it to her. Emily gagged profusely when she tried to smoke it. The smoke from the fire had done so much damage to her lungs that her body just couldn't handle any more pollution.

“Are you all right?” Abby said concerned about her best friend. Emily had been through so much in the past thirty-six hours. She looked at her friend's tear-stained face and couldn't begin to fathom all that she had been through. Abby was having a hard enough time with it. They were only twenty-four and much too young to be going through this. Abby didn't have any children of her own, but Michael and Leslie were like her niece and nephew.

Still coughing, Emily said, "Yeah, I'm fine."

As Abby was getting on the Interstate, she asked, "So, what happened in there?"

"I don't want to talk about it," Emily said as the image flooded her brain again.

When they arrived at Terri and Marvin's house, everyone was sitting around talking. Emily walked in and took a seat on the chair in the corner of the living room.

She didn't know what to think and she didn't feel anything at all. Then she saw Terri in the kitchen and went to join her.

Leaning on the counter, looking at her mother, she said, "Where are Rachel and I going to live, Mom?"

"You can stay here in Jason's old room until we figure something else out," Terri, continuing to wash the dishes, said.

"All right." Emily hesitated before continuing. "Uh, Mom, I have another problem, Mom. We have no clothes. Sheila bought me this sweat suit today, but this is all I have. Rachel is still wearing the same clothes she wore to school yesterday."

Terri stopped doing dishes and turned to look at her only daughter. "We will worry about that tomorrow. We have to go buy something for Michael and Leslie to be buried in anyway, and we have to be at the funeral home at two o'clock to give them the clothes and to make all of the funeral arrangements. Try not to worry. Okay, honey?"

"Do you think anyone would mind if I slip off to bed?"

"No, you go on. I'll take care of it." Terri was worried about Emily.

"Thanks, Mom." Emily went straight to bed and left the explaining up to her mother. She was sure Terri would handle it for her. Her mother always kept her word.

Emily lay in bed, eyes filling with tears again as her mind began to fill with good memories of Michael and Leslie. She had to laugh as she remembered one day not too long ago, when she and the kids had been in the yard playing with the hose when the phone rang. She ran into the house, grabbed the phone and looked out the window to see Michael holding the hose toward the car. A steady stream of water was going right in the open window of the car.

She ran out the door screaming, "Michael!"

He looked at her and proudly announced, "I'm washing the car, Mommy!"

She grabbed him in her arms and gave him a big hug, thanking him for washing the car. She couldn't help but laugh as she spent the next thirty minutes cleaning up the flood. Tears began to escape and a lump formed in her throat as she saw Michael proudly standing there in her mind's eye. Oh, how she longed to hold him. Her gut wrenched as the tears began to flow freely.

A memory of Leslie crept in next. She had to have shots when she was fifteen months old and was scared, so Emily had made a deal with her. "If you are a big girl when you get your shots, then Mommy will take you to Dairy Queen."

Leslie didn't cry at all when they stuck her. She puckered out her bottom lip, but fought the tears.

Emily asked, "How are you doing, sweetheart?"

Leslie smiled with her lip quivering, "Me have ice cream?"

Emily cried and laughed and cried some more. *What goes around comes around!? I have never done anything to warrant THIS coming around, have I?* She began recalling her life, searching for an answer to that question.

Chapter 13

Emily and her brothers had been raised in the suburbs of Chicago, Illinois. She had never been popular, but always had some very close friends. She had her share of acquaintances as well.

Her childhood was easy. Her parents were still married after all of these years. She had seen them argue a few times, but nothing major. They did their best in raising her and her brothers. They had lived in a nice middle-class part of town in one of the best school districts in the country. Marvin worked a lot so that Terri could be home every day when the kids got home from school.

When Emily was seven and Jason was starting Kindergarten, Terri suggested that they start taking care of foster kids. They did that for ten years. It was an interesting experience for the whole family. There was always a new person in the family, but they learned not to get too attached because there was no telling when that child would leave and another would come. They got Larry in the summer of 1982 when he was just a few days old. He was a little black boy whose parents were intercity teenagers. They had him for two years when they decided to adopt him since he had been with them since birth and they were the only family he had ever known.

Terri and Marvin raised the kids in a non-denominational Christian church. They went every Sunday, rain or shine, Emily's whole life. Her parents were always telling her about Jesus; how He was born of a virgin, lived a sinless life, performed miracles, and died for her sins. They made sure she knew that God loved her enough to send Jesus to die on the cross for her. They made a big deal of it when Scott and Jason accepted Christ as their personal Savior and were baptized. She felt a little left out and knew that her parents were disappointed that she hadn't accepted Christ, too. When she was twelve, she said the prayer, was saved and baptized. She still wasn't really sure what to think of it all. It sounded a little far-fetched, but it made her parents happy. She did all of the things they asked her to do and memorized Bible verses that didn't really make sense to her.

It was a devastating blow when her father announced that his company was going to transfer them out of state. That news came in the summer between her junior and senior year of high school. She had gone to school in the same district, with the same group of friends since Kindergarten. All of a sudden, her father told her that she wasn't going to graduate with all the kids that she had grown up with! She tried to talk her parents into letting her live with friends but they wouldn't allow it. She asked if the move could be delayed one year so that she could graduate with her friends. Marvin checked with the company, but was told that to take the promotion he would have to move immediately.

Emily didn't understand why this was happening. Why wouldn't her parents let her stay with friends? Why wouldn't they let her stay with Scott, who was nineteen and had a place of his own? Why couldn't Marvin go and let the rest of the family stay for a year? In her confusion, Emily blamed her parents and began rebelling that summer. She got in trouble with authority, began smoking cigarettes, marijuana and drinking. It was during her farewell party when she was drunk, stoned, and not thinking clearly that she got pregnant.

They moved to Nashville before Emily knew she was pregnant. When she found out, she thought she would just get an abortion and no one would have to know, but abortions cost money. She tried to force a miscarriage by not eating, doing more drugs, smoking more, drinking more, and punching herself in the abdomen as often as possible. She would pick fights at her new school trying to lose the baby. She saved every penny she got her hands on so that she could get an abortion if all else failed. For her seventeenth birthday, her parents gave her plane tickets to Chicago for a weekend. She was going to stay with Scott, but her parents would check in often. She saw this as the perfect opportunity to deal with the pregnancy. She had quite a bit of money saved up before the trip, and her parents gave her more for spending money.

When she arrived in Chicago, she made some phone calls and found out she had enough to abort the pregnancy. She made the appointment and then she called her friend, Sandy, to tell her the good news. Deciding to celebrate, she went out and got drunk. The next morning, as she lay passed out and hung over on the couch, the phone rang.

"Hello?" Emily said groggily as she answered Scott's phone on the fourth ring.

"Emily! Wake up!" Terri yelled.

"Yeah, Mom, I'm up. What's wrong with you?" *Oh, my head!*

"Are you pregnant?" Terri demanded.

"What?!" *How on earth does she know?*

"You heard me. Are you pregnant?"

"Yes, Mom. I am pregnant and I have an appointment this afternoon to change that fact, so don't worry about it," Emily said defensively.

Terri took a deep breath trying to calm down. Sounding much more in control, she said, "Emily, don't do anything, all right? Please come home first and let's talk about it before you do something that you'll regret."

"Okay," Emily agreed to get her mother off the phone. This conversation was making her head hurt even more. *Hangovers suck!*

Emily had gone right back to sleep, vaguely remembering the conversation. She overslept, missed her appointment and went home. Her parents were totally supportive of her. They talked with her as an adult, presented her options to her, and told her that what-ever she decided they would back her up one hundred percent. They told her that her friend, Sandy, had called and told them about the baby and Emily's plans to terminate her pregnancy. Six months later, Rachel was born. Amazingly, she was a robust eight pounds and very healthy.

When Rachel was one, Emily met Henry. They began dating right away. A year later, Henry rented a white stretch limousine and proposed to Emily. He took her out to a wonderful dinner and show. Emily was in love. She was happy for the first time in a long time. They were married in a nice, small church wedding. Rachel, at two and a half, was the cutest flower girl!

It was a rough marriage. They loved each other, but they weren't ready for that kind of commitment. Emily's parents tried not to interfere or help too much, while Henry's parents couldn't seem to back off or keep their noses out of it. To top it all off, Emily got pregnant with Michael just two months after the wedding. He was born three weeks before their first anniversary. Four months later, Leslie was conceived. Emily's family lovingly began calling her "Fertile Myrtle". Henry and Emily decided it would be best for her to stay home with Rachel and Michael, and the new baby after she delivered. His parents had a fit. They had never really liked Emily and now they thought she was using Henry. They began accusing her of planning this before she and Henry got married. Henry tried to tell them that it just didn't make sense to pay for daycare for the boys so that Emily could work during the pregnancy. The daycare alone would cost more than half of Emily's wages. But, eventually they convinced Henry that he was he was being taken advantage of and they talked him into leaving her. When he walked out the door, Rachel was four, Michael was almost one, and Leslie was due in three months. The divorce was final a month after Michael's second birthday, one month before Leslie's first birthday.

Since the divorce, Emily had been working second shift as a check processor at a bank. Henry paid his child support very sporadically. He would keep a job until they started taking the child support out of his paycheck and then he would quit. She got fed up with not being able to depend on it and called her attorney five months prior to the fire. Henry appeared in court and was found guilty. He was sentenced to ninety days. He had only visited the kids once since the separation.

She continued to rack her brain trying to figure out what she had done to deserve this fate. Eventually, she slipped off to sleep.

Chapter 14

"Here, this is a nice shirt." Scott said as he handed Emily a red polo at the store on Saturday morning.

"Yeah, Michael would like that one. Now we need to get him some jeans."

"Emily, why don't you come over here and help me find a dress for Leslie," Terri said trying to hurry them along.

"All right," Emily said over her shoulder. "We'll be right over here in the girls' department, Scott. Size 3T should fit Michael just right.'

"Okay."

Emily joined her mother in the girls' department. After a few minutes of rummaging through the racks, Emily said, "I don't see anything that Leslie would like, Mom."

"Well, they have put out all of the winter clothes now."

"Leslie loves flowers, though. I want a dress with big, beautiful flowers." There was a lump forming in Emily's throat, though she fought back the tears.

"How about this one?" Scott said holding up a deep maroon dress with faint flowers and a white ruffled collar.

Emily said quite loudly, "You didn't know her. She wouldn't like that one. She didn't like ruffles and frills. She was a simple girl who liked things simple."

Scott did his best to hide his hurt. "Okay, well, let's see if we can find something simple."

Terri grabbed Emily's arm. "Do you have to yell? I mean the whole store heard you."

"So, what! My kids are dead and we have to find something to bury them in. Do you really think I care what people are thinking right now? Excuse me for embarrassing you."

Emily stormed off. Before long, she felt bad about hurting Scott and embarrassing her mother. She worked her way back over to them and said, "I'm sorry, Mom. It's just that I am really stressed out right now. Scott, that dress is beautiful and the closest one to what Leslie would like. Will you guys forgive me?"

"Yeah, we will. Won't we, Mom?"

"Yeah, we will," Terri said.

"I was wondering if we could go by the house before we go to the funeral home."

"The house? You mean the one that burned down? Why would you want to go there?" Terri exclaimed.

"I would like to see it and look around for stuff I might want to get from there."

"I don't think you will find anything useful," Terri said. "Scott, would you mind taking her? I don't think I could handle that."

"Sure, Mom."

~ ~ ~ ~ ~ ~ ~

After they dropped Terri off at home, Scott and Emily went to the duplex that Emily called home before the fire that claimed the lives of her two youngest children. Scott drove very slowly as he approached the house to give Emily time to absorb the reality of it. Emily sat there numb as the house slowly came into view. She thought that having seen it on TV would have prepared her for this, but she was wrong. She was speechless as they approached.

They pulled into the driveway as Scott looked lovingly at his only sister staring at what just two days ago was her home, but now was just a brick frame around black piles of ashes. He put his arm around her shoulders and pulled her into him. She relaxed onto his shoulder. They sat like that for a few minutes. Finally, Emily said, "Well, let's get this over with."

"Are you sure you are up to it?"

"Yes, I'm sure. I have to do this or I will regret it forever."

"All right. We will move at your pace and whenever you are ready to go, you let me know."

They walked slowly up the steps and into the doorway that used to be the front door. The living room was nothing but a pile of ashes. As they walked through the room toward the hallway, something pink in a pile of ashes where the desk used to be caught Emily's eye. She made her way over to it. "Scott, look at this!"

"What is it?" Scott asked joining her.

Emily brushed ashes off of the Bible that her father had given her for Mother's Day just four and a half months ago. It was in perfect condition except for some discoloration of the pages. The desk was gone. The TV that sat on top of the desk was gone. Everything in the living room was gone except for the Bible.

"Where was that?"

"It was in the desk drawer!"

"Wow! How cool! God saved His Word! That is awesome."

Emily rolled her eyes and handed the Bible to her oldest brother. "I'm going to check out the other rooms," she said as she turned away. Scott stood there in awe examining the Bible.

As she entered the kitchen, all she found was total destruction—ashes, melted plastic, or broken glass. The bathroom was completely smoke and water damaged.

Emily went into what used to be her bedroom. Her waterbed had exploded from the heat and flooded the room along with the water from the fire hoses. All of her furniture was totally destroyed by water and smoke. She opened her dresser drawers. She was able to salvage a few outfits, but not many because apparently she hadn't closed all of the drawers completely the morning of the fire and the clothes were destroyed by smoke and water.

Scott met her in the hallway as she was headed into the kids' room. He put his arm around her and escorted her in. The room was in the same condition as Emily's room. Emily sat on the floor next to the toy box and began going through the toys. It was all too damaged to save, except for a little stuffed car at the very bottom. It wasn't Michael's favorite toy, but she wanted to take something of his to save. She moved over to Leslie's bed where she found the stuffed doll that Leslie slept with every night. It was in pretty rough shape, but Emily didn't care. It was Leslie's and that is all that mattered.

It appeared that the fire itself had been contained to the living room but smoke and water had destroyed the remainder of the house. They stood there surveying the damage for a few minutes when all of a sudden Emily pulled away from Scott and almost ran back into the living room. As Scott entered the living room, he found Emily on her hands and knees in front of a pile of ashes across the room from where they had found the Bible.

"What are you looking for?"

"My wedding rings. They were in my purse, which was on this table. Diamonds are rocks, right? They can't burn, right?"

"That is right, but gold melts and so it is probably gone."

"The gold, yes, but not the diamonds."

While Scott thought it was like looking for a needle in a haystack, he got on his hands and knees beside Emily and they looked for two quarter-karat diamonds and one half-karat diamond. They searched for hours to no avail. Emily sat down, exhausted with soot all over her face, hands and clothes. "It is almost like God didn't want anything from that marriage to survive."

"Oh, Emily, don't say that."

"Well, Michael and Leslie are gone, my wedding rings are gone, and all of the pictures are gone. Everything is gone. I had the rings at Mom and Dad's house for a long time. I had just put them in my purse the day before the fire so I could show them to a friend of mine. Ironic? Coincidence? Who knows? Seems strange to me, that's all."

"Come on. Let's go. You need a shower," Scott said helping Emily to her feet.

"Oh, and you don't?" she said laughing. "Making a fashion statement? Your sandy blonde hair has black soot highlights."

Chapter 15

Emily had driven past East Ridge Cemetery and Funeral Home countless times in the past, but this was the first time she had ever come inside. It dawned on her that this is the first time she had ever been in any funeral home. All four of her grandparents, both of her parents, and all of her brothers were still alive. In fact, she still had one great-grandmother living. Sure, she had heard about some of the kids she went to school with dying in car accidents and it was just last week when one of her friends from high school called and told her that her best friend from high school was murdered a few months back, but she hadn't spoken to Angie in years. *My first real experience with death has to be my children. How is THAT for luck?*

Emily looked around the big white building. It was very pleasant with comfortable sofas and chairs in the lobby area. There were beautiful wooden end tables and coffee tables with hand-painted lamps and attractive flower arrangements decorating them. It was very quiet and had a somewhat peaceful feel to it.

"Hello. Are you the Payne family?"

"Yes, we are," Marvin answered.

"My name is David Murphy. I am the funeral director. Please step in here." Mr. Murphy was a fairly young man, early thirties maybe. He had dark hair and blue eyes. The family all filed into a conference room with a large oak table and office chairs surrounding it.

Once everyone was seated Marvin said, "I am Marvin, Michael and Leslie's grandfather. This is my wife, Terri; my daughter, Emily, the children's mother; my sons, Scott and Jason," pointing to each as he said their names.

Mr. Murphy shook hands with everyone. "Thank you for coming in. Do you have the clothes?"

"Yes, sir," Emily said as she handed Mr. Murphy the bag full of clothes.

"Great. Thank you. We need to discuss a number of things today and then there will be paperwork to sign. I know this is very hard on you, so I will make it as easy as possible. You'll have to pick out the burial plots today. This large map right here is the entire cemetery," he said, using a wooden pointer to point to a large laminated map on the wall. "All the green plots are available. This section here is our children's garden. You may choose from any section you wish, but if you choose the children's garden, you cannot be buried in the plot next to the children." Mr. Murphy pointed to another section. "This area here has the most vacancies, making it easiest for you to purchase a number of plots near each other."

Emily walked up to the poster map for a closer look. "I want them to be in a section where I can be buried next to them. Leslie loved the shade trees so I want them under a tree."

"This section here has a few plots next to each other and is the only place where there is a tree close by," Mr. Murphy said pointing to a tree.

"That's fine. I want Leslie closest to the tree, then Michael, and the plot next to him for me."

"Are you sure you only want three plots? What about your daughter?"

"Hopefully, she will live long enough to get married and will be buried with her husband. No, three will do." Emily sounded as if she was thinking out loud.

"All right. You might want to think about that, so we will leave it open. I mean if you ever get married again, you would want your husband buried with you," sounding like a true salesman.

"I'm not getting married again," Emily said flatly.

"Moving on..." Scott said coming to his sister's rescue.

Mr. Murphy and Emily took their seats at the table. "I typed up a tentative obituary." He slid a piece of paper across the table to Emily. "Read this over and tell me what you think. Please make spelling corrections between the lines and use the bottom to add other names or information you want listed in the newspaper."

Reality sunk in a little more as Emily looked at her children's names on a piece of paper entitled "Obituary". She couldn't read it, so Marvin took it, read it over, made some changes and conferred with Terri.

"Can we take a break?" Emily asked, wiping the tears from her eyes.

"Sure. Actually, that would be good and then we will go into the next room where the coffins are so you can pick those out."

Chapter 16

"Hey, Em." Scott caught up with Emily just as she was coming out of the restroom. "Do me a favor and let me do the talking when we are looking at the coffins. This guy is a salesman and he is trying to sell you things you don't need. When I worked at Johnson Funeral Home, I learned a lot about this stuff. You don't need to buy another plot for your future husband. You can be buried double-depth."

"What does that mean?" Emily asked.

"Well, typically the vault and coffin are placed six feet underground, right?"

"Yeah, I suppose."

"When you choose double-depth that means the first spouse's vault and coffin are placed twelve feet underground and then when the other spouse dies, their vault and coffin are placed six feet under, on top of the first spouse."

"So, you are saying that even if I do get married again, I can purchase one plot for both my husband and I?"

"Yes, I am saying that if you buy one today, you and your husband can both be buried in that plot."

"So then why can't we do that today with Michael and Leslie?"

"You could, but the problem would be that the ground won't have time to settle on the first one before putting the second casket in place, but we can ask about it."

"We'd better get in there." Emily said when she saw Marvin look out the door of the coffin room for the second time.

"All right. This is about what you want. Don't let this guy talk you into anything."

"Then I'll just tell you and you can tell him."

"Sounds good to me." Scott and Emily were whispering to each other as they slipped into the room. Terri, Marvin, and Jason were looking at the coffins on display.

"Ah, here they are," Mr. Murphy noted as Scott and Emily entered the room.

Emily's eyes immediately fell on a beautiful metallic baby blue coffin that was full-sized. She walked straight to it.

"We have coffins especially for children over here."

Emily looked at Scott. "I really like this one."

Mr. Murphy interrupted, "That one is nice, but it's for adults. Please come look at our children's coffins."

Emily followed Mr. Murphy over to the children's section. There were some nice coffins, but she really liked that blue one. She gravitated towards one that was similar to the blue one, but it wasn't as nice. Emily noticed the prices on the children's coffins were not much less than the one she wanted. She looked at Scott with tears welling up in her eyes.

"Here we have a very nice oak coffin. Don't you want your children to be buried in the best possible coffin?" Mr. Murphy quipped.

Scott looked furious. He looked Mr. Murphy in the eye and pointed to the door. Mr. Murphy got the hint and led Scott out of the room.

"What is it, Emily?" Terri asked.

"I like that blue one best," she said pointing back over to the adult section while choking back the tears.

"I didn't look at that one. Why don't you show it to me?" Emily and Terri walked back over to the blue one. "Oh, I like that one. I can see why you want it. Oh, look, here is a matching pink one."

"I like that idea," Emily said losing the battle the with her tears.

Mr. Murphy re-entered the room with Scott right behind him. "But, Ma'am, those are full-size coffins. I mean I can sell them to you, but they cost more than the children's coffins."

Scott pulled Emily off to the side and whispered in her ear, "You decide what you want. Don't worry about anything else."

"I really like that blue one and Mom suggested we get the matching pink one for Leslie. And they are the cheapest," Emily said to Scott, ignoring Mr. Murphy's ever-annoying presence.

"You could do that, or since they are both so small, you could have them placed in the same coffin. They would both fit. Then you only have to purchase one vault, one coffin, and one plot," Scott suggested.

"Let's do that. I want the blue one."

When Scott told the others, Terri suggested a dove gray full-sized coffin that was just like the blue one so that they were not in a gender-specific coffin together. Emily agreed.

They returned to the conference room to set the dates and times for the wake and the funeral and to discuss the funeral itself—the program, the set up, which room, and so on. The remainder of the funeral arrangements went without any problems. Emily was emotionally drained by the time they left there.

~ ~ ~ ~ ~ ~ ~

Later that evening, Emily walked in the living room, just as Scott was telling Uncle Joe about the funeral home experience. "So, I watched for awhile, but then when he tried to lay a guilt trip on Emily, I was livid. I signaled him to meet me in the hallway. When we got out there, I told him, 'this is my niece and nephew that we are burying and that is my sister you are scamming. I am not going to stand here and watch this go on any longer. I used to work in a funeral home. I know what is legal, I know what her options are, and I know that she can put the kids in whatever coffin she chooses. I, also, told her about double-depth, so you can knock one of the plots off of the list of things you think you sold her today. Now, you go back in there, answer all of her questions truthfully, and only sell her what she picks out. No sales tactics. Got it?' You should have seen the look on his face!"

"Great! I'm sure Emily appreciated that."

"Well, she knows that we talked in the hallway, but she doesn't know what was said. I just don't want to upset her anymore than she already is."

"Upset me?" Emily asked. Scott turned with a look of surprise.

"I didn't know you were standing there."

"Well, if you think that I am upset about my big brother coming to rescue me from that sleaze ball of a salesman, you are sadly mistaken. I didn't get the chance to thank you for that, so thanks." Emily hugged her brother tightly.

Chapter 17

Emily slept well. She was numb to all that was going on. She was simply going through the motions of life.

She was breathing a lot more easily. Occasionally, she would have to take a deep breath to get enough oxygen, but during discharge from the hospital, the nurse told her that may happen for a few weeks. She still couldn't smoke, but needed to hold a cigarette sometimes. That was the only peace she had left.

She was dressed and ready to go her children's wake long before anyone else. The family was all at the hotel still. She sat waiting in silence.

As people began to arrive, Emily visited with them like she didn't have a care in the world.

Terri watched Emily for a while. She asked Marvin, "How can she not care? They were her children and she is mingling and socializing like this is a party!" Others noticed also, but no one said anything to Emily about it.

There was a knock on the door and Jason jumped up to answer it. "Emily, Katherine is here," he called through the house.

Katherine was one of Emily's closest friends. They had met during Emily's senior year in high school. Emily was pregnant with Rachel then and had a hard time making friends. Katherine had had no problems accepting her. Katherine had been there for Emily through her pregnancies with Rachel and Michael, her wedding, and her divorce. Katherine's husband had been transferred out of state while Emily was pregnant with Leslie. She had moved back to Nashville when she and her husband divorced just after Leslie's first birthday.

"I have something for you." Katherine handed her a large cardboard envelope.

"What is it?" Emily asked, curiosity getting the best of her.

"Just open it," Katherine answered with a grin on her face.

Emily opened the envelope to find studio pictures of Michael and Leslie. She had received the pictures from the photographer just days before the fire. She hadn't had the chance to distribute them yet and lost them all in the fire.

"Where did you get these? I thought they were burned up in the fire!"

"They were. I called the studio and told them what happened. They reprinted them and sent them to me by overnight mail."

"Oh, Katherine! Thank you!" Emily threw her arms around Katherine, almost knocking her over.

"And look here," Katherine said. "They sent all the negatives. This letter here gives you full rights to the pictures; no need to worry about copyright infringement."

"Katherine, that is wonderful. You think of everything. Hey, Mom…" Emily took the pictures in the kitchen to show her mother.

~ ~ ~ ~ ~ ~ ~

At the funeral home, people were milling all around. Emily took her seat in the front row. She sat just watching as people walked up to the casket to see her children's bodies. She knew they weren't in their bodies anymore, but she didn't know where they were. She couldn't think about that right now. That was just too deep.

There were so many people that Emily didn't know. *What are all these people doing here? I have never seen half of these people.*

One of Emily's co-workers, Rebecca, came out of nowhere and handed her a card. Emily had seen her around at work, but they had never talked. Rebecca was the quiet type that no one ever talked to. Rumor had it that her husband wouldn't allow her to talk to anyone. She was the butt of many jokes at work. "There is a box at the back of the room for cards and stuff," Emily said.

"I wanted to give it to you personally," Rebecca said firmly.

"Oh, Okay. Well, thank you." Emily sat there holding the card for a long time, just watching people.

She was going to put the card in the box, but decided to go ahead and open it. It was absolutely beautiful. Big pink and white roses

adorned the front along with the words, "In your time of loss..."
Emily opened it up. "...My heart goes out to you. May God keep you
and bless you in all that you do. I know it's hard to understand, but
it's all part of His master plan. Just trust in Him, keep your faith, and
He will be with you day to day." *How nice! That was really sweet of
her.* Rebecca had written a Bible reference on the bottom under her
signature. Emily picked up the King James Bible that was on the end
of the row of seats. She looked at the table of contents and found the
book of Isaiah. She turned to chapter forty and read verses twenty-
eight through thirty-one. It said, "Hast thou not known? Hast thou
not heard, that the everlasting God, the LORD, the Creator of the
ends of the earth, fainteth not, neither is weary? There is no searching
of his understanding. He giveth power to the faint; and to them that
have no might he increaseth strength. Even the youths shall faint
and be weary, and the young men shall utterly fall: But they that
wait upon the LORD shall renew their strength; they shall mount
up with wings as eagles; they shall run, and not be weary; and they
shall walk, and not faint." Then she turned to chapter forty-three and
read verses one through five and verse seven. "But now thus saith
the LORD that created thee, O Jacob, and he that formed thee, O
Israel, Fear not: for I have redeemed thee, I have called thee by thy
name; thou art mine. When thou passest through the waters, I will be
with thee; and through the rivers, they shall not overflow thee: when
thou walkest through the fire, thou shalt not be burned; neither shall
the flame kindle upon thee. For I am the LORD thy God, the Holy

One of Israel, thy Saviour: I gave Egypt for thy ransom, Ethiopia and Seba for thee. Since thou wast precious in my sight, thou hast been honourable, and I have loved thee: therefore will I give men for thee, and people for thy life. Fear not: for I am with thee: I will bring thy seed from the east, and gather thee from the west; Even every one that is called by my name: for I have created him for my glory, I have formed him; yea, I have made him."

Emily was totally confused. She thought *I guess it is saying that God is with me right now. That he is going to help me through this. He put me in this boat and now he is going to help me? Whatever! That's exactly why I don't even believe God exists.* She got up to go to the restroom and stuck the card into the box on the way out.

Chapter 18

Emily couldn't stand the thought of sitting in that funeral parlor any longer. The wake was scheduled to last six hours. She found a clock and discovered she still had three and a half to go. She slipped outside and found some of her friends. She walked up and asked Katherine for a cigarette.

"Here." Katherine handed her a cigarette and lit it for her. "How are you doing?"

"I'm fine. What are you guys doing out here?" Emily inquired.

"Just hanging out. We want to be here for you, but it is too hard to sit in there." Abby pointed toward the funeral home.

"It is tough to sit in there. I don't know what my parents were thinking when they scheduled this thing for SIX hours!"

"Well, they may have done that so that all of your friends could come. I mean if they scheduled it from twelve to three, the ones who work first shift couldn't have come. If they did it from three to six, the ones who work second shift wouldn't have been able to make it." Marsha glanced at her watch, "I gotta leave here myself in about a half hour so I can go to work."

"Well, you have a point, I suppose. I don't even know half of these people."

"I was wondering about that," Abby said. "Don't look now, but here comes Henry."

Emily turned to look just as Henry reached her. "Hey, ya'll. How are you?" Henry asked in a cordial voice.

"Fine," Abby said in disgust.

"As well as can be expected. You do remember what we are here for right?" Emily said in a very degrading tone of voice.

"Yeah, Em, I do. They were my children, too," Henry said obviously hurt.

"Oh, is that what you call them? I thought they were just a product of your donation," Emily retorted.

"Look, I didn't come over here to fight with you. I came over here to see how you're doing. I can see that you are doing just fine and that you haven't lost one touch of your sarcasm. But, I also wanted to tell you that my family has asked everyone they know to help with the funeral expenses. A number of these people are from my parents' and grandparents' churches. They will be making a donation to the fund, but I need the fund information."

"My dad has all that and it will be printed in the funeral program tomorrow," Emily said matter-of-factly.

"Fine. Thank you. I know you don't believe me, but I loved them too," Henry said with a lump in his throat. He turned and walked away. The tears welled up in his eyes as he struggled with the regret of never having had a relationship with his kids. He always thought there would be time for that later on. Now, he knew that you can't take one moment for granted.

Emily was so livid. After he was out of earshot, she said, "You loved them enough to deny fathering Leslie. Oh, yeah, you did visit ONE time after you left. I guess that constitutes a relationship, right? A father who loves his children pays child support, visits them regularly, and is part of their lives."

"I don't get men," Katherine said.

"You ain't the only one," Emily said. They all laughed.

"You gotta love what Emily put on the birth announcements when Leslie was born," Abby said, chuckling.

"What was that?" Marsha asked.

"Henry left her right after she got pregnant with Leslie. Then, when she told him she was pregnant, he said it wasn't his baby and someone else must have knocked her up. So, on the birth announcements, it says 'Mother: Emily Payne Carter' then she crossed out 'Father' and wrote 'Sperm Donor: Henry Carter'. She sent them to everyone including his family and friends."

"Oh, my gosh... how funny! Good one, Emily," Marsha said, laughing hysterically.

"Yeah, well, his family and friends didn't think it was a good one," Emily said with a sly smile on her face. Laughing made her feel a little better.

As Emily made her way back into the funeral home a little while later, she ran into Brandon.

"Hey, girl. How are you doing?"

"I'm surviving. I don't know. It's like reality hasn't set in. I mean, I know they are dead in my head, but I am just not feeling anything at all. Does that make sense?" Emily always felt comfortable talking to her next-door neighbor.

"Yeah, it does. I know we don't know each other extremely well, but if you need anything, call me." He handed Emily a piece of paper with a phone number on it.

"You are homeless now, too. Where are you staying?

"I am crashing at a friend's until I can find another place to live."

"Ah, well, good luck."

"What are you going to do?"

"I am staying with my parents for the time being. I haven't even thought about where I am going to live – just taking it one day at a time for now."

"Well, you are dealing with enough. I just hope everything works out for you."

"Thank you, Brandon."

~ ~ ~ ~ ~ ~ ~

Emily tried to go to sleep to no avail. She finally gave up and wandered outside to hold a lit cigarette. *It is such a beautiful night* she thought as she looked up at the stars. "Michael. Leslie. I love you guys. I am going to miss you so bad. I don't know how I am going to live without you." She sat on the deck in her parent's backyard for hours crying and talking to Michael and Leslie. Thoughts of suicide crossed her mind, but she decided she could never do that. Rachel needed her too badly.

Chapter 19

"Emily. Emily." Marvin whispered loudly trying to rouse his sleeping daughter. "What are you doing out here?" Emily had laid her head down on the rail of the deck and fallen asleep.

"I came out for a cigarette because I couldn't sleep," Emily said groggily.

"I'm glad you got a little rest, but it would have been better in bed, don't you think?" he said smiling. He sat down next to her and put his arm around her. "How are you feeling?"

"My neck is a little stiff and I'm very tired," Emily replied, resting her head on her father's shoulder like she did when she was a little girl.

"You said you couldn't sleep. Do you want to talk about it?"

"I don't know, Dad. I feel like I'm living in a haze; like this is all a bad dream that I am going to wake up from, but then I can't sleep. It doesn't make sense."

"Well, you have been through a lot. Let's just take it one day at a time. We'll get through this together. I'm always here for you. Just lean on me and I'll do what I can to help you," Marvin felt the need to be the rock for the whole family. Someone had to remain strong and help everyone else. Terri was taking it a lot harder than she would let on. Marvin knew, though. He would push his own feelings aside for now to tend to the rest of the family. He would deal with it when everything had calmed down.

"Thanks, Dad," Emily smiled up at her father.

"Come on in. Your mom is making some coffee. Then you need to get ready for the funeral. Everyone will be here in a few hours."

~ ~ ~ ~ ~ ~ ~

The funeral parlor was packed full of people. All the seats were full and there were people standing all along the back and sides. Emily was surprised to see so many. She was seated in the front row to the right of the aisle with her parents, all three of her brothers, Scott's wife and Rachel. In the front row to the left of the isle were Emily's grandparents, uncles, aunt, Henry, and his parents. Emily's closest friends and Brandon sat in the row behind her, with her co-workers and Terri and Marvin's church members filling up the remainder of that section. The section behind Henry's family was mostly Marvin's co-workers with some of the congregation of Henry's parents' church. The media had not made an appearance at either the wake or the funeral.

The media had been relentless all weekend. Every other time the phone rang it was another reporter. The street in front of the Payne residence was full of news vans with their camera equipment non-stop. Whenever family and friends were coming or going from the house they had to sneak in and out the back door. The back yard had become a parking lot. On Saturday morning, the day after the kids died, Marvin talked to Marc Johnson, the spokesman for the hospital, and told him what the media was doing. They had been hounding the hospital for more information, also. Mr. Johnson gave the media a statement Saturday evening. He, then, told them that they had better not even think about showing up at the funeral home, or they would never get another statement from Vanderbilt Hospital again. They hadn't shown up at the funeral home.

The service was very nice. It was short, sweet and to the point, which is how Emily wanted it. Marvin, Scott, Jason, Larry, Uncle Joe, and Uncle Jack were the pallbearers. Only immediate family and close friends were invited to the graveside service, so all of the co-workers and church members left after the funeral service. The pastor from Terri and Marvin's church led the graveside service. It was very moving. The pastor said something about Michael and Leslie going to heaven because they hadn't reached the age of accountability yet. Emily didn't know what that meant. *I don't doubt that they are in heaven, if there is such a place. They were good kids and they were just kids. They hadn't had time to do anything bad enough to keep them out of heaven. Well, maybe that's what 'age of accountability' means.*

When the graveside service was over, Katherine asked her if she wanted to come over to her house for a little while. She didn't spend much time on goodbyes, but she figured everyone would understand. She did let her parents know that she was going to Katherine's. Terri was none too happy. She thought Emily should go back to the house with the family. Emily told her mother she needed some time with her friends, but that she would be there before long. Terri reluctantly dropped the subject. Emily took Rachel and they hopped in the car and headed away.

Chapter 20

When Emily returned to her parents' house a few hours later, the house was full of people who were sitting around eating, talking and laughing.

"What is going on here?" Emily yelled as she walked in the front door. All fell silent and turned to look at her. "You are all sitting here in this house eating and drinking, laughing and joking around like this is a wedding or a vacation. Have you all forgotten that we put my kids in the ground today? Or do you just not care? You didn't come here to party. You supposedly came to help me through the hardest day of my life."

Uncle Jack rose and put his arm around Emily. "Come here and let's talk."

Emily reluctantly walked with Uncle Jack out onto the back deck. She didn't really know her Uncle Jack very well. He was Terri's oldest brother, but he lived in California and didn't come around much. The only other time Emily could even remember seeing him was when she was ten years old.

"Look, sweetie, we are not partying. We know what we did today. We haven't forgotten that, but we can't mope around all weekend without being able to relax a little. For a long time after the funeral we were talking about the kids and how special they were. It made me wish that I had been around more. I never even met them, but after listening to your mom telling stories about them, I feel like I know them well. There were a lot of tears shed. I'm sure you had your share of tears and memories during that same time frame at your friend's house."

"I'm sorry about that, Uncle Jack, but it just didn't look like anyone cared very much," Emily said. She and Katherine did laugh and joke a little, as well as tell stories about Michael and Leslie.

"We do care, honey. You know, people grieve in different ways and for some it takes longer for reality to set in about what is really going on."

"I didn't know that, but it makes sense. We aren't all the same," Emily said beginning to understand.

"No, we aren't. Some people may cry, others may be numb, and some may get mad, but we are all grieving."

"I am mad!" she said looking down, kicking the deck with her foot. "I am mad at the kids for leaving me. I am mad at God, if there is one, for taking them. I am mad at my parents for expecting me to act a certain way. I may have overreacted when I came in and everyone was sitting around here acting like this was a party, but that really upset me." Emily looked at her uncle.

"I understand that. That is how I have always handled grief, too. I get mad. I used to get mad at God, but now I don't think he exists, because of all the evil in the world, but maybe he does. Your mom and dad think so."

"You said you used to get mad at God, but now you don't think he exists. So, why don't you believe in him anymore?" This peaked Emily's curiosity. She thought everyone in her family believed in God except her.

"Yeah, I used to believe. See, I was raised in the same church as your mom and Uncle Joe. We went to church every time the doors were open. I used to be very involved in it, but then I got drafted and went to Vietnam. Living the sheltered life I had lived, I believed in God because that is what my parents told me to believe. But then, when I got out there in the real world and saw all the killing and the drugs and the evil – well, I just don't believe all the superstitious religious crap anymore."

"I don't know what to believe about God. Mom and Dad always took me to church, so I heard all the cute little stories about Jesus, but I think that is all they are – cute little stories. I mean, are we really supposed to believe that Jesus put mud in a blind guy's eye and made him see again? I believe that like I believe Winnie the Pooh can talk and Tigger can bounce." Uncle Jack couldn't help but laugh.

"They tell us to believe that Jesus rose from the dead, but 'don't believe everything you see on TV, young lady'," Uncle Jack said sarcastically.

Before long Emily was laughing. It actually felt good to laugh. "Now I feel like a hypocrite, going off on everyone else and now here I am laughing!"

Emily hadn't even realized the sun had gone down. It didn't seem like she and Jack had been out there that long. She glanced into the house and noticed most of the people were gone.

"It looks like everyone is pretty much gone. I want to apologize to the people who are still here and say goodbye before they leave, too," Emily said getting up.

"Actually, that is probably what they are waiting for. Most of us are leaving in the morning," Uncle Jack said, rising to join her.

"Thanks, Uncle Jack. Where have you been all my life anyway? I am going to miss you."

"I have been in California, but hopefully, we'll be able to stay in touch now," he said as he put his arm around her shoulders.

"I hope so. Well, I am ready to go in now."

They went in the house. All three of Emily's brothers, Tammy, Emily's parents, all four of her grandparents, Uncle Joe, Aunt Rhonda, and Rachel were present. Everyone else had gone home. "Can I have everyone's attention please?" All eyes turned to Emily and even Rachel was quiet.

"I am really sorry about the way that I acted when I got back from Katherine's. I don't know what got into me. It has been a difficult weekend, though. I hope you will all forgive me."

Everyone said, "We forgive you and we understand."

Then they all said their goodbyes and headed off for their hotels. Their planes were all leaving first thing in the morning so this was the only time to say goodbye. Scott and Tammy had the car, so they would be driving back home tomorrow.

Emily was so glad that she had the opportunity to apologize before anyone left town. That thought and remembering her conversation with Uncle Jack comforted her as she drifted off to sleep.

Chapter 21

After everyone left, Emily did her best to resume a normal lifestyle.

Two weeks after the fire, Emily decided to take a vacation. She took Rachel out of school for a few days and headed to Florida. It was relaxing and a much needed escape, but as soon as they returned to Tennessee, so did reality! Michael and Leslie were gone.

There was a permanent lump in Emily's throat that just wouldn't go away. She had cried a few times, but all that did was give her a headache and didn't help the lump so she tried not to cry.

Three weeks after the fire, Emily returned to work. All of her co-workers were very glad to see her back and very understanding of everything she was going through. Katherine pulled her off to the side and sat down with her. "If you need anything at all, will you let me know? I know what you are going through. I know how you feel."

"You don't know what I am going through!" Emily snapped. "No one can possibly know what I am going through or how I feel unless they have been where I am right now!"

"I have been," Katherine said quietly.

"What? What are you saying?" Emily was confused. Katherine had never said anything about this before.

"I am saying that I have been through the death of a child. That's why I didn't call you when I was living in Missouri. I had a son in St. Louis. He died of crib death when he was three months old."

"Oh, Katherine! I am so sorry. I had no idea. I can't believe you didn't tell me!" Emily was shocked to hear about this and a little hurt that Katherine hadn't ever told her about it.

"I know. I'm sorry I never mentioned it before, but it is just so hard to talk about," Katherine said apologetically.

Feeling free to really talk about it now, Emily asked, "So, does it get any easier?"

"Yes and no. I mean the pain won't be as intense as it is right now, it will eventually subside some, but it will never completely go away. You just learn to live with it. Actually, it kind of becomes a part of you. Oh shoot, Em, I don't know how to explain it, but you know what I mean."

"Yeah, you mean I had better get used to this lump in my throat," Emily said sarcastically.

"No, that will go away." Katherine struggled to explain. "Look, the first year is always the hardest because just when you think you are 'over it' there will be something else to deal with. Like right now you are probably really upset that they aren't here for Halloween and you are thinking about the costumes you had pictured them in and the plans that you had made."

"Yeah," Emily said surprised that Katherine had hit the nail on the head.

"Just when you get past Halloween, it will be time to deal with Thanksgiving, then Christmas, and so on. But once you get past all of the 'firsts', it will get easier. Goodness gracious, it hasn't even been a month. You have to grieve in your own way and you have to give yourself time to heal. You have been dealt a major blow and it will take time to heal from that. Trust me, you don't want to rush it or you will start over later when the wounds get re-opened somehow. You have to allow yourself time to heal thoroughly or it will always be there under the surface, just waiting to rear its ugly head again."

"So that explains why you thought about pictures when no one else did."

"Yeah, we hadn't even gotten Matthew's first pictures taken yet when he died. It is the one thing I have always regretted. I didn't want you to be in the same boat," she said, touching Emily's arm.

"Thanks, Katherine," Emily replied.

"Not a problem."

"Oh, by the way, Mom went to Chicago," Emily said changing the subject.

"What? Why? When?" Katherine was clearly surprised by this announcement.

"She said she couldn't handle it here. She said there are too many memories in the house. She can't go to the grocery store or Wal-Mart for the same reason. Then, one day last week she informed us that she is going to Uncle Joe's for awhile, got in the car and left."

"Wow, Em. I'm so sorry to hear that."

"I don't know what to think or how to feel about it. I mean I know she is grieving too, but I need her here," Emily said trying to comprehend.

"Well, I know I'm not your mom, and no one else can be your mom, but I am here for you if you need me. If you need anything at all, just let me know, even if you just need a shoulder to cry on or an ear to talk off. I have two shoulders and two ears, and you are more than welcome to both."

Emily couldn't help but chuckle. "Thanks, Katherine."

"Emily, I have a question, but if you don't want to talk about it right now, that is fine. We can talk about it later."

"What is it, Katherine?" Emily could tell that whatever she was getting ready to ask was something that had been bothering her for quite awhile.

"Did they ever determine the cause of the fire?" Katherine asked.

"Well, originally, they said it was the couch being placed to close to the baseboard heater. That's what the media reported. I asked the fire investigator what he thought. He said that he believes it started across the room from the heater. He said based on the way the roof beams fell, it had to have started by the front door," Emily explained.

"Really? So, then how did it start?" Katherine asked curiously.

"We don't know. There was nothing by the front door that could have started the fire. The only thing near the door was the light switch right inside the door and they have completely ruled out anything electrical, so there is no way the light switch is the culprit. So, for now, we just don't know. They are still investigating it. I have pictures of the house at home. I looked to see what the fire investigator was talking about, and I see what he means about the beams. I'll bring the pictures tomorrow and show them to you. I don't like to look at them, but I am glad I have them."

Katherine seemed distracted as she said, "Yeah, would you do that? I would like to see them."

~ ~ ~ ~ ~ ~ ~

Emily and Brandon had talked on the phone a few times and decided to be roommates since they were both in the same boat – homeless. They figured they would both benefit from rooming together and splitting the bills. The three-bedroom places that they looked at were just too expensive. They settled on a two-bedroom townhouse with an attached garage. Emily took the smaller room upstairs, Rachel was given the larger room and Brandon turned the garage into his room.

Rachel had asked a lot of difficult questions that Emily didn't know how to answer. She didn't want to lie to her, but she also wanted to provide her with the answers she was seeking. Where is heaven? Who is in heaven? Where will I go when I die? Why did Grandma leave? Is she coming back? When is she coming back? The hardest question was why did Michael and Leslie die? *How do I answer her when I am searching for the same answers myself?* Emily wondered. She answered the best that she could. She was totally honest with Rachel and when she didn't know the answers she told her she didn't know.

Chapter 22

Brandon was born and raised in the Nashville area. He had lived in Nashville most of his life. His parents were hard working, middle class citizens who did the best they could for their three children. Brandon's father was an executive in a marketing company that specialized in promotions for the music industry. Brandon's mother was a fulltime housewife and mother.

Brandon was the oldest. He was four and a half when his brother Christopher was born. Brandon was extremely jealous of Christopher and felt rejected by his parents. Six months after Christopher's birth, they started sending Brandon to Kindergarten which Brandon figured was his parents' way of getting rid of him so they could spend more time with Christopher. Brandon began acting out in violent ways, first towards his baby brother and then to other kids at school.

The school that Brandon attended was racially diverse. His class consisted of four Mexican kids, seven white kids, and fourteen black kids. Brandon got in his first fight when he was in first grade. One of the colored children called him a name. Brandon didn't know what the name meant, but he knew by the boy's tone that it wasn't nice. He severely beat the child and was suspended from school for a week. During that week, his parents told him that they were going to be having another child. Jill was born seven months later.

The feelings of rejection were growing stronger with each day. First his parents had rejected him by paying so much attention to Christopher. Then they rejected him by sending him to school every morning. Then his teachers rejected him by making him sit alone in the hall. They made it clear that they didn't want him at school at all when they told him he couldn't come back for a whole week. The kids at school picked on him all the time. And now, his parents brought their "darling daughter" home from the hospital.

Mr. and Mrs. Brooks were very good parents, totally devoted to all of their children. They never really neglected nor rejected Brandon. They couldn't figure out why their little boy was turning on them like he was. They sought counseling but Brandon wouldn't talk. He didn't know how to say what he was feeling. They tried spending time with him, but the younger kids had to be cared for. They even took turns taking Brandon out by himself while the other parent stayed home with the younger kids. Brandon misunderstood this, too, and thought they were getting him out of the way for the parent who had stayed home to get closer to the other children.

When Jill was about six months old, a family moved in next door with a son few months older than Brandon. Mrs. Brooks introduced herself and Brandon to Steve and his mother. Steve and Brandon became really good friends. They did everything together. Where Steve was, Brandon was. Steve was an intellectual child who had a passion for learning. Brandon quickly caught on and absorbed information like a sponge.

When he was learning about the slaves he thought so *that is what they are here for. I knew they had to have some kind of purpose, but what are they doing in school. They should be working.* When he found out that President Lincoln led the North in the fight to free the slaves, hate for that man rose up in him. He idolized John Wilkes Booth for killing Lincoln that night at Ford's Theatre and wished that killing him would have undone what Lincoln accomplished. During the study of the civil rights movement, Brandon loathed all that Martin Luther King stood for. He detested all people of color.

He kept his hate for the blacks buried deep inside. He didn't breathe a word of it to anyone, not even Steve.

~ ~ ~ ~ ~ ~ ~

As Brandon moved the last box into the garage, which would now be his bedroom he stopped and looked around the room. He set the box down and opened it. He pulled out a big tube with a pipe stuck in the side and walked into the kitchen. He put water in the tube and went back in the garage, put some weed in the pipe and began to smoke it. *Ah, I have been waiting to do that all day. I wonder if Emily wants some. Eh, forget it. I'll share with her later. This one is for me. I am kinda glad we got this place together; makes it easier to keep tabs on her that way. And I know she'll pay most of the bills. She is so kind. Ha! Stupid broad.*

The Red Cross and people that Emily knew donated everything they needed to furnish a house and then some. They had two couches, two loveseats, a recliner, two televisions, a dinette set, and bedroom furniture for each. They also gave them dishes, cookware, linens, and everything else a household needs. They put the extra couch in the garage for Brandon and the extra loveseat in Emily's room.

Rachel liked having the bigger room. She had been given more toys than she had ever had in her life. She loved her new room and all her new things. She even liked her new bed. She missed climbing up on the top bunk, though. She decided not to think about her bunk bed because it made her think about Michael sleeping under her. She wiped a tear away as she jumped up and ran over to her new toy box full of treasures.

Emily was organizing all of her donated clothes in her closet. It felt so good to have a closet again. At her parent's house, she had been living out of a suitcase and a couple of laundry baskets. She had never had a chair in her room, let alone a love seat. She loved the idea. *Now, I can sit here and write in my journal. I can hang out in my room and relax without people bugging me constantly, and I won't be in anyone else's way either, but I'll be right across the hall if Rachel needs me.* She sat down on the loveseat to try it out. She pretended like she was writing in her journal when she realized she didn't have a table to place her drink on. Later, that night she mentioned it to Brandon. He took a box, sealed it, and put a sheet over it. "There you go." She smiled, thanked him and took it up to her room. It worked perfectly. *He is so smart. I think I'm going to like this living arrangement. And with him paying half of the bills, I'll have money to do things with Rachel, like the zoo, the fair, and stuff like that. Shoot, I can even start saving for the future.*

Chapter 23

"Hello?" Emily said picking up the phone on the second ring.

"Hey, Em. How are you?" Emily looked out the window at all the bear trees. *Winter is just around the corner*, she thought.

"I'm fine, Dad. How are you?" Emily replied.

"I'm good. I am going to go to Chicago for Christmas to see your mother, Uncle Joe, and Aunt Rhonda. I was wondering if you and Rachel would like to go to with me," Marvin said.

"Oh, Dad, I don't know. I really wanted to go to the grave on Christmas," Emily said sadly.

"Whatever you think is best." Marvin didn't want to push his daughter. "Do you think Rachel would like to go with me even if you don't go?"

Emily told Marvin she thought it would be best for Rachel to go. She needed to see her grandma and ask her all the questions about her leaving and when she would be coming back. After hanging up the phone she called Rachel into the living room.

"Honey, do you want to go with Grandpa to see Grandma for Christmas?" Emily asked her daughter.

Rachel's face lit up. "Yeah!"

"All right. Well, you only have a half day of school on Friday, so Grandpa is going to pick you up after school. You'll leave right away. Then you'll come back home next Wednesday, okay?"

Rachel's face fell as she realized what her mother was saying. "Aren't you going with us, Mom?"

"No, sweetheart, I have to work. You go and have a good time. We'll celebrate Christmas together when you get home. All right?" Emily lovingly touched her daughter's cheek.

"Oh, Okay." Rachel agreed reluctantly.

When Friday finally arrived, Rachel was extremely excited about seeing her grandma. "Grandpa!" she screamed in excitement when Marvin entered the house and threw her arms around his waist.

"Hello, Rachel. Are you ready to go?"

Rachel picked up her suitcase which had been sitting by the door. "Yup! Let's go!"

"Are you sure you don't want to come too?" Marvin asked as Emily put Rachel's suitcase in the trunk.

"Yes, Dad, I'm sure." Emily crossed her hands and shivered from the cold. She hadn't put a jacket on to walk them out to the car.

"Well, what are you going to do for Christmas?" Marvin inquired.

"I don't know. I'll be working most of the time that you are gone. On Christmas Day, I want to go to the grave for a while. I love

Rachel and all, but I really need a break from her and all her questions, anyway. I think it is best for both of us this way," Emily said quietly out of Rachel's earshot.

"All right. Well, you take care and if you need anything, call Uncle Joe's," Marvin said walking around to the driver's door as Emily made her way to the passenger side of the car.

"Okay. I'll be fine, Dad," she said over the top of the car. Leaning into the backseat, she said, "You be a good girl, Rachel." She put the seatbelt around her daughter.

"I will, Mom. Merry Christmas."

"Merry Christmas. I love you." She hugged Rachel before shutting the door.

"I love you, too."

Emily spent the next few days working so much she didn't have time to think about all that should have been going on but wasn't because of that terrible fire. When she wasn't working or sleeping she was writing in her journal.

On Christmas morning, she dressed in layers of clothing because it was freezing outside. She grabbed a thick blanket and headed toward the door.

"Where are you going?" Brandon caught up with her just as she reached the door.

"I'm going to the grave," Emily said impatiently.

"When are you going to be back?" Brandon asked.

"When I get back," Emily retorted. "I'm in no hurry. This is all I have planned for the day, so don't worry about me." Emily didn't mean to give him an attitude, but she was tired of the way he was treating her lately. He had been supportive for about a month after they moved in together and then started making subtle little remarks about her getting over it and moving on.

"I'm concerned about you spending Christmas alone. I was wondering if you wanted to go to my parents' house with me."

"Sorry, I'm spending the day with my kids," Emily said trying to brush past him and escape out the door.

"Yeah, your dead ones! You should be with the kid that's alive, but you shipped her off to Chicago," Brandon said in a hateful, judgemental tone.

Emily said a few choice words as she slammed the door in Brandon's face.

When she arrived at the grave, she spread the blanket on the ground and made herself comfortable. She had been there for about an hour when the cold got to be almost too much to bear.

I don't want to go home, but I don't know where else to go. Maybe he is right. Maybe I should have made Rachel stay home. Or, I guess I could have gone to Chicago with them. Then I would at least be with my family, instead of all alone. Have I been a bad mother to Rachel? In a way I guess I have neglected her. I have been so wrapped up in my guilt and my grief that I haven't paid much attention to her since the fire. Too much has already been destroyed by that fire.

Emily resolved not to let the fire destroy her relationship with Rachel, too. She vowed, "Michael and Leslie, I am going to be the best mother I can be to Rachel. She has been through too much. She misses you and Grandma really badly, but I think she misses me, too. Even though I have been there physically, I haven't been there emotionally. I left that poor little six-year-old girl alone to deal with her grief all by herself. I promise you that I won't do that anymore."

Realizing she only had two days to deal with it all before Rachel came back, she decided to pack up her things and go back home. She had a lot of work to do.

Chapter 24

When she arrived home, Brandon was gone. She grabbed a beer, a pack of cigarettes, and a pen. She went to her room and locked the door. She set the stuff down on the end table box next to the loveseat. She went to her nightstand and got the ashtray, her journal and the blanket off her bed. She settled down on the loveseat and lit a cigarette. She read over the last few entries in her journal detailing how Brandon had been treating her. She wrote her vow to be a better mother to Rachel and wrote out what she was going to do to try to accomplish that. She poured her heart out in writing.

She only left her room long enough to use the restroom and grab another beer. She heard the door open when Brandon got home, but she pretended she hadn't heard it.

"Emily," he called. "You up there?"

She didn't answer. She just kept writing.

A few hours later, she heard laughter from downstairs. She wandered down to get another beer and to see who was there. Brandon was sitting there smoking a joint with a couple of friends.

"Hey, hermit, you want some?" Brandon said holding the joint out in her direction. Emily totally ignored him as she walked into the kitchen. She didn't want to be derailed from the mission she was on. She had a lot of healing to do and not much time to do it.

"Man, she has been a royal female dog lately," Brandon said under his breath.

"Well, come on, man," Emily heard Jeff say. "She has been through a lot lately."

"She should be over it by now. I mean moping around here and treating me and Rachel like crap ain't gonna bring her kids back anyhow," Brandon said jealously.

"No, but darn, dude, don't you have any compassion?" Jeff asked.

"Not when she's treating me like the worst thing that ever happened to her. I have done everything I can to help her and what does she give me in return? An attitude!" Brandon tried to sound like Emily's victim when in reality it was the other way around.

"If you've been treating her like that, maybe you are the worst thing to happen to her. She needs support, help and sympathy right now, dude," Jeff said boldly. No one else said a word.

Emily wished there was another way to go back upstairs without walking through the living room. She took a deep breath and walked as fast as she could. She decided to block out everything he said to her. She wasn't going to let him distract her. She was on a mission for her daughter and she wouldn't let Brandon stop her.

She locked the bedroom door behind her again. She grabbed Leslie's doll and Michael's car that she had gotten from the house and sat back down on the loveseat. The doll and car were stained with smoke and still smelled like smoke, but Emily didn't want to wash them or she would wash away the faint smell of her children that remained. She sat there for an hour hugging the toys to her chest, rocking back and forth as she wept for her children. She missed them so intensely.

Suddenly, there was a light rapping at the door.

"What do you want?" Emily snapped trying to hide the tears in her voice.

"Can I come in?" It wasn't Brandon. It was Jeff.

"Yeah." Emily reached over and unlocked the door.

Jeff came in and sat on the corner of the bed. "Does he talk to you like that all the time?"

"Yes," Emily said fighting the tears.

"I'm sorry, Em. I talked to him about it. I hope it helps," Jeff said sympathetically.

"Where is he?" Emily inquired.

"He and John went to get more beer."

"Jeff, I really don't feel right talking to you about this. You're *his* friend. But thank you for standing up for me the way that you did," Emily said feeling uncomfortable confiding in Jeff.

"Not a problem. It's just that it really made me mad the way he talked to you. I have gotten to know you since ya'll have been room-mates and I care about you, too."

"Well, thank you, but it still doesn't feel right discussing our problems with you. No offense."

"No offense taken. I better get back downstairs before he gets back anyway. I would hate for him to get even more upset with you for talking to me. I just hope my little talk with him works," Jeff said going back out the door.

"All right. Thanks again," Emily said as he shut the door behind himself. She reached over to lock and saw that Jeff locked it on his way out.

Jeff's brief visit helped Emily out of her depression. She picked up the journal to read what she had written. She kept flipping back-wards. She had written thirty-three pages! She began reading what she wrote and eventually drifted off to sleep.

1994

Chapter 22

Emily had fully expected Brandon to treat her better after his discussion with Jeff on Christmas night, but she was wrong. It had gotten worse – much worse. Emily was working very hard on her relationship with Rachel, and being the best mother she could possibly be. Emily had decided to work overtime every chance she got so she could save up as much money as possible. Brandon complained constantly about everything. It was as if Emily couldn't do anything right. She didn't know why he acted like that, but she didn't even like coming home anymore. She had more important things to do than be concerned with what Brandon was upset about from one minute to the next. What Brandon didn't know is that she was saving so that she could move out. She was ready to be on her own. She didn't need a roommate who complained and nagged all the time. She had roomed with him to save money, but this wasn't worth it.

She called the townhouse in mid-January and the answering machine picked up. She heard Brandon's voice. "You've reached Brandon and Emily. Sorry, we aren't in to take your call right now.

Please leave a message and we'll get back in touch with you." Emily was furious!

The message had been her children – all three of them. Rachel said, "Hello. Please leave a message." Michael said, "and we'll call you back." Then Leslie said, "bye, bye."

When she got home, Emily confronted Brandon about it.

"You had no right to change the greeting on MY answering machine!" Emily screamed.

"The phone is in my name," Brandon responded.

"Then buy your own answering machine. That was the only recording I had of their voices." Emily began tearing up.

"Well, it is time for you to move on and if you aren't going to do it on your own, I'll help you," Brandon said arrogantly.

"I don't need your help, nor do I need you telling me when it is time for me to move on. I was planning on keeping that tape forever," she yelled fighting the tears. She did not want him to see her crying.

"Well, you're a loser and you need to get a freaking life!"

The river of tears began to flow as Emily stormed out of Brandon's room and slammed the door behind her. She had to tell someone about it or she would go nuts. She went up to her room and dialed Katherine's number.

"Hello?" Katherine answered on the third ring.

"Hello," Emily said flatly.

"Emily, what's wrong?"

"Brandon erased the answering machine message!" The tears began to flow again.

"What?!" Katherine said shocked.

"He erased it and put his stupid voice on it."

"I was afraid something like that would happen, or that you would lose it somehow, so I called you and recorded it."

"What?! You have a copy of it?"

"Yes," Katherine said smiling.

"Oh, Katherine. That's great!" Emily wiped the tears away. "Thank you so much!"

"Not a problem. That's what I'm here for... to think of things that you won't think of." Katherine laughed and so did Emily.

Emily felt much better when she got off the phone. She was glad she called Katherine and extremely grateful that Katherine had thought to record it.

The following week, Brandon was really drunk and high when Emily got home from work. There were beer bottles littering the coffee table, the ashtray was overflowing with cigarette butts, and the tray Brandon used to roll joints was on the floor.

As she was walking past him, he grabbed her arm. She pulled away. "I want to talk to you, Em!"

"Sorry, Brandon, I don't have time right now. I have things to do."

"You never have time. I don't know what you do with all of your time, but it sure isn't spent taking care of your kid. She left this," he slammed a doll's shoe on the coffee table, "on the floor. I stepped on it and really hurt my foot."

"I'm sorry, Brandon. I'll talk to her about keeping her toys picked up, which she usually does. She is only six." Emily rolled her eyes.

"It is your responsibility to teach her right from wrong. Leaving her toys around for others to step on is wrong."

"I said, I'm sorry. I know she didn't leave it laying around just so you would step on it." Emily was getting angry.

"You can't cover for her for the rest of her life. She has to answer for this. Where is she?"

Now, Emily was furious. "Her whereabouts are none of your business. I'll have you know that Rachel is my daughter. You will not make her answer for anything. You are my roommate. Nothing more, nothing less."

"Someone needs to discipline that child and it's obvious you're not going to do it," Brandon yelled accusingly.

"Well, *you* certainly are not going to discipline my daughter, especially when you are all doped up." Emily took a deep breath to calm herself. "Look, there is something that I need to discuss with you. It is nothing personal, but I am trying to get my life back in order and I just don't have time for this crap. I have decided that it is time for me to look for another place to live." Emily began to walk out of the room. Brandon took another swig of his beer. Then, he said something that stopped her cold.

"This is the same crap that Suzie pulled before I set her house on fire. No one burns Brandon."

Emily was shocked. Luckily she had her back to him and he didn't see the look on her face. *I have to stay calm if I am going to get him to talk.* She took a deep breath and turned around.

She sat down on the chair across from him and lit a cigarette. "What are you talking about, Brandon?"

"Suzie decided one day that we were no longer going to live together and asked me to move out. I told her that if I couldn't live there no one would, so I set the house trailer on fire." Suzie was Brandon's ex-girlfriend in Georgia.

Emily was thinking about a time a few weeks before her house caught on fire. Emily was sitting on the porch watching the kids play in the yard when a sheriff came by and asked if Steve was home. Steve was Brandon's roommate in the duplex but he moved out about a month after Emily moved in. Emily told the sheriff that Steve didn't live there anymore and that Brandon wasn't home. He asked if she knew Brandon's last name. Emily told him what it was. The sheriff thanked her and left. A week before the fire, an envelope from the sheriff's office was on Brandon's door with his name on it.

"...It was actually her uncle's trailer, but he was always trying to kick me out. I figure they both deserved what they got; killed two birds with one stone." Brandon paused reflecting on his victory. "Anyway, I found out she was cheating on me and that is why she wanted me out, but that's beside the point."

"So, what are you saying?" Emily wasn't sure if he was threatening her.

"I'm saying that you are not kicking me out," Brandon said matter-of-factly.

"No, I am not kicking you out. I told you, I am moving. I don't know when, but I will let you know when I find a place."

"And just what am I supposed to do?"

"I guess you could find another roommate. If you start looking now, you should be able to find one before I move out."

"And you don't know when you are moving?" Brandon slurred.

"No, I haven't started looking for another place yet. I just wanted to let you know that I am going to start looking." *And based on what you just told me, it will be sooner rather than later.*

"Well, thank you for the warning and thanks for not putting me out," Brandon said sarcastically.

If he only knew what was going through Emily's mind right then, he wouldn't be thanking her. He would be looking for a way to get rid of her – permanently.

Chapter 26

Emily laid in bed that night tossing and turning. She couldn't fall asleep. She tried reading, writing in her journal, counting sheep. She even tried drinking a beer. Nothing worked. Memories and thoughts kept running through her mind.

"The fire started right inside the front door, Ms. Payne," the fire investigator had told her five days after the fire.

"The only thing right inside the front door was the light switch," Emily had said.

"I don't know how to explain this. We don't know what DID start the fire, but we do know what DIDN'T. It wasn't the light switch. In fact, the fire was not electrical in nature."

"Then, what could it have been, Mr. Allison?"

"We are not sure." Mr. Allison paused. He wanted to comfort her somehow. "We are still investigating and we will let you know if we find anything else." No one ever called her.

Then Emily remembered that she had been told that Brandon disappeared shortly after fire started and, if she remembered correctly, it was before the fire had even been put out.

The next image that Emily's mind conjured up was two days before the fire. She was standing on the front porch talking to Brandon. He had moved his coffee table from inside his living room to the outside of the house. He put it against the house underneath the kids' bedroom window.

"Why did you put your coffee table there?" she had asked.

Brandon had grabbed his back and said, "I was moving it around back to the trash when my back started hurting, so I put it there for now. I will move it the rest of the way tomorrow." Why he brought it out the front door and decided to carry it all the way around the house, on her side of the duplex, was beyond her. Brandon did a lot of things that didn't make sense. She decided to just drop it. *The table was still there the morning of the fire. Was that intentional?*

She had overheard a conversation at the funeral home that flooded her brain next. Emily didn't even remember this until now, but then again she was quite disconnected at the funeral. Brandon had been talking to one of the neighbors. "I put the cats in a cage the night before the fire. I just had a feeling something bad was going to happen. Thank God I did, or they would be dead, too." *He told me that he was busy rounding up the cats and that is why he didn't even realize my side of the duplex was on fire. He said that is why he didn't try to help me and the kids get out.*

When the next image re-surfaced in her mind, she knew what she was dealing with. Brandon's mother had come to the house once and as she was leaving she gave Emily a look that made no sense, until now. The look on her face was definitely one of compassion and worry combined. *Oh my god, she knows!!! She knew back in November.*

Just before Christmas, after Brandon and Emily had lived together for almost six weeks, she had overheard a conversation between Brandon and Jeff about an eviction notice. Now, she knew what that envelope was about, too.

Emily got up and began to pack quietly. She only packed what Brandon wouldn't notice was packed. She didn't want him to discover her plan before she even finished making one.

~ ~ ~ ~ ~ ~ ~

On the third ring Terri finally answered the phone. "Hello?"

"Mom! I need to talk to you!" Terri could hear the combination of fear and relief in her daughter's voice.

"What is it, Emily?"

"I have to get out of here. I have to get out of Nashville! If he finds out that I figured it out, he'll kill me!" Terri was concerned that Emily was going to hyperventilate.

"Take a deep breath, Emily." Terri could hear Emily breath in deeply. "Now, what're you talking about? If who finds out what? What did you figure out?"

"Mom, I think Brandon started the fire," Emily bluntly stated.

Now it was Terri's turn to get hysterical. "What?! Why?! Why do you think that? Why would he do that? What is going on?"

Emily filled her mother in on the conversation that had taken place the night before. Then she went over all the memories that had gone through her mind. "Mom, all the little things that didn't make any sense, now make perfect sense. There are no more unanswered questions." Emily paused to let this all sink into her mother's head.

As hard as she tried, Terri couldn't think of one question that this scenario didn't answer.

"Emily, you have to get out of there."

"Yeah, I know, Mom. I don't know where to go, though."

"Come up here."

"The only problem with that idea is that I don't think the car will make it that far."

"Call your dad. Tell him you need to use his credit card to rent a car. Tell him you are coming up here, but do not tell him about this. I don't want him doing something rash. Tell him if he has any questions to call me."

"Would you call the school up there and find out what all I need to get Rachel registered?"

"Yeah, I didn't even think about that. Where is Rachel? You didn't..."

Before her mother could even finish the thought, Emily jumped in, "No, Mom, she isn't with Brandon. She is at Katherine's tonight while I try to figure all this out and stuff."

"Thank goodness for that," Terri said relieved.

"You didn't really think that I would leave her with Brandon knowing what I just told you, did you?"

"No, I'm sorry, honey. I didn't mean to, well, you know."

"Yeah, I know," Emily said, obviously hurt.

"Where are you calling from? He can't overhear..."

"No, Mother. I'm not stupid. I'm at a payphone."

"I'm sorry. I'm just freaking out a little bit here."

"Well, you calm down and I'll call Dad. I'll call you back."

"All right. And remember..."

"Yeah, don't tell him."

Emily called her father and told him the whole story.

"I'll pick you up at 7:00 in the morning and we'll go get a rental car."

"All right. I'll see you then, Dad."

"Are you all packed and ready to go?"

"No, but I will shove what I can into boxes and suitcases tonight while Brandon is sleeping. I'll have to hide them until we get back with the rental car so he doesn't figure out what is going on."

"Well, pack as much as you can. I'll see about getting you a van instead of a car so you can take as much as possible," Marvin suggested.

"Okay. I won't be able to go back, so I have to get it all in one shot."

"It'll be all right. If you want to come to my house and sleep for awhile before hitting the road..."

"No, Dad. I need to get out of town right away. He knows where you live. I'll stop along the road if I have to."

"Honey, if you are up all night packing, you will need to."

"Depends on my stress level. Right now, sleep is the last thing on my mind. Brandon should go to bed soon, so I need to go."

"All right. Hey, do me a favor. Do not to tell your mother about what you suspect. It would upset her too badly and she is going through enough."

Too late. Emily thought, but didn't say a word. She disagreed with her parents, thinking that they each had a right to know. *I just won't tell Dad that Mom knows and I won't tell Mom that Dad knows.*

Chapter 27

Brandon sat in his room waiting for Emily to get home. *Where could she be at this hour of the night?*

"Yoo hoo! Earth to Brandon."

"Ah, sorry man," Brandon said as he took the joint from Jeff and hit it. The room stunk of all the weed they had been smoking and the smoke was thick like a cloud around the lone light bulb hanging from a wire in the middle rafter. Brandon had hung bandanas advertising many different bands, drugs, alcoholic beverages, and money from the rafters which formed the ceiling. There were rock band posters decorating the walls. The table and floor were covered with empty beer bottles. The ashtrays were overflowing. Judas Priest's *British Steel* album was blasting from the stereo speakers.

"Where were ya, man?" Jeff said as he exhaled.

"Just thinking," Brandon said while trying to hold the smoke in his lungs.

"Obviously! What were you thinking about?"

When Brandon finally exhaled, he answered, "Just wondering where Emily is. She is never out this late; especially on a weeknight. She has to work in the morning." The red glow of the clock read twelve thirty-seven.

"What does it matter? Thought you didn't care about her?"

"I don't!" Brandon snapped. He stood up and walked out of the room.

Gee, I wonder what brought that on. I'll bet he likes her. Whatever the case may be it's obvious he cares, Jeff thought. Jeff lit up a cigarette and relaxed on the sofa in Brandon's room and just marveled at the musical talent of Judas Priest.

Brandon returned a few minutes later. He sat stiffly on the other end of the couch and lit a cigarette. They listened to two songs without saying a word before the album ended. They sat in silence for a few more minutes when Jeff said, "So, what's up, man?"

"Nothin' really. We got in a big fight last night and she hasn't been home much since. I mean she slept here last night, but then left early this morning without a word. I haven't seen her since."

"What were you fighting about?"

"That's just it, man, I don't remember. I was pretty trashed when she came home and I told her about a toy that Rachel had left lying around. I don't remember what all was said, I just know that it got really heated. I have been racking my brain all day trying to remember and I just can't."

Brandon remembered everything that was said, but he didn't want to tell Jeff. Jeff knew him well enough to know something was wrong, but he didn't know that Brandon was lying about how much he remembered.

What does Emily think about what I told her last night? I know I said too much, but how far over the line did I go? I wish she would get home so I could quit worrying about it. Where the heck could she be? What on earth am I going to do about it?

Brandon got up and put in Led Zeppelin's *Houses of the Holy.* "Oh, cool," Jeff said as the tape started playing. He started tapping the arm of the couch in beat with the first song. "This is my favorite Zeppelin record, man."

"I like it, too, but I think Zeppelin II is better," Brandon said.

"Yeah, all the Zeppelin albums are great, man. I wish I could have seen them live, but John Bonham had to…" Jeff stopped midsentence when he heard a car door slam. They both sat there listening for a second one that didn't come. They heard the front door open, close, and footsteps going up the stairs.

"Guess she's still mad," Jeff offered.

"Oh, well, screw her. Hey, man, I'm beat. I think I'm gonna crash," Brandon said hinting that it was time for Jeff to go.

"Oh, yeah, sure." Jeff stood up. He picked up his beer and chugged the rest of it. He put his cigarettes in his pocket. "Later, dude. I'll come by tomorrow after work. I'll have some killer stuff with me."

"Cool, dude. Have a good night." Brandon raised the garage door and let Jeff out. Then he closed it and locked it. He turned the stereo up and walked into the house. He watched out the living room window as Jeff pulled away. Then he walked slowly and quietly up the stairs. He stood in the hallway just outside of Emily's door listening.

He snuck back down and into the garage. He laid down on his bed, staring at the bandana ceiling and began deciding what to do about this little problem.

Chapter 28

Emily worked all night gathering together the things she thought they would need the most. She tried her best to be very quiet. It was hard walking around on the second story of an old house quietly. Brandon was just downstairs and the floors kept creaking. Of course, he was in the garage and her room was above the kitchen and Rachel's room was above the living room, but she was paranoid. She just knew he was going to hear her and come up wanting to know what she was doing. She had been trying to think of something to tell him just in case. She finally decided to tell him that her mother was sick and needed her help, so she was going to go up to Chicago for a while to care for her.

She had brought boxes home from work. She filled up box after box. She numbered the boxes in order of necessity. She wanted to bring them all, but knew that wouldn't be possible.

Once all the boxes were packed up, she put them in Rachel's room and closed the door. She only left out the things that she used every day and night in case Brandon came in her room before they got back with the rental vehicle. She was exhausted and Marvin wouldn't be there for a few hours yet, so she decided to lay down and get some rest.

When she awoke to her alarm, she hit the snooze button. Something didn't feel right. She rolled over groggily and half-opened her eyes. Her eyes flew open in terror when she saw Brandon sitting on the loveseat in her room.

"Sleep well?" he asked.

"Yeah, I did," Emily lied.

"Ah, I see. Even though you only slept for" he stretched to see the clock "two hours and fifteen minutes?"

"Uh, yeah." Emily tried not to panic. *How much does he know? Why is he sitting here questioning me? Did he hear me packing?*

"Can we talk about this?" Brandon asked.

"Talk about what?" Emily asked, trying not to let him hear the fear.

"You know. Now, come on. I heard you moving around up here all night. Then when you stopped moving around, I waited awhile and came up here. I found you asleep and a number of boxes in Rachel's room. All of her clothes are packed up and most of her toys are. Speaking of Rachel, where is she?"

"She is still at Katherine's. I told you she was going over there last night to spend time with her daughter." Katherine didn't even have a daughter. Her son was a few years younger than Rachel, but Brandon didn't know that.

"Who is this Katherine chick? Why doesn't she ever come around? I don't think I've met her. If she is such a good friend of yours, you would think she would come over once in awhile." Emily didn't want to discuss this. She just wanted him to go away so she could get dressed and be ready when Marvin got there.

"She is a friend of mine. Now, if you don't mind, I have things to do today." Emily slid up into a sitting position and leaned against the wall.

"Actually, I do mind. I want to know what is going on here. What's up with all the boxes?"

"I have to go to Chicago. Mom is sick and..."

Brandon cut her off. "Your mother is just fine, so don't even try it. Look, I know that you are still having a hard time dealing with the whole fire thing. I am, too, but don't you think we could work through this together?" Emily didn't like the crazed look in Brandon's eyes. She reached for the phone to call Marvin and tell him to come now, but the phone was not on her nightstand. Terror began to set in.

"No, Brandon..." Brandon held his hand up to hush her.

"I'm talking, you're listening. Do you think you can do that? Just shut up and listen?" Emily took a breath. "Don't answer. Just listen."

Emily started to move like she was going to get up. Brandon quickly, but casually, moved over in front of the door, which Emily noticed was locked. If she didn't lean on something she was going to faint from the weight of the terror that was gripping her heart. She settled back against the wall.

"I know that you were dealing with a lot. I mean, single-parenthood is tough, so you decided to kill yourself. You thought if you set the house on fire it wouldn't look like a suicide. You thought that your parents would handle an accident better than suicide. You couldn't figure out a way to do it and protect all three of the kids, so you decided to take Michael and Leslie with you. Rachel was your favorite and so you planned it when you knew she would be safe at school. I know that you loved Michael and Leslie. In fact, you loved them so much that you thought it would be better for them to die, since growing up in this racist society would be so hard on them. Isn't that right, Emily? You did what you thought was best for your children?"

He is accusing ME of starting the fire?! Emily couldn't believe what she was hearing. All fear turned to anger. She wanted to kill him with her bare hands. She tried to get up to do just that, but something was holding her against the wall. She couldn't move. It was as if a strong man had his hands on her shoulders holding her down. She could feel the hands of a non-existent person on her shoulders. Brandon didn't seem to notice.

Emily couldn't believe she was hearing this. *I have to get out of here. Dad should be here soon. Oh, I hope he is early.* She stole a peek at the clock. Marvin was due in fifteen minutes. *Please hurry, Dad. Please hurry.* Emily begged silently.

"I thought of a way that you can finish your plan." Brandon pulled a piece of paper from behind his back, "See, all you have to do is copy this in your hand-writing and then I will help you finish what you started. I know you're nervous and scared, and that is why I'll be here for encouragement. You know it's what you want. It is what you've always wanted. And it is best for everyone in your life. Rachel doesn't need a mother like you. No, you pawn her off every chance you get so that you can go out whoring around. She would be much better off with your parents. Your parents would be better off without you to support financially or emotionally. I mean, haven't you put them through enough? Your friends don't need you. You don't really have any friends, just stoner buddies. I sure as hell don't need you. There are plenty of other fat, ugly sluts like you that I can split the bills with. So, why don't you do us all a favor and finish what you started."

He walked over to the bed and handed her the note he had written, a pad of blank paper and a pen. He sat back down on the loveseat. Emily was appalled by what she was reading.

Mom and Dad, I am so sorry, but I just couldn't take it anymore. I can't live without Michael and Leslie, so I am leaving this earth. Please take care of Rachel for me. I have packed all of her clothes and favorite toys for you. Tell her that I love her and that I will see her in heaven someday. Please forgive me for all the grief and pain that I have caused everyone. Tell Brandon that I appreciate all that he has done for me. I will miss you. Love, Emily.

Emily knew that her parents would never buy this note. Even if she hadn't told them what was going on, just the fact that the note said she was going to heaven would tell them that she didn't write it. They knew she didn't believe in heaven.

Emily sat staring at the note for as long as possible. She was trying to kill time. *Dad should be here soon. I hope he hurries.*

"Come on. I don't have all day. I have some boxes in Rachel's room to unpack; I'll have to unpack all of your stuff. And then I have some important phone calls to make. Your parents are going to want to know about your death right away."

She took the pen in her hand and poised it over the paper. *I don't want to write this. I don't want to die this way. I want to be here for Rachel.* Tears began to well up in her eyes.

Chapter 29

S he heard a knock on the door.

Brandon heard it, too. He moved back in front of the bedroom door. "You had better hope that they are knocking on the neighbor's door." Emily sat there stunned. She didn't know what to do. She didn't want to write the note. She knew it was Marvin at the front door and she was in the back bedroom on the second floor. How could she get his attention? She tried to act like she was so upset about what was going on in the bedroom, that she didn't notice the knocking.

The pounding on the door got louder and more persistent. Brandon cussed. "Don't even think about leaving this room. I'm going to get rid of whoever is at the door." Emily kept looking at the suicide note he had given her, as if she wasn't aware of the world around her.

When Brandon left the room he closed the door behind him. Emily snuck over to it quietly. She opened the door very slowly, peering out. She didn't see anything. She could hear Brandon talking to her father through the closed front door, "She is sleeping right now."

She couldn't hear what Marvin's response was, but it was obvious he wasn't buying Brandon's excuses. Brandon was getting irate. Marvin wasn't giving up and going away. Of course, Brandon didn't know that Marvin knew the potential danger that his daughter was in. The more Brandon refused to open the door, the more determined Marvin was to get in the house.

Emily slipped out into the hallway. There was no way she could sneak downstairs because the front door was at the bottom of the stairwell.

Finally, Brandon ignored Marvin and bounded back up the stairs. He was going to grab Emily, kill her and then himself, but Emily had other plans. As Brandon reached the top of the stairs, Emily hit him in the face full force with an aluminum baseball bat she had gotten from Rachel's room. She had positioned herself behind the wall at the top of the stairs, waiting for Brandon to come back up.

Brandon went flying back down the stairs and landed in a heap against the front door. Marvin started pounding frantically, not knowing what was going on. Emily ran down the stairs. She knew she couldn't move Brandon's limp, unconscious body, so she just stepped over him. She yelled, "Go to the back door, Dad!"

Marvin ran around the house as quickly as he could. Emily was standing at the back door, bloody baseball bat in hand, shaking like a leaf. Marvin put his arms around his daughter. "Are you all right?"

"I will be as soon as I get out of here."

"Well, I got you a van. It's in the driveway. I thought it would be better for me to go ahead and get it and then let you take me back to the airport to get my car."

"That was a good idea, because there would've been no way for me to come back with the van if you hadn't. Once I leave, that is it." Emily paused, a look of fear clouding her eyes, "unless, of course, he's dead. I may have killed him, Dad."

Marvin let go of his daughter and walked through the house. He found Brandon lying still against the door, but he was breathing. "He isn't dead, honey. It looks like he is going to have a serious headache when he wakes up, though." Emily saw the bloody lump quickly forming on his forehead, and his right eye was already swollen shut.

"Guess the girls' little league's finally paying off," Emily said under her breath relieved that she hadn't killed him.

Marvin took Brandon by the ankles and pulled him into the middle of the living room. He opened the door wide and said, "help me move the big stuff while he is still out cold. Then, if he wakes up, you can get the other stuff moved while I watch him."

There weren't very many heavy boxes. Once those were loaded up, Emily carried the lighter boxes down the stairs and handed them to Marvin who put them in the van while keeping a close eye on Brandon. As they were loading one of the last boxes, they heard Brandon moaning. "You finish, I'll watch him."

"All right, Dad."

Emily tried to ignore Brandon as she carried the last of the boxes down the stairs and out the front door. She glanced over and saw him sitting on the floor propped up against the couch with Marvin watching him closely. Brandon was looking at the puddle of blood in the middle of the living room floor and holding his shirt against the wound on the back of his head. He was obviously confused.

"I'm done," she announced coming back in the house.

Brandon looked at her for the first time. The hatred in his eyes was unmistakable. Emily broke the eye contact as soon as it was made.

"Would you like me to call an ambulance for you?" Marvin asked Brandon as he made his way toward the door.

"No. I'll be fine," Brandon mumbled.

"Good answer. There is no need to get the police involved in this, right?" Without giving Brandon time to respond, Marvin put his arm around Emily and escorted her out of the townhouse for the last time.

On the way to the airport to pick up Marvin's car, Emily told him all that had happened before he arrived.

"So, you are telling me that if I hadn't gotten the van first, I would have been there in time to prevent that?"

"Yeah, and I would have NOTHING! I couldn't have gone back. He would have destroyed it all before I got back there."

"You're right, but as your father, I feel like I should have done more to save you from what you went through this morning."

"Well, if you were a mind-reader I would have expected you to do more. How could you possibly have known what he was up to? Don't feel guilty and beat yourself up about it, Dad."

"You know, I could say the same thing to you about the fire." That comment hit Emily like a ton of bricks. She had been blaming herself for the fire – feeling guilty that she hadn't seen what kind of person Brandon was and therefore, did nothing to prevent the death of her children.

After dropping Marvin off at the airport, Emily headed to Katherine's house to get Rachel. They didn't waste any time there. Emily wanted to hit the road as soon as possible. It was only a matter of time before Brandon completely regained his composure. Then what would he do?

She had plenty of time to think and to worry. It was an eight-hour drive to Chicago.

Chapter 30

After Emily left, Brandon sat hunched against the couch thinking. It was slowly coming back to him. *She hit me with something and knocked me down the stairs. What did she hit me with? I didn't think she had it in her.*

Brandon sat there for hours trying to figure out how much Emily knew and how he would go about finding out for sure if she knew anything. He couldn't threaten her. If he did that, than she would know something was going on worthy of the threats. He couldn't start asking questions because that, too, would make him look suspicious. Besides, she wouldn't tell anyone everything except her family and they definitely wouldn't tell him anything.

Something was bothering him about the way that Marvin had said, "There is no need to get the police involved in this, right?" *Why did he sneer when he said the word police? How much did Marvin know?*

He had to come up with a plan. He was still a little light-headed when he stood up. He went to the bathroom and gathered some towels. He tried to clean up the blood but it was dry so he couldn't get it out of the carpet. He washed the blood off of the door. He tried to think of something to tell his friends to explain the big blood stain on the carpet. He couldn't come up with anything but he remembered a throw rug Emily had had in her room. He found it rolled up against the wall in the corner. He struggled to get it down the stairs and laid it out on the floor.

Geez, my head hurts, he thought as he put his hand on the back of his head. He felt matted blood and decided to shower. As he caught a glimpse of himself in the bathroom mirror, he remembered about his eye. It was now solid black and almost swollen shut. *How did I not notice that?* He was so intent on figuring how much Emily knew, he didn't even realize his eye was swollen!

As he showered he tried to think of something that would sound good but not give him away. He hadn't told anyone about starting the fire and he wasn't going to now.

He still hadn't come up with a plan when there was a knock on the door. Brandon looked at the throw rug on the way to answer the door. It wasn't obvious at all. The only thing that might catch someone's attention, other than the eye, of course, was that the welcome mat was now inside the front door instead of outside, but he had to cover that blood somehow, too.

"Hey... Oh, dude, what happened to your face?" Jeff asked as Brandon let him in the house.

"Emily flipped, man! She just totally snapped on me this morning and smacked me with a freaking baseball bat, man."

"Where is she now? I saw her car out front." Brandon looked and sure enough Emily's car was in the street in front of the house. He hadn't even noticed.

"She loaded up a van and left; said she was going to see her mom in Chicago."

"Well, that's good. She needed to get away from here."

"Obviously! Look what she did to my face! She's gone off the deep end, I tell ya." The more Brandon talked along these lines, the more he liked it. If he could make it sound to everyone like Emily was crazy; then even if she did start talking, no one would believe her. *Even if she calls the police, they will question people AFTER I have already convinced them that Emily is crazy. People will tell the police that Emily flipped. The police are going to believe them over a crazy grieving mother who feels the need to lay the blame somewhere – a coping mechanism that many grieving people subconsciously use. Ah, this is going to work out better than I thought it would.*

"What did she say?" Jeff asked.

"I asked her what was wrong because she was still giving me the silent treatment. She told me not to talk to her. I said, 'We can't live together if we can't even speak to each other.' She said, 'fine, I'll move out.' I said, "Oh, Emily, you don't have to move; we can work this out.' She started screaming at me and calling me names.

Then she said something that blew my mind! She said, 'Get out of my face and get out of my life, you murderer.' I was stunned."

"She called you a murderer? Why would she say that? Who does she think you killed?" Jeff was flabbergasted.

"Get this! She thinks I started her house on fire! She thinks I killed her kids and that I was trying to kill her! Do you believe that?" Brandon said incredulously.

"Wow, she really did flip! Why did she hit you?" Jeff was interested in what was going on with Emily, but he didn't want Brandon to know that he cared about her. He made it sound like he was just interested in the gossip. "Tell me the rest of the story."

"She went upstairs and I followed her. I told her not to go, that we could work this out. She said there was nothing to work out, unless I could bring her kids back. She carried a box of toys down the stairs. I touched her arm and asked again if we could talk about this. She grabbed the baseball bat out of the box and whacked me upside the head with it."

"Holy cow! That doesn't even sound like Emily," Jeff said half under his breath. He couldn't believe what he was hearing. *Well, it's good that she is going to be with her mom then. At least her mother will get her the mental help she needs.*

"I know. I know," Brandon said shaking his head as if in disbelief.

Chapter 31

Wow, I hadn't realized that I was being so hard on myself until Dad said that I should stop beating myself about the fire. How could I have known what Brandon had done? He seemed like a really nice guy when we lived next door to each other. I needed help with the bills and so did he, so we moved in together. In a way, I'm glad we did, too, or I wouldn't know what I know now. I don't understand why he decided to live with me knowing what he had done to me, though. And all because he was being evicted. That's an extremely strange reason to risk the lives of three people. I don't think I have ever seen such selfishness. Dad is right, there is no way I could have known that Brandon was a psychopath.

Emily had been driving for almost three hours, her mind going non-stop the whole time. Rachel was sitting in the seat beside her quietly watching the state of Kentucky go by. "Mommy, I have to go potty."

"All right. I want to get a snack. Do you want something?"

"Yeah! Ice cream!" Rachel said excitedly.

"Ice cream?!" Emily said, laughing. "It is twenty degrees outside and you want ice cream? Why don't we get some cookies and milk?" Emily suggested.

"Okay, but I want chocolate chip," Rachel cheered.

Emily got off at the next exit. They found a mini market and parked close to the front door.

They walked around for a while. Emily stopped to look at the books. Rachel saw a row full of toys the next isle over. "Can I look at the toys, Mom?"

"Yeah, I guess, but if anyone comes in the isle you come back over here."

"Okay, Mom."

Emily was looking at the novels. She needed a new book to read. She didn't see anything that interested her. Just as she was walking away a Bible caught her eye. It was just a simple red leather bound Bible. She picked it up. It was marked five dollars. *New King James Version. I think Mom likes this one. Oh, what the heck.*

She went to the toy isle and found Rachel looking at some travel games. "Whatcha got there?" she asked.

"Look, Mom, this is neat." Rachel held the toy up so her mother could see it. "It is a little park with ponds and paths and stuff. It is made of metal and the people have magnets on them so I won't lose them in the car. Can I get it, please? Please?" she begged.

"How much is it?" Emily asked.

Rachel turned it over, "five ninety-nine. Please?"

"Yeah, I guess," Emily agreed.

"Cool." Rachel said jumping up and following her mother to the register. She placed the cookies, milk and Bible on the counter.

"That park thing she has is five ninety-nine," she told the clerk.

When they got out to the van, she told Rachel to get in and put her seatbelt on. Emily unwrapped Bible and opened it to the very beginning. "In the beginning…" She read just a few verses. *I'll have to read that part that Rebecca put on that card when I get to Mom's. I can understand this one better than that one at the funeral home.*

Emily stuck the receipt from the gas station where she was just reading, closed the Bible and started the van. As she drove, she thought about God. *I don't know why, but since Michael and Leslie died I have been curious about God. Does he really exist? Does heaven really exist? If so, how does a person get to heaven and how do I know that Michael and Leslie are there?* She looked over at Rachel snoring on the seat beside her. "All right, God, you got my attention," she said out loud. "I am really not sure if you exist or not, but Mom and Dad think you do. Rebecca thinks you do and for some reason thought that I needed to know that your Bible says you will help me deal with my kids'…" She stopped. She couldn't bring herself to say the word 'murder'.

As she drove and thought, the desire to read more of the Bible grew stronger and stronger. But she didn't want to stop. She wanted to get as far away from Nashville as she could, as quickly as she could.

Rachel was sound asleep in the seat next to her as she approached Indianapolis and realized she hadn't gotten any gas since leaving Nashville. She pulled off the Interstate and into a gas station. Rachel didn't wake up when she stopped the car, so she decided to read the Bible again for a few minutes.

She held it on her lap and as she was trying to open it where the receipt was, it fell open in Psalm. She began reading chapter thirty-seven. "Do not fret because of evil-doers, nor be envious of the workers of iniquity. For they shall soon be cut down like the grass, and wither as the green herb. Trust in the Lord and do good; dwell in the land and feed on his faithfulness. Delight yourself in the Lord and He will give you the desires of your heart. Commit your way to the Lord. Trust also in Him and He shall bring it to pass. He shall bring forth your righteousness as the light, and your justice as the noonday. Rest in the Lord, and wait patiently for Him; do not fret because of him who prospers in his way, because of the man who brings wicked schemes to pass. Cease from anger and forsake wrath; do not fret – it only causes harm. For evildoers shall be cut off; but those who wait on the Lord, they shall inherit the earth. For yet a little while and the wicked shall be no more; indeed, you will look carefully for his place but it shall be no more. But the meek shall inherit the earth, and shall delight themselves in the abundance of peace."

She stopped there at the end of verse eleven. *Wow, I am not quite sure what all of that means, but I can tell that if I have to chose sides, I don't want to be on the evil-doers side. But it says, "He shall bring forth your righteousness as the light".* I haven't been righteous by any stretch of the imagination. I mean, I could be worse, yeah, but I'm far from righteous.

She continued to think about this as she put gas in the van. She woke Rachel for another bathroom break and they quickly hit the road again. Rachel fell back to sleep as soon as they passed through the city of Indianapolis and the scenery became flat, boring, corn fields with an occasional barn off in the distance.

Some of the verses she memorized in church when she was a kid came flooding back.

Not by works of righteousness, which we have done, but according to His mercy He saved us, through the washing of regeneration and renewing of the Holy Spirit. Titus 3:5.

For by grace you have been saved through faith, and that not of yourselves; it is the gift of God, not of works, lest anyone should boast. Ephesians 2:8-9

For all have sinned and fall short of the glory of God. Romans 3:23

For the wages of sin is death, but the gift of God is eternal life in Jesus Christ our Lord. Romans 6:23

He has shown you, O man, what is good; and what does the Lord require of you but to do justly, to love mercy, and to walk humbly with our God? Micah 6:8

I remember the verses I memorized, but I don't know what they mean now any more than I did when I was a kid. I guess I will have to break down and ask someone. I don't really want to ask Mom. She will get all fanatical thinking that I am ready to be 'converted'. No, I can't ask Mom. Maybe Uncle Joe will answer my questions and keep it to himself, for the time being anyway.

Chapter 32

"Uncle Joe?" Emily and Uncle Joe were unloading the van into the storage unit that Terri had rented for her.

"Yeah, Em."

"I was wondering if you and I could talk, you know, confidentially, sometime. I have some questions about the Bible, but I don't want to ask Mom. You know how she is."

"Sure, Emily. I would like that." Joe paused before adding, "You know, your mother means well."

"I know she does, but she gets so worked up about it every time the subject comes up. I get worn out just trying to ward her off. I am not getting converted or anything. I just have some questions. That's all." Emily was grateful for the time that she and Uncle Joe were getting to spend together. Uncle Joe was a big part of her life when she was growing up. He used to work at the bakery at the end of the road that she lived on when she was a kid. He would come over almost every day after work.

Rachel and Larry were playing together at Terri's and Rhonda was cooking dinner while Joe and Emily were unloading the van and then returning it to the rental car company. They were going to meet at Joe and Rhonda's for dinner.

"I understand. We can either talk on the way back home or we can go out tonight after dinner."

"I think I would rather go out after dinner. I don't know how long it will take and I would really like to spend some time with you. You know, like we used to," Emily said grinning.

"Sounds good to me," Joe said as he picked up another box and began to carry it into the storage unit.

"I bought a Bible at a gas station on the way here." Emily didn't see the surprised look on Joe's face. "I don't want Mom to know about it. Can I leave it in your car until morning? Then I'll get it from you while she's at work."

"That's fine with me. I just wish you weren't so paranoid about your mom knowing you are reading the Bible. There is nothing wrong with that."

"I know there is nothing wrong with it. It's just that Mom will say things like, 'Oh, this is just what I have been praying for' or 'are you ready to accept Jesus?' and she'll be so excited, she won't answer my questions without getting all emotional about me asking them. I have tried to ask her stuff before and all she does is confuse me."

"I understand. Really, I do. I could talk to your mom, if you want me to."

"No, Uncle Joe," Emily said firmly. "I really just want to ask some questions without Mom even knowing I am asking at this point. I'll tell Mom when I am ready to." *If I am ever ready to,* Emily added silently.

~ ~ ~ ~ ~ ~ ~

"I told them we were going to Papa Passero's Pizza like we used to do when you were a kid," Joe said as they got in the car.

"Cool. Just like old times. Except that there isn't a race tonight," Emily said feeling like they were sneaking out.

"They don't know that," Joe said laughing.

After they were finished shooting the breeze for a little while, Emily told Uncle Joe everything that had happened with Brandon and what she came up with when she put two and two together. "So, now I have to get on the phone tomorrow and call the police in Nashville and tell them."

"Wow, Emily. I'm so sorry to hear all of this. And I am mad – mad at him for killing Michael and Leslie, but more mad at him for putting you and your family through all of this. He really did Michael and Leslie a favor, because now they don't have to put up with the crap that we have to put up with on this earth, but what he did to you was cruel. You are the real victim here."

"Well, I don't think that he has done Michael and Leslie a favor, but that kind of opens the door to what I wanted to talk to you about." Emily told Uncle Joe about the card that Rebecca had given her.

She opened the Bible that she bought to the passage in Isaiah that Rebecca had written in the card and let Uncle Joe read it.

"Wow! So, this is what prompted you to go buy a Bible?" Joe said when he finished reading.

"Yeah. I was trying to figure out what it means," Emily said curiously.

"It means that you can find strength in God. If you trust in Him, He will be with you through it all. Romans 8:28 says 'And we know that all things work together for good for those who love the Lord and live according to His purpose.' So, He can take this and make it good."

"Well, I wasn't, and still am not, a Christian and I don't know if I will ever be one," Emily stated.

"Well, we'll just have to wait and see what God plans to do with this, but I can guarantee He will do something with it, because your parents and brothers are Christians. Do you have any more questions?"

"Yeah," Emily turned to Psalm 37. "What does iniquity mean?"

"Sin. It's just another word for sin."

"Okay. Well, when I was reading this, I'll tell you, I don't want to be an evil-doer or worker of iniquity. I don't want this," she pointed to the passage, "to happen to me!"

"Well, honey, you might want to seriously consider becoming a Christian then. If you don't, that is exactly what is going to happen to you."

"But, I'm a good person. I don't think I'm an evil-doer!" she said defensively.

"Oh, Emily, I know you are a good person, but no one is good enough to get into heaven by doing good. The Bible says in Romans 3:23 that everyone has sinned and fallen short of the glory of God."

"I know, which leads me to my next question. I memorized a number of verses when I was growing up and they were swimming around in my brain on the way up here. I didn't understand them back then, and I don't understand them now. Maybe you could explain them to me."

They sat in the restaurant they had sat in many times when Emily was in her early teens. She felt very comfortable there and with him. They talked for hours. Uncle Joe explained the verses that Emily had memorized when she was a child. She understood what they were saying now, but she still didn't quite understand the whole accepting Jesus thing. It kind of made sense, but she was still somewhat confused.

"Thanks, Uncle Joe. I really learned a lot tonight. I am still not ready to be 'converted' as Mom puts it, but I have some stuff to think about. If I have any more questions, I'll let you know."

"Good. I am glad I could help. Maybe we'll have to make this a regular outing again. I miss watching the races with you."

"Me, too," Emily said smiling.

Chapter 33

Emily spent the next day on the phone. She called the police in Nashville first. After being transferred countless times, she was finally talking to a homicide detective. *Maybe he can help.*

"Homicide. Detective Caruthers, can I help you?"

"I hope so. I have talked to six million people today. I am calling because my children were killed in a fire back in September. At the time, the cause was unknown, but now I have reason to believe that the fire was intentionally set. I believe the man who lived next door to me at the time is the one who did it." Emily proceeded to tell him everything she knew, why she suspected him, and where she was now.

Detective Caruthers listened attentively and took vague notes. He told Emily he would check into it and would get back with her within a week. They exchanged phone numbers and hung up.

Emily felt better now that someone in authority knew what she suspected and was checking it out.

~ ~ ~ ~ ~ ~ ~

Emily spent the next few weeks looking for a job and hanging out at the library. She checked out a number of books on grief, especially those dealing with the death of children. She talked to someone from Compassionate Friends, a nationwide self-help group of parents who have lost children due to many different causes of death and want to use their experience to help others. It was helpful just to talk to someone who knew the pain she was experiencing. It was also helpful to talk to someone who didn't know Brandon or the whole situation. Emily also called Gale, Angie's mom. Angie was the friend of Emily's from high school who had been murdered just under a year ago. She was a graduate student at an out-of-state college. She had been seeing a guy for about six weeks and when she went home with him for the first time, he raped and strangled her to death. He hid her body, which was discovered five weeks after the murder.

Gale and Emily met for dinner one night. Gale said that she still hadn't cleaned out Angie's room.

"Well, I wasn't given the option as to when to clean out rooms. The fire took care of that for me," Emily stated regretfully.

"That's where I feel closest to Angie. I'll go in her bedroom to cry and remember her. I don't go in as often as I used to, but I still like to have it just how she left it."

"That place for me would have to be the grave, but it's in Tennessee, so I can't go there now. Maybe that is why I feel so far away from them."

"It might be. It is really soon for you to have left. I mean, I understand why you did, but that has to be tough on you," Gale sympathized.

"It is. Do you find yourself wanting to take care of Angie's things? Like cleaning her room even though she isn't there to dirty it?" Emily asked.

"Yes, why do you ask?"

"It's just that every time I go to the grave, I bring a rag and clean the grave marker really good. I try to keep nice, fresh flowers in it at all times. Before I left to come up here, I brought some artificial flowers so they would stay nice for a while. I just feel the need to take care of it for them, but I feel like a nutcase," she confided.

"That is your maternal instinct. It's normal. It was your job as their mother to take care of them, clean up after them and all that stuff. You still feel those urges. Don't feel like a nutcase."

Emily asked some questions about the legal system. Gale had a really hard time with those because Angie's murderer still hadn't gone to trial.

"But at least he is behind bars while we wait. I can't imagine what you are going through, knowing he did this and is free as a bird. Has he tried to come after you since you left Nashville?"

"No. Now, my biggest fear is that he will get away with it."

"I can understand that. Luckily for us, there was no question about it being murder or who did it. Now it is just a matter of proving it. They will get him, Emily. Just give them time."

Gale had encouraged Emily more that words could express. One of the books that Emily had picked up ended with a sobering thought. "Do you want to live or just exist?" *I can't answer that yet. Right now, I just want to find some kind of normalcy in my life while I wait for the police to do their job.*

~ ~ ~ ~ ~ ~ ~

A few more weeks went by. Emily had found a temporary job working in an office. She was doing filing and answering phones, but that was fine with her. It was money coming in and she didn't have to think real hard. She wasn't sure if she could handle work that was mentally taxing.

She had called Detective Caruthers a number of times and left messages. He rarely called her back and when he did, it was always when she wasn't home.

Occasionally, the phone would ring in the middle of the night and when Emily would answer, the other person would hang up. She was having a hard enough time sleeping. She didn't need that. She suspected it was Brandon. He could have an old phone bill that had her mother's phone number on it. And they couldn't figure who else would do that.

Chapter 34

In mid-March, Emily sat Terri down. "Mom, I need to talk to you."

"What's up?"

"I need to go to Nashville."

"Why?" Terri sounded concerned and frustrated at the same time.

"Because the police haven't called me other than those few times that he left a message. I need to find out what is going with this."

"Oh, Okay. I thought this was some big news you had to tell me the way you sat me down and said 'we need to talk'," Terri said sounding relieved.

"Well, it is big news. I'm not talking about taking a trip. I want to move back to Nashville."

"Oh, Emily. Why? Why do you want to uproot Rachel like that again? She's finally settled here. She has friends here. Why can't you just go to Nashville for a week, do what you have to do, and then come back here?"

"Mom, I don't want to live here for a few reasons. I am finding out that I can't solve the problems from here. I can't stay on the police from here. I can't plant myself in the police station there and say 'I'm not leaving until I get answers' if I am here. Nashville is my home. I don't like it here anymore. Yes, I was raised here, but this isn't where I belong anymore. And the grave is in Nashville. I need to be able to go to the grave whenever I need to be near the kids."

"Well, that is just ridiculous! The kids aren't in the grave..."

Emily cut her off. "I know, I know. They're in heaven," she said very sarcastically. "I don't want to start that again. Look, I have found out that a lot of parents need something or some place tangible to feel their kids' presence. For me that place is the grave, regardless of where their spirits are."

"I don't like the idea. I think you should stay here."

"Well, I don't like it here. I'm sorry, Mom. It isn't you. It's Chicago. Actually, other than the cold, it isn't even Chicago. It is the fact that this isn't home anymore."

"Well, I don't understand that. Chicago has always been your home. You were raised here. You have family here – family that loves you. All you have in Nashville is your dad and he isn't home most of the time anyway," Terri reasoned.

"I have a lot of friends in Nashville, too. And they love me. If home is where the heart is, then Nashville is home. I, also, have a job there, which I absolutely love. I need to go back." Emily didn't know how to express the loneliness she had felt the whole time she was in Chicago.

"You can get a better job here. You just took the first one that was offered to you. All you have to do is look some more," Terri argued.

"I don't want to, Mom, and I don't want to discuss it anymore. I'm sorry, but I am going home," Emily stated firmly.

The next few days were very awkward around the house. Uncle Joe took Emily out to eat again and tried to talk her into staying. She knew immediately that Terri had put him up to it, because he was saying all the same things she had said. It wasn't as difficult to explain to Uncle Joe why she wanted to go home. Just before they left the restaurant, he said, "I understand why you want to go back. My only concern is Rachel. She needs stability and she has that right now. That, and I am going to miss the Papa Passero's nights again."

"I will miss the Papa Passero's night's, too, but I have to go on with my life and I have to get justice for Michael and Leslie."

When they returned home, Uncle Joe, Terri and Emily sat around Terri's dining room table discussing the move.

Uncle Joe said, "I understand why she wants to go back to Nashville, Terri. My concern is Rachel's safety and emotional well-being."

"Well, that is one of my biggest concerns, also," Terri replied looking at Emily.

"I agree that it wouldn't be in Rachel's best interest to move her again at this point in time," Emily said. "She has been through enough this school year and moving her again in the middle of school won't help. I'm also concerned about her safety. If Brandon should find out where I'm staying and come after me, I don't want Rachel to get hurt in the process. I was thinking that maybe it would be best if Rachel was to stay here with you, Mom, at least until summer. That will give me time to find a place and get settled. And she wouldn't have to change schools until after she is done with first grade."

"I think that would be better than moving her again now. She needs some stability. I would like you to at least think about moving up here when you are done doing what you feel you need to do in Nashville," Terri pleaded.

"I will think about it, but I won't make any promises. Are you staying here forever? What about Dad?"

"That's neither here nor there at this point." Terri made it very clear that her relationship with Marvin was a closed topic for now.

After much discussion, they finally agreed, albeit reluctantly, that Emily should go back to Nashville.

Emily made all the arrangements. She would be leaving in two weeks.

Chapter 35

Katherine picked Emily up at the airport and took her to her house where Emily would be staying. She thought Katherine's was probably the safest place in Nashville, simply because Brandon didn't know Katherine, let alone where she lived. Emily got her old job back and started working immediately. She would have to wait for a few weeks before she would have the money to get a vehicle, but since she and Katherine worked together it would be fine.

She called the police again two days after her arrival and left Detective Caruthers another message with her new phone number. Another week went by with no reply. Katherine asked Emily if she wanted a ride to the police station.

"I hate to impose on you. I don't know how long I will be there. I am planning on going when I get a car," Emily explained.

"I think you should go as soon as possible," Katherine said.

"Well, when I go I'm going to camp out in the waiting room until he'll hear me out."

"I will sit with you for awhile. If it will be too long, I can leave and come back when you are ready to be picked up."

"Thanks, Katherine. What would I do without you?"

Ten days after her return to Nashville, Emily walked into the police station. "I need to see Detective Caruthers," she announced to the woman in a police uniform behind the window.

"He isn't in right now," the uniform stated.

"I'll wait."

"Well, ma'am, he may be a few hours," she said trying to talk Emily out of waiting.

"That's fine. My name is Emily Payne and this is regarding an arson, which resulted in the death of my two children back in September. I have left numerous messages over the last month and he has yet to call me back. I'll wait," she said firmly.

As Emily walked away, she heard the receptionist call Detective Caruthers on the radio and let him know that she was there. She joined Katherine in the waiting room.

About a half an hour later, Emily looked up to see a small, serious looking man enter the waiting room. He had short, dark hair circling the bald dome on top of his head. He was wearing blue jeans and a white button-down shirt with a dark blue tie. "Ms. Payne?" he said looking back and forth between Emily and Katherine.

"Yes, Sir," Emily said standing and offering her hand.

"Detective Caruthers. Nice to meet you."

"Nice to meet you, too. This is my friend, Katherine." Emily pointed to Katherine who had also risen and offered her hand.

"Hello, Katherine." Turning back to Emily, Detective Caruthers said, "Come on back and let's talk." Emily followed Detective Caruthers to his cubicle. It was a small hole in the middle of a big room. There was barely room to move around. Detective Caruthers pulled a thin file out of the file drawer labeled "Carter, Michael and Leslie 9/30/93."

"This is what I have..." Detective Caruthers read all of his notes to Emily. Every single piece of information he had in the file, Emily had given him.

"Well, that answers my first question right there. You haven't discovered anything new since the first time I talked to you."

"No, I haven't. I don't know what you thought I might find, because there is nothing to find," Caruthers stated sounding as if Emily was interrupting his day and he didn't want to spend this time talking to her.

"What about the arrest from the fire in Georgia?"

"Non-existent."

"I don't think he was arrested under his real name. I think he used an alias," Emily said.

"Then the only hope we have is to get his fingerprints so we can match them up with the national data base."

"So, how are you going to get his prints?"

"That's the problem. I don't have any way of getting of his prints. Unless you could bring something in that has his prints on it, but it would have to be a whole print, not smeared and preferably only his print on the item." Detective Caruthers looked off into space in deep thought. "Actually," he began thinking out loud, "that probably wouldn't do though, because an officer would have to collect the sample to identify that the print on the object actually belonged to him. No, the only way we could get them is if he's arrested for something."

"So, you have done nothing on this? Have you even looked for more evidence?" Emily concluded.

"Like I said, I don't know what you think we might find. This case is six months old, all the evidence is long gone."

"So, there is nothing that can be done?" Emily began to tear up.

"I'm sorry. There just isn't enough. I understand where you are coming from. Every grieving mother needs someone to blame. That's normal, but it'll pass. You'll see."

"You think I am sitting here just because I am grieving!? You think I am wrong, don't you? You don't think he did it, do you?"

"It wouldn't be the first time someone came in here falsely accusing an ex just because she needed fault placed somewhere. Look, Ms. Payne, I believe this fire was an accident – a tragic accident, but nevertheless, an accident."

"He wasn't, I mean isn't my ex. He was my neighbor. That's all."

"Oh. I thought you lived together."

"We lived together *just as* roommates for a few months after the fire. Then he made comments and did things that made me begin to wonder. Brandon setting the house on fire intentionally is the only thing that fits all of the loose pieces together."

"Well, we need more of those loose pieces first. We just don't have enough right now. If you find out anything new, let me know."

Emily was furious and crying as she entered the waiting room. Katherine didn't ask. She just put her arms around her friend knowing that Emily would open up about it all when she was ready.

Emily called Mr. Allison, the fire investigator who worked on the case. They went out to lunch one day and Emily expressed her concerns to him.

"I'm sorry, Emily. I didn't find anything to support the arson theory. True, we don't know what started the fire, but we can't just automatically assume that it was arson. We always look for signs of arson when the cause of ignition is unknown, which we did in this case. There was no accelerator, like gasoline, for instance, used. There were no explosives used. There were no signs of breaking and entering. There is really nothing at all to indicate that arson was the cause."

Emily felt crushed. She didn't know what to do or think. All she knew was that she was going to do everything in her power to make sure that he didn't get away with it. One way or another, Emily was determined to see that justice was served. She knew in heart that he did it, now all she had to do was convince the law enforcement officials that she was correct.

Chapter 36

One night, Emily was out at a local bar and happened to run into Kim.

"Hey, Girl, what's up? Haven't seen you, well, since January," Kim said when she saw Emily sitting at the bar.

"Not much. I haven't been around much since January." Kim was one of Brandon's friends who Emily actually got along with.

"Well, he is doing about the same. He moved in with Greg after you left and..." Kim began filling Emily in on Brandon.

Emily interrupted her. "No offense, Kim, but I really don't care what Brandon has been up to."

"What made you leave so suddenly anyway?" Kim asked curiously.

Emily had been wondering what he was telling people. "What did he tell you?"

"He said you just freaked out one day. That you were going to kill yourself, but your dad showed up and talked you into moving in with your mom in Chicago. He said your parents thought it was being around here that was driving you crazy."

"Well, that is partially true, but not entirely," Emily said somewhat surprised that Brandon had said anything true.

"So, what is the truth?" Kim inquired.

Emily proceeded to tell Kim the basics of what she knew. She didn't reveal any of the evidence she had other than Brandon telling her about starting Suzie's house on fire. She, also, told her about the meetings with Detective Caruthers and Mr. Allison.

Kim got excited. "Hey, I have an idea! A way we can get him arrested."

"Really!? What's that?" Emily was intrigued.

"I will call the police and tell them he's stalking me. We'll get a restraining order and then I'll get him to come over and they'll pick him up. Once they have his fingerprints, I'll just tell them I want to drop the charges."

"Sounds like a plan to me, but are you sure you want to do that? I mean, he's your friend and he's dangerous," Emily said.

"If he really killed those babies, he is no friend of mine. Those kids were adorable, Em. I have to do my part in trying to get him off the street."

"You may be risking your life," Emily warned.

"So? I don't think he will hurt me, but if he does, he does. Avenging Michael and Leslie is more important. He has to pay for that. There's something I have to tell you, Emily."

"What?"

"This isn't going to be easy for you to hear, but I think you should know. When I heard Brandon say this, I was ready to kill him with my bare hands."

"What did he say, Kim?" Curiosity was killing her.

"He said, 'Those kids were nothing but half-breeds anyway.'"

Emily was speechless as this sunk in. "That bastard," was all she could say.

Kim got the restraining order against Brandon. A few days later, she had her sister, Connie, call him and tell him that she had some killer weed. He jumped on the opportunity for good drugs until he heard he had to pick it up at Kim's house. Connie convinced him that Kim wasn't home and that the restraining order said he couldn't be anywhere near Kim, not her home, which of course was a lie, but he fell for it. When Connie hung up the phone, Kim called the police and said that Brandon had been riding by watching her house. The police were waiting at the end of the road when Brandon came over. He was arrested, taken downtown, and booked.

Kim found out that she couldn't drop the charges against him. Brandon spent the night in jail. Emily called Detective Caruthers and told him the whole story about how Kim got the restraining order and that Brandon was in custody and his fingerprints were on file.

"We can't use those fingerprints," Detective Caruthers said.

"What? Why not?" Devastation hit Emily like a ton of bricks.

"Because they were obtained illegally. You can't have someone falsely arrested and then use the fingerprints to associate that person with another crime. It doesn't work that way."

"So, we did that for nothing and we still have nothing on him?"

"I'm afraid so, Ms. Payne."

~ ~ ~ ~ ~ ~ ~

Emily went to Chicago in August and got Rachel. They moved to an apartment in a town fifty miles outside of Nashville. She was close enough to the grave to visit when she needed to, but yet far enough away where Brandon wouldn't find her. Rachel started second grade and Emily was the best mother she could be. She learned important lessons when Michael and Leslie died, one of which was to make a lot of memories, because someday that may be all you have left. She and Rachel started doing all kinds of things together. She bought them both bikes and they would go riding together. They went swimming, camping, out to eat, and just spent a lot of time hanging out together.

In November, one year and six weeks after the fire, Emily made one last attempt at getting someone to do something. She sent a letter to the district attorney along with the list of all the reasons she suspected Brandon had done it. He sent her a letter back saying the same thing that she had been told all along – not enough evidence for an indictment.

She had tried her best to get someone in authority to at least check into it, but no one would. She had to accept the fact that it was over. There was nothing more she could do. She and Rachel went on with their lives, doing their best to just put the unsolved murder behind them.

2000

Chapter 37

"**G**ood morning, Lisa." Emily walked passed the receptionist's desk on her way into work all bundled up on this late-January morning. "Sure is cold out there today."

"It is definitely a bitter one this morning," Lisa said laughing. "Oh, some guy called for you late yesterday afternoon. You were already gone, so I took a message. Here." Lisa offered Emily a pink slip of paper.

"Thanks." Emily's brow furrowed as she read the message. "Detective James Tomarano? Who the heck is that and what does he want with me?" Emily asked herself under her breath as she made her way to her desk.

She sat the note down on the desk as she unwrapped herself. She couldn't figure out who he was or what he could possibly want. She was little apprehensive about calling him. It just isn't every day that a detective calls and leaves a message for you to call him. There wasn't even any indication as to what it could be about or even what squad he was with. She pondered all of it for a few minutes before dialing.

"Domestic violence, Detective Tomarano speaking. May I help you?"

Domestic Violence? "Yes, this is Emily Payne. You called my work and left a message for me to call you?"

"Ms. Payne, thank you for calling me back. I really appreciate it. I assume you have a few minutes?" Detective Tomarano said.

"That depends on what this is regarding," Emily said apprehensively.

"Well, actually, it's regarding the death of your children, Michael and Leslie."

"What? That was almost six and half years ago," Emily said more loudly than she had intended.

"Yes, Ma'am, I know, but there are some things about that that I would like to discuss with you. Is now a good time?"

"Not really. I mean, I am at work. I am very curious, but at the same time I don't want to discuss this with ears all around," she said feeling that she had already said too much.

"I understand. Do you have any lunch plans today?"

"No, not yet, but I could have some."

"All right. Well, I will pick you up at 11:30 and we'll do lunch. Sound good?"

"Yes, that is fine." After giving him the address and directions to her office building, Emily hung up the phone. For the remainder of the morning she couldn't concentrate on her work. A number of different thoughts were going through her mind. *What on earth has prompted a detective to start asking questions about Michael and Leslie's deaths? Have they finally decided to believe it wasn't an accident? If so, why after all of these years? I haven't even thought about pushing the arson thing anymore since 1995!*

~ ~ ~ ~ ~ ~ ~

Emily was more than ready to find out what was going on when an unmarked white Ford Crown Victoria pulled around the circle drive in front of her office building. Emily had been waiting for him in the lobby and saw his badge on his belt as soon as he walked in the door. She approached him, "Detective Tomarano? Emily Payne," she said offering her hand.

"Hello, Emily. Or do you prefer Ms. Payne?" he said shaking her hand.

Emily liked Detective Tomarano immediately and felt very comfortable with him. "Emily is fine." Detective Tomarano was relieved. She was about the same age as his daughter and he felt a fatherly kind of warmth for her. He couldn't imagine his daughter in Emily's shoes.

As soon as they were in the car Emily said, "All right, Detective, the anticipation has been killing me all morning. What *is* going on?"

"Please, call me Jim. We have reason to believe that the fire that killed your children was not an accident after all. We believe it was arson."

"Really!? Well, it is about time." Emily couldn't hide the attitude in her voice.

"What do you mean by that?" Tomarano asked.

"I tried to tell you people, I know not you personally, but other police officers, that this fire was arson shortly after it happened."

"You did?" *Why didn't I know that?*

"Yes, I did. I was relentless about it. I talked to fire investigators, police officers, homicide detectives, and even sent a letter to the district attorney. Every single one of them said the same thing, 'if it was arson, you are going to have to come up with more evidence than just your suspicions and circumstantial evidence.' One detective even told me he wasn't surprised I wanted to blame someone because most grieving parents need to place the blame somewhere."

"Do you have any idea who you talked to? I mean, if I could get my hands on those original files, it may be very helpful to my current investigation." *And I'd really like to know who it was that was so cold. We just don't treat people like that.* Tomarano was completely flabbergasted that one of his fellow officers would actually say that to a grieving mother.

"I don't know the names right off the top of my head, but they are in a file at home. I'll get them for you."

Once they arrived at the restaurant and had placed their order, Emily asked, "So, what happened to get you looking at this, finally, six and a half years after the fact?"

"There was a fire last week in South Nashville. You may have seen it on the news," Tomarano stalled waiting for Emily's reaction.

"I don't watch the news," she stated.

"Oh, okay, well, there was a fire in South Nashville last week. No one was home at the time except for a few pets that died. The investigators were clueless as to what could have caused it. When Mary, the woman who lived there came home, she started freaking out and kept saying, 'it's just like when the kids died' over and over again. They didn't know what she was talking about and couldn't get anything else out of her. They ended up taking her to Vanderbilt Psychiatric Hospital. Eventually, she told the doctors that her boyfriend, a guy named Brandon, had accused her of cheating on him and so she told him to move out. That is when I, a domestic violence detective, was called in on the case. I asked her what she meant by what she said about kids dying. She look petrified as she told me that this Brandon character had told her about a fire that occurred six years ago. He told her that he lived next to this woman and her house caught on fire because the couch was too close to the heater. He said that two kids died in that fire. I started pulling files and soon discovered that there was, in fact, a fire six years ago in which he lived next door and two kids died – yours!"

"Wow, so he did it again. I was wondering how long it would be before he did."

"Well, we pulled this guy's record. It is pretty long. No convictions of arson, but there is a history of domestic violence, kidnapping, driving under the influence and misdemeanor drug charges."

"That is exactly why I don't watch the news anymore. Every time I would see a fire, if they said the cause was unknown or intentionally set, I would wonder if Brandon was involved. I finally got tired of that torment. I, also, learned the hard way that you can't believe everything you see on the news."

"Well, hopefully we will get this guy off the streets and then you can watch the news again," Tomarano said laughing.

"I don't know about all that," Emily said still skeptical about reporters. Just then the food was brought to the table. They ate silently as Emily absorbed all that she had just been told.

Chapter 38

When they finished eating, Emily asked, "So, what happens now?"

"Well, I will have to do a full investigation. There's no telling how long that will take since this case is so old. I'll have to find all of your old neighbors, the doctors that treated you and the kids at both hospitals, the police officers, fire investigators, and so on. Then, I'll have to interview each of them to see what they remember. I'll pull old files and reports. I'll contact your old landlord and his insurance company. Once all that is done, I'll have to write up a report and submit it to the district attorney who will review all of it and then let me know if we have enough to take it to the grand jury."

"I have names of most of those people you just listed. So, you are telling me that it may be quite a while yet before this is over?"

"Yes, Emily. I'm sorry, but it is going to be awhile. I wish I could give you some idea as to how long, but I really don't know at this point. I just made a connection to your case yesterday. I will say that if finding the others is as easy as it was to find you, and if and they cooperate, it will go faster."

"You know, I waited six and half years for your phone call, and now I am not so sure I wanted it after all," Emily said half to Detective Tomarano and half thinking out loud.

"Why do you say that?" Tomarano asked.

"You have to understand, Detect, ah, Jim, that was a long time ago. I have gone on with my life and so has my family." Emily paused trying to figure out how to express what she was feeling right then. "Let me see if I can explain this. You see, I have put all of those feelings in a box and put the box in a cabinet. Every once in awhile, I'll open the cabinet and look at the box, but you're asking me to open the cabinet, open the box, and go through the emotional content piece by piece by piece countless times in front of many total strangers. I just don't know if I can do that."

"That makes sense," Tomarano said understanding as well as anyone who hasn't been there could understand. "How about this? I'll give you a couple of days to process all of this. I know this has come out of nowhere and broadsided you. Here's my card." Detective Tomarano handed Emily a business card. "You think about it and call me in a couple of days. Deal?"

"Deal," Emily agreed as she put the card in her purse.

~ ~ ~ ~ ~ ~ ~

Emily was not very productive for the rest of the day. She wanted to talk to her mother and Abby about it all, but she didn't want to talk at work. People were asking her all afternoon if she was all right. She would nod or just say yes as she went about her business.

When she arrived home, she went straight to Rachel's room. She wasn't there. She found the usual "Mom, went to Sue's. Be home at 6. Rachel," written on the dry erase board by her desk. *Good, that means I have almost an hour to tell Mom the whole story.*

After listening to Emily tell her everything, all Terri could say was, "Oh, my gosh. Well, it's about time."

"That is what I said at first, too, Mom, then it hit me what this means."

"What does this mean? That Michael and Leslie will finally get justice? That you can finally rest knowing that this psycho will spend the rest of his life in prison?"

"Wow, aren't you the optimistic one? He hasn't been convicted yet. He hasn't even been arrested yet, and we have no clue how long it will be until he is, *if* he is ever. No, Mom, this means we have to go through it all again. Are you really up to answering all the questions that they may ask and dragging all of this to the forefront of your mind again?"

"Well, hopefully, I won't have to testify. I mean, I don't know what I could tell them anyway. But, yeah, if I had to, I would do it without hesitation."

"Okay, well, I *will* have to testify. There is no doubt about that. In fact, I am the key witness. I don't know if I want to do this."

"I don't think you have a choice in the matter. Besides, if you do have a choice and you decide NOT to do this, how are you going to feel when he sets another fire? And he obviously will. What if he kills more kids? Then what, Emily? It is your duty to society to do this."

"You kill me the way you go from optimism to pessimism, Mom."

"I am just being truthful, dear. These are things you need to think about." Deep down, Emily knew her mother was right.

"Well, I didn't say I wasn't going to do it. I just said I don't know if I can or not. I guess I have a lot of thinking to do now."

"Well, you think and I'll pray."

Emily rolled her eyes. "Okay, Mother. I have to get dinner going. I'll talk to you later."

Terri knew that Emily only called her "Mother" when she was disgusted with her about something. She also knew that Emily still refused to believe in God, so it didn't take a genius to figure out that she must be disgusted with her comment about praying. Terri was beyond caring what Emily thought about her relationship with Christ. She wanted Emily to find God, but she didn't shove God down her throat. At the same rate, she wasn't going to pretend that she didn't have a relationship with Him and part of that was prayer.

"All right. Tell Rachel I love her."

"All right, Mom. Oh, and I don't want Rachel to know anything about this, okay?"

"I understand." Terri didn't agree with keeping it from Rachel but she had begun to respect Emily's wishes as Rachel's mother a few years ago. "She won't hear about it from me."

"Okay, good. Have a good night. Bye, Mom." Emily hung up the phone.

There, I let Mom know. Now, I need someone who will sympathize a little.

Chapter 39

Emily picked the phone up again and called Abby.

"Hey, Em. How are you?" Abby asked answering on the second ring.

"Not good, Abby. Could you come by for coffee later? I need to talk and I may need a hug." Emily felt tears welling up in her eyes.

"Sure, what's up?"

"I don't want to get into it right now and I gotta get dinner going. Rachel will be in bed by the time you get off of work, so we'll talk then."

"All right. I'll come by on my way home," Abby said curiosity creeping up inside of her. *What could be going on?* she wondered.

Emily felt better just knowing that Abby was going to come by. She had just finished making dinner when Rachel came in. "What's for dinner?"

"Spinach and cheese tortellini and it's ready so go wash up."

After dinner, Emily helped Rachel with her homework and then they watched TV together for a while. Abby called at eleven to let

Emily know she was on the way. Emily started some coffee and waited patiently for Abby. She arrived just as the coffee pot groaned a last attempt to brew. They sat at the dining room table as Emily unloaded all that had happened that day. Abby listened intently making mental notes of questions she had. She didn't want to interrupt because it was obvious that Emily needed to get all of this out of her system first.

"What do you think?" Emily asked.

"I think it is a good thing and I have to agree with your mother, it is about time. I have a lot of questions, though. I need you to refresh my memory on some things," Abby said. Abby and Emily had lost touch when Emily moved to Chicago. During that time, Abby accepted Christ. When Emily returned, she was so determined to get the police involved, that she didn't contact all of her friends. It wasn't until three years ago that they hooked back up. By then, Emily didn't want to discuss the fire anymore. She had "moved on".

"Fire away."

"First of all, you said you have the pictures of the house back then? Have you looked at them recently? Has this Detective Tom..." Abby stumbled over the name.

"Tomarano, but just call him Jim. Ironically enough, I looked at them last week. No, I have not showed them to him yet, but if I go through with this, I will."

"You have often mentioned a list of circumstantial evidence. What is on this list?"

Emily got up and walked over to the desk in the corner of the dining room. She opened the file drawer and pulled out a rather thick file marked Fire/Funeral. She opened it on her way back to the table. "Here," she handed Abby a worn, faded piece of paper. "This is a copy of the list I sent to the District Attorney and this is the cover letter." She handed her another paper.

Abby tucked the letter behind the list as she read in silence. Her face registered surprise as she read the list. Then she read the letter. "Wow, Em. I really had no idea that you had this much evidence. I don't understand how the district attorney could decide that this wasn't enough to warrant an officer at least looking into it! What exactly did he say in response to this?"

Emily silently handed Abby another piece of paper. *Ms. Payne, I am sorry to hear about the death of your children in such a horrible tragedy as the one you described in your letter. Unfortunately, however, there isn't enough evidence listed here to justify reopening a case that has been closed for over a year. It was investigated at the time by one of Nashville's best fire investigators. While the cause of ignition is listed as unknown, there wasn't then, and isn't now, enough evidence to substantiate an arson accusation. Please let me know right away if you obtain any more evidence and we will consider reopening the case again at that time. Sincerely, Toby Jackson.*

"I agree that there isn't a smoking gun, but it is definitely suspicious. It sounds as if he expected you to continue investigating it yourself."

"That is the impression I got too. So, now what am I going to do, Abby?"

"You know I love you and I know this is going to be hard for you, but you have to do whatever you can to help get this guy. He has to pay the consequences for his actions."

"I believe he has been paying the consequences by living with it every day for the last six and a half years."

"And you think that is enough? Besides, you need closure on this."

"I have closure. I had closure in 1995 when I forgave him. I don't know if he has paid enough to learn his lesson, but he has paid enough in my book."

"But he hasn't learned his lesson, or we wouldn't be sitting here right now. He set another fire... that is what reopened this, right? Em, you have to think about the rest of society. Is anyone safe in Nashville while he is free?"

"But, I tried all of this six years ago. It didn't work. I moved on with my life. Rachel is doing much better now and I don't want to bring all of this back up again for her, or for my parents, or my brothers. I mean, why can't we just let sleeping dogs lie?"

"He isn't sleeping anymore. He did it again, and he'll do it again until you do your part in stopping him."

"Thanks, Abby. Lay it all on me..." Emily said with a slight grin on her face. "You're right. Once again, you're right. I'll call Jim in the morning. Thanks, Abby! You always manage to make me smile while telling me exactly what I don't want to hear. I love you." Emily hugged Abby.

"I love you, too," Abby said opening the door. "If you need anything..."

"You know darn well I'll call you," Emily said grinning.

Abby sat in the car in Emily's driveway and prayed. She prayed for Emily to do the right thing and for the strength that she will need to do this. She prayed that Brandon would not set any more fires while they were investigating the case and she prayed for the police to find the evidence that they need. She also prayed that God would help her know how to help Emily.

Chapter 40

"**D**omestic Violence, Detective Tomarano speaking."

"Hello, Detective. It's Emily Payne."

"I thought we had agreed on Jim and Emily?" he said chuckling.

"Yes, actually, we did. Sorry, Jim." Emily smiled. "Well, I was calling to let you know that I have thought about things. I have decided that while this is extremely difficult for me, I will help you the best that I can, but I will not allow this to consume my life again. I don't want my family involved until, and unless, it's absolutely necessary. Oh, and I do not, under any circumstances, want to talk to the media about it." Emily felt more in control by laying out all of her demands right up front. She knew that Detective Tomarano would do whatever he could to make sure her wishes were granted.

"That is fine. None of those things will present a problem, but I do want you to know that it is going to require some of your time."

"I understand that, but I am not doing to the leg work this time. I am not a detective and have no desire to pretend like one."

"All right. Now that that is established, do you have those names for me?"

"Yes, I do." Emily had gone through the file after Abby left last night. She copied them all down on one piece of paper. "I have names and phone numbers or addresses on everyone except one of Brandon's friends. His mother owned a house though. I'll bet she still lives there."

"Which friend?"

"Jeff."

"Well, I will need to speak with him. Do you have his mother's address?"

"No, but I can go by her house and get it off of the mailbox for you."

"I have a favor to ask. That is, if you don't mind... and if it's too much to ask, just tell me... okay?" Tomarano asked.

"What?"

"I would appreciate it if you would come with me to look at the house, the grave, and then we can go to Jeff's mother's together."

"The house? You mean the one that he set on fire? I haven't been there in years." Fear was apparent in Emily's voice.

"Like I said, if you can't do it, just say the word."

"How can I say no to you? You are so nice and so understanding."

"So is that a yes?"

"Yeah, I suppose it is. We may have to take it slowly, but, yeah, I'll go. I have decided that I will cooperate with you as much as you need me to. I wouldn't be able to live with myself if he killed someone else. I don't want blood on my hands. I can do it Friday evening. My daughter will be spending the night at her friend's house. She doesn't know about this and I don't want her to know yet."

"Rachel? How old is she now?"

"She is twelve. Getting big and doing well. I really don't want to mention this to her until we know if Brandon will be arrested. I don't want her losing faith in our justice system. I think I have lost enough of that for both of us."

"That is understandable. I'll call you on Friday afternoon and we'll set up a time."

"All right. You have a good day."

"I will. And, Emily?"

"Yes?"

"I want you to know that I am proud of you. I know this is hard, but it's for the best. Just think about your kids. Remember, this will bring justice for them and closure for yourself."

"No, Jim, actually, I am doing this for prevention purposes only. It isn't about revenge. It isn't about justice. It isn't even about closure. You have to understand, I forgave Brandon back in 1995. I had my closure then."

"You forgave him?!"

"I had to. I couldn't have gone on with my life, if I hadn't. Trust me, Brandon being free or being behind bars for the rest of his life...

neither makes any difference to me, personally. Nashville will be safer with him behind bars. That is the only difference it makes."

"Well, I have to say, you are more of a man than I am. I could never forgive the man who killed my children."

"I don't expect you, or anyone else, to understand it, but that is the fact. Look, I have to run. I'll talk to you on Friday."

"Friday it is." Tomarano sat there stunned after hanging up the phone. *She forgave him? How did she do that?* Emily puzzled and impressed him more and more every time he spoke with her.

Emily picked the phone up again immediately. It was answered on the third ring. "Abby, I'm sorry... I didn't realize how early it is. Just call me when you get up."

"It's all right. What's up, Em? You okay?"

"I'm fine for now, but I may need you Friday night." Emily filled her in on the plans she had just made with Tomarano. "It is the first step in ripping open all these old scars."

"You know I'll always be there for you. Just call me when you are close to being done and I'll take my lunch. I can take as long as you need."

"Thanks, Abby. Now, go to sleep. What are you doing up at this hour of the morning?" Emily said laughing.

"Glad to hear the sarcastic Emily that I love, and laughing at that. Goodnight."

"Goodnight." It felt strange saying that at 8:30 in the morning, but Abby works until 11:30 pm, and goes to bed at about three in the morning, so 8:30 am is the middle of the night to her.

Chapter 41

Tomarano picked Emily up at her house at seven o'clock. She took him by Jeff's mother's house first since that was the easiest, both emotionally and geographically. She waited in the car while Tomarano went to the door. He knocked and waited. He knocked again. Just as he was turning to leave he heard the door open behind him.

"May I help you, sir?" a frail old woman's voice said. He turned to face her. Her appearance matched her voice. She was a very small woman who appeared to be in her seventies, hunched over a walker standing behind the screen door.

"Yes, ma'am, I hope so. I am looking for a Jeff Carlisle. His mother lived here six years ago. Would you happen to be Mrs. Carlisle?"

The woman had noticed the badge attached to Detective Tomarano's belt. "That depends on why a Nashville police officer in street clothes and an unmarked car wants to know?"

He took a step closer. "My name is Detective Tomarano, ma'am. I am a domestic violence detective. I need to ask Mr. Carlisle a few questions." He noted the worry and concern that flashed through the old woman's eyes before she masked them. "I assure you he is not in any trouble with the law, nor is he a suspect, but he may be a witness."

"A witness to what?"

"A crime that happened six and a half years ago," Tomarano said not wanting to give away too many details.

His reply peaked her curiosity. "I'm Mrs. Carlisle. Please, come in. It is cold out there," she said opening the door and letting him in. Tomarano looked at Emily and gave her a thumbs-up as he walked in the house.

Emily watched as Tomarano went in. *Must be the right place.* Emily tried not to imagine what may be going on inside the house. It didn't take long before Tomarano came back out.

"Score one for the good guys," Tomarano said as he got back in the car. "That is still her house and that was her that I talked to. She called Jeff and I talked to him on the phone. He said he would be more than willing to come in and give us a statement. Said he wanted to help in anyway that he could. Said he had always wondered about the possibility of Brandon setting that fire, but never said anything because he didn't want to upset you any more than you already were."

"He suspected it!? I wonder who else suspected and didn't bother to tell me. Now, I wish I had seen Jeff when I was trying to convince Detective Caruthers to check it out. I really didn't think he would know anything and if he did, I didn't think he would turn on Brandon," Emily said more to herself than to Detective Tomarano.

"Well, he sure sounded fond of you." Emily looked surprised. "He asked how you were doing. I told him you were fine. He asked me to give you this." Detective Tomarano handed Emily a piece of paper with a phone number on it. She slipped it in her purse without looking at it.

Tomarano backed out of the driveway. "Where to now?"

"The grave, I guess. We'll be back tracking, but I ..."

Tomarano cut her off before she could finish. "Hey, I have a full tank of gas and all night. We are doing this your way – in your order and as fast or slow as you want me to go."

"The grave it is, then," she said in a tone of finality.

They rode in silence to the grave. *Jeff asked about me? That's strange, but then again, he did always seem to care about me. I don't think I am going to call him, though. I don't think it would be wise for us to talk about the case before the trial. The case? That is the first time I have ever referred to Michael and Leslie's deaths as a case. Maybe I can do this after all. I guess I'll know by the time tonight is over. I think this is going to be the hardest part – the grave and the house. I have been to the grave a few times, but I haven't gone to the house since the day after the fire when Scott and I were digging through the ashes looking for my wedding rings.* Emily remembered that day vividly – finding the Bible on top of the ashes that had been the desk, retrieving Michael's car and Leslie's doll from the toy box, and the ashes they dug through in an unsuccessful attempt to find her wedding rings. She remembered joking with Scott about making a fashion statement with soot all over his face and in his hair. That brought a smile to her face as she watched the trees go by.

Chapter 42

As Tomarano pulled the car into the graveyard, he glanced over at Emily. "You need me to stop here for a minute?"

"No, you're fine." Emily began thinking aloud. "I haven't been here in almost two years now. Hard to believe that." She turned to look at Tomarano. "I mean one of the main reasons I moved all the way back from Chicago was to be near the grave and now I don't even come here anymore."

"Where is their grave?" Tomarano asked.

"Go around the circle and then follow the signs to the Garden of Peace. They are along the back side under the only tree back there."

As he began to work his way to the Garden of Peace, Tomarano said, "You moved to Chicago after the fire?"

"Yeah, when I first found out he did it. I was scared to death and my mom was up there so I went to live with her. I only stayed a few months though. I couldn't get any cooperation from the police over the phone. Of course, now I know the phone wasn't the problem. I, also, wanted to be close to here." She pointed in the direction of the grave. "I had talked with other parents who found it therapeutic to spend some time in their dead child's bedroom. I didn't have that. All I had was their grave. I used to spend hours just sitting here."

Tomarano stopped the car under the tree. Emily sat in silence for a few minutes with tears welling up in her eyes. She slowly opened the car door and got out. The cold January wind was kicking up the thin layer of fine snow that had fallen that afternoon. Emily was oblivious to the cold as Tomarano pulled his collar up over his ears. She led the way to the grave.

She stopped abruptly and stood frozen staring at the marker displaying her children's names. She had chosen a two-foot by two-foot slab of pink granite with a large heart-shaped bronze marker. The name 'Carter' was in large letters on the top center of the heart. On the left side, it said 'H. Michael' with his date of birth and death under his name. On the right side, it said 'Leslie L.' with her date of birth and death. Pictures of the kids had been imbedded in the granite on either side of the point of the heart. Above 'Carter' on either side in the humps of the heart were bronze ribbons. The one on the left said, 'together forever' and the one on the right said, 'in God's loving care'. Emily noticed that the pictures were rather faded. Tomarano gently touched her arm. She turned to look at him as he handed her two long-stem red roses. That was enough to break the dam. The tears started to flow as she took the roses and laid them on the marker, one on Michael's name and one on Leslie's.

She lingered for only a few minutes before the cold made its presence known. She turned to tell Tomarano she was ready to go back to the car, not realizing he had already done so. She removed the frozen tear from her eyelash as she moved slowly back to the car. Tomarano had the heater up all the way.

"You all right?" he asked as she sat down.

"Yeah, just go. I want to get this over."

Tomarano offered her some McDonald's napkins. "This is all I have."

"Thank you," she said, taking them from him.

They rode in silence for the next five minutes. Tomarano stopped the car at the end of the street on which the house sat and looked at Emily. "You ready?"

"Just go slowly if you would please," Emily said bracing herself.

"Okay." Tomarano inched down the street at five miles per hour. Emily stared out the window waiting for the house to come into view. The last time she was here the roof was gone in the middle, there were sheets of plywood in place of the windows, and a flower arrangement had been placed under the window that Emily had tried so desperately to open. As the house slowly came into view, she realized that time had gone on here as well. The house was very attractive looking. The black smoke had been cleaned off of the beautiful tan brick. The roof had been replaced with green shingles and the trim was painted a dark red. Emily took a deep breath. In her mind's eye, it was a beautiful fall day in 1993. She saw Michael and Leslie running in the yard kicking a ball around. They were laughing. She saw herself sitting on the front porch with a magazine in her hand, which was being ignored as she watched the kids play. Rachel came out of the house and touched her back with a box of Popsicles. She jumped and laughed as she pulled her oldest child to her in a hug. "Michael, Leslie... you want ice cream?"

"Yay," Michael yelled.

"Me, ice cream, too," Leslie screamed running behind her big brother.

A tear had escaped and hung on Emily's top lip. She turned to Tomarano, "That window there is the one that I tried to open." Emily pointed out the layout of the house from the safety of the car.

When she was finished, he asked, "Would you like some coffee?"

"Sure. I'm ready to leave here."

They didn't talk much on the way to the coffee shop. Once they were seated and sipping on steaming hot coffee, Tomarano said, "Do you think you could draw me a blueprint of the house?"

"Yeah, I think I can do that."

"No rush, but I'll need it all labeled. I need to know where the furniture was placed, where the heater was, where the outlets were, and if you can, where they found you and the kids."

"I'll do my best. I am not sure if I remember where all the outlets were, but I'll try."

"Like I said, there is no rush on it, but it will help down the road. One thing we are going to have to do is disprove the heater theory and I think your blueprint will help with that."

"Okay. Well, I have some pictures of the house after the fire."

"You do?" Tomarano was pleasantly surprised.

"Yes," Emily said matter-of-factly.

"Emily, that is great. Wow. I thought we were going to have to wait for the insurance company to go through their archives before seeing any pictures."

"Well, I have some. I don't know how helpful they will be, but my dad thought it would be best to have them in case I ever wanted to see them. Of course, when they were taken we had no clue it was arson, or that these pictures might someday become evidence in a murder trial. I guess things do happen for a reason."

"Wow. I am really glad your dad thought of that."

"I have them at my house. I will give them to you when you drop me off, but I want them back."

"Oh, that is fine. I'll take them to the station and scan them into the computer. I'll have them back to you by next week."

When they got to her house, Tomarano walked her to the front door.

"Come on in," Emily said.

Tomarano stepped inside the door and waited as Emily went to get the pictures. He looked around her living room. It was a simple, but attractive home. She had hardwood floors with a big area rug.

The coffee table, end tables, and TV stand were all oak, matching the floor. The furniture was beige. The walls were painted a light brown with white trim. She had chosen oak and black wrought iron decor. It was a very comfortable setting.

"Here you go." Emily handed him an envelope marked 'fire pictures'.

"Great. Thanks. I'll call you when I am done scanning these in."

After Tomarano left, Emily decided a nice hot shower might help her shake all of the negative emotions that this night had drudged up. Tears mixed with the water from the showerhead as she stood there with steam rising all around her.

"Why would God do this to me if he loves me so much? Why? Why? Why?"

Chapter 43

E mily was laying on the couch when a soft rapping on the door interrupted her thoughts. She looked at the clock on the wall. 11:45 pm. *Who could be knocking on my door at this hour of the night?*

"Oh, hi, Abby!" Emily was pleasantly surprised to see her best friend at the door. "What are you doing here?"

"I was worried about you. You called me the other day and said you were going to the grave and the house with Jim tonight. I thought you were going to call me when you were done. I called you a few times and you didn't answer the phone, so I thought I would come by and see how you are doing."

"Well, come on in. I'll start some coffee."

While Emily was making the coffee, Abby made herself comfortable on the couch. She began praying for her friend and for the words to say. She wanted to comfort Emily. She wanted to make sure she didn't say anything that would upset Emily in any way.

"All right. Coffee is going," Emily said returning to the living room.

"Are you all right?" Abby asked.

"I will be. It wasn't easy, but I made it through." Emily sat down on the chair across from Abby.

"Do you want to talk about it?"

"I don't know. I mean, what is there to talk about? I feel like the kids just died a month ago and that I haven't made any progress in the last six and a half years. Tonight just brought it all right back up to the surface."

"I'm sorry, Emily. I wish I could have been here for you when you got home," Abby said soothingly.

"I wanted a hot shower, which I thought would make me feel better. It did, in a way. I have just been laying here thinking for the last," she glanced at the clock, "three hours."

Emily stopped talking as she slipped into deep thought again. Abby didn't say a word. She just sat there waiting for Emily to go on. Abby had learned that asking Emily questions would just make her defensive and cause her to shut down, but if she just made herself available than Emily would eventually pour it all out.

"Oh, doesn't that coffee smell good?" Emily said heading for the kitchen. Abby joined her. Abby was putting sugar in her coffee when all of a sudden Emily threw her arms around her and began sobbing. "I just don't understand all of this. Why did he kill them? That is the one thing I have never figured out. I know he did it, but I

246

could never figure out why! For all these years I have thought it was about him being evicted. That is still the only explanation that has been offered, but it just doesn't make sense. Setting fire to a house where three innocent people are inside is a bit extreme just because the landlord is kicking you out. Don't you think?"

"It is extreme and, I agree, it doesn't really make sense. What has Jim said about that?" Abby asked holding her friend.

"Nothing really. He thinks that Brandon set Suzie's house on fire because they had been dating and were living together when she had had enough of his crap and kicked him out. He had told me that was why he set the one in Georgia, too; they broke up and she kicked him out. But, we were never dating. I wasn't trying to kick him out. We didn't live together until after the fire. I just can't figure it out."

"I don't know. If this works its way through the system maybe we'll find out why he did it. Wouldn't it be really sweet if he confesses and explains it all?"

"Yeah, it would be sweet, but I don't see that happening. Brandon is evil. He isn't going to go down without a fight and he will try to bring as many down with him as possible."

"I know, but a girl can wish, right?" Abby said with a chuckle. They went back into the living room and settled back down on the couch.

"I don't think I'll ever understand all of this, even if we do find out what Brandon's motive was. I mean if you believe in God, which I know you do, everything happens for a reason. Others say it is karma or fate, but I never did anything to deserve this. I just don't get it and I have a hard time believing that these things just happen. I don't know how to explain it. All kinds of things are going through my mind. I am not asking for an explanation. I am just thinking out loud." Emily sat there in deep thought as Abby prayed silently.

Abby finally broke the silence. "Well, Em, I don't know what to say."

"Then, let's change the subject." They started talking about what new movies were coming out. Abby thought maybe she would treat Emily to a movie tomorrow night to get her mind off of things.

~ ~ ~ ~ ~ ~ ~

There were a number of things in Brandon's file that Detective Tomarano had not told Emily. He had mentioned the other fires, but he said nothing about the three domestic abuse arrests, or the one kidnapping arrest. All of that happened in Alabama. Tomarano was still trying to find the victim. She had hidden herself well. If he couldn't find her, there was no way Brandon would.

He would tell Emily about all of that when he found and talked to the victim and even then, only if she would be a witness in the case. There was just no need to worry Emily with anything else right now. He had located Brandon before he contacted Emily. He was keeping a close eye on him.

Tomarano had tracked Brandon's residences all the way back to Emily's fire. He began looking at any and all suspicious fires anywhere near those locations. He found a few, but couldn't connect

Brandon to them. He knew he was grasping at straws, but he wanted this guy and he wanted him bad. He had told other detectives working with him, "I want this guy so far under the prison that he will never see the light of day again." No one could blame him. They all felt the same way.

Chapter 44

The following week, Tomarano called Emily and told her that he was done with the pictures. He could either deliver them or mail them, whichever she would prefer. She told him she would prefer it if he would deliver them so they wouldn't get lost or destroyed in the mail. They agreed to meet for lunch.

"So what happens now?" Emily asked as the waitress walked away.

"Now, we wait," Jim said as he took a bite of food.

"Wait? For what?" She had to wait for Tomarano to swallow before he could answer.

"Well, I have calls in to all of the potential witnesses and we have to wait for them to call me back. There are a lot of people that I need to talk to about all of this. We really don't know who saw what. Sometimes, what people think is insignificant is just the thing that breaks the case. Also, just because no one came forward doesn't mean no one saw him doing it. Does that make sense?"

"I suppose." Emily was picking at her food.

"I have spoken with Mr. Rutherford, the investigator that the insurance agency had hired at the time of the fire. He said that he never bought the heater/couch scenario, but couldn't figure out what else it could have been, so eventually he filed the pictures and other evidence and had to just let it go. He is pulling all of that out of the archives. When he gets it pulled he will call me and we will go over it all. Until then, we wait."

"How long will that take?" Emily was beginning to feel anxious.

"I don't know. I assume a month maybe to talk to everyone. I will get on the phone again next week if people haven't called me back."

"Then what?"

"Well, once I talk to everyone that I need to talk to and see all the evidence that I need to see, I will present it all to a district attorney. They will then decide if we have enough evidence to get an indictment. If we don't, I will keep digging. If we do, they will take it to the grand jury and get the indictment, Brandon will be arrested and a trial date will be set. Brandon will probably not be able to post bond so he will stay in custody until the trial. At that time, you among others, will testify to what you know. A jury will decide if he is guilty or not. If they convict him, a sentencing hearing will be set at which time the judge will determine how long Brandon will have to serve and where he serves his time."

"Sounds like a long, drawn out process. So, how long do you think all this is going to take from beginning to end?"

"Unfortunately, I have no idea. I have seen these things take a few months or a few decades. I wish I could give you a more solid answer than that, but I can't."

"Well, you know, it's been six and a half years already, what is a few more?" Emily couldn't hide the sarcasm in her voice.

"I understand your skepticism, but at least now we are working on it. That is good news, right?"

"Yeah, I suppose it is encouraging. I just wish this was over so I could really go on with my life. I waited for someone to take me seriously and no one did, so I moved on. Then out of the blue, here you come disrupting my life and stirring all of this up again, only to sit here and tell me that you have no idea how long this is going to take. Do you have any idea what you have put me through?" The disgust in her voice was very apparent.

"Emily, I have been with the police force for a very long time, so I have an idea what you are going through, but as for first hand experience, no, I don't know what you are going through. And to be perfectly honest with you, I don't want to know first hand what you have been through or are going through. I cannot even begin to imagine it. Please accept my sincere apologies and my word that I will make this as easy and painless as I possibly can."

"Thank you so much for saying that. I mean, I hate it when people say 'I can just imagine what you are going through'. No one can possibly imagine it. I am extremely glad that you got this case because I believe that you will make this as painless as possible. Detective Caruthers could take some pointers from you."

"He is no longer with the force. In fact, I don't think he is even still in Nashville. I really don't know where he is now."

"I am just glad it wasn't given back to him when it came back up again. So, I guess I should look forward to hearing from you in, what? A month?"

"Something like that. Do you want me to keep you informed every step of the way or only when major things occur?"

"I really don't know. I guess for the time being tell me only when major things occur and then if I have any questions along the way or want an update, I'll let you know. That way I can continue on with my life as much as possible. Will that work?"

"Yes, that works for me."

Tomarano hesitated before continuing. "There is one more thing."

"What's that?" Emily was curious.

"If you don't mind, I need to talk to Rachel."

"Rachel? What do you need to talk to Rachel about?" She couldn't hide the surprise on her face.

"Well, we need to cover all of our bases."

"What do you mean?"

"Rachel was there shortly before the fire started. I just need to make sure that she didn't do anything that may have started it."

"What? What are you saying? I thought you were convinced it was Brandon?"

"I am, but, again, I need to cover all of my bases. There is a possibility that the defense will say that Rachel did something that started it before she left for school. If I talk to her first, we can nip that in the bud before he even tries to go there."

"Is that really necessary? I mean, haven't you put me through enough? Now you want to put my daughter through even more. She has been through plenty. I don't think that it's necessary for you to question her. She doesn't even know that you are looking into this and I told you last week that I don't really want her to know. Either you believe that Brandon did it or you don't, but leave Rachel out of it."

"Well, I can hold off on that until later."

"Why can't you hold off on that forever?"

"I don't know. We may be able to. Let's just drop that for now. We can readdress that later if we need to."

"Whatever. Again, I don't see what Rachel has to do with this. I seriously doubt I will change my position on the matter," Emily said firmly.

"Well, we'll cross that bridge when and if we come to it."

"Fine."

"Are you about ready?"

"Ready for what? Ready for my past to be in my past once and for all? You'd better believe it."

"Unfortunately, it isn't time for that yet, but it will be soon enough. I meant are you ready for me to take you back to work."

"I suppose."

Emily did her best to resume her normal lifestyle. It would be so much easier if she didn't even know about the investigation that was going on in the background of her life. *I wish that they had called me right before arresting him instead of at the beginning of the re-opening of the case.* She had begun looking over her shoulder constantly again. *What if he figures out that they are looking at it and decides to come after me? I am as good as dead.* She changed her phone number to an unlisted number and put all of her bills in her brother's name. He wouldn't look for Jason or think that she might live with Jason, so he wouldn't pursue anything he found in Jason's name.

It was almost as if she had gone back in time to right after she received the letter from the district attorney telling her that there was nothing they could do. *How long am I going to have to live like this again?*

2003

Chapter 45

Emily had gone on with her life. Brandon was free, but he hadn't made an attempt to contact her in any way. Emily had moved to third shift at work so that she could spend more time with Rachel. Rachel was in high school. She was popular and making good grades. Marvin and Terri had gotten divorced. Because they both dealt with the murders in different ways, it drove a wedge between them. Terri and Emily were closer now than ever, but Marvin had pretty much faded out of Emily's life.

When the World Trade Centers were bombed in September of 2001, Emily felt the pain of the victims' families. She still hadn't found the spiritual comfort or answers she had sought. Watching the firemen and soldiers putting their lives on the line, and in some cases dying, for total strangers hit Emily in a strange way. She couldn't comprehend the sacrificial actions of those heroes. All she had been told about God's love began to sink in. Jesus Christ dying on the cross for her began to make a little more sense and she decided it was time to give Him a chance. She had searched everywhere else to no avail. She called Abby one day in October and asked if she could go to church with her. She sat in the sanctuary every Sunday for two months. One day in December she was tormented again by the pain of grief. Another Christmas was approaching—another Christmas without Michael and Leslie. She lay in bed crying when she began thinking about God. All of a sudden, she felt a comfortable presence. It was almost as if he said to her, "I know, Emily. I know. I know what you have been through. I know what it is like to watch your child die. I know what it is like to wish you could do something, but knowing you can't. I know I could have stopped My Son from dying, but if I had, I would have lost you forever. Don't you see? I did it for you!" That night, Emily decided to give her life to Jesus Christ. As soon as she said the words, meaning it this time, it was as if a light bulb went on and she began to see clearly all that Abby, her parents, Uncle Joe and others had been saying all along. She still didn't fully comprehend why Michael and Leslie were dead, but she knew that God didn't take them.

During the summer of 2002, Tomarano called and said that he had gathered all the evidence that he could and presented it all to the district attorney, but was told that there still wasn't enough evidence to get an indictment. He told Emily that they were turning it over to a cold case detective. Detective Pritchett had been assigned to the case. He was a very nice man in his late forties with twenty plus years of homicide experience. He had been a cold case detective for the previous five years when this case was handed over to him. His determination was contagious as he began working the case. He told Emily that he would not retire as long as this case was unsolved.

"You think it is going to take at least fifteen more years?!" Emily asked flaberggasted.

"No, I don't. Hopefully, we'll be able to solve it soon. I just want you to know how dedicated I am to solving this for you."

The ten-year anniversary came and went. It had begun to feel like the case was never going to be solved when Emily's phone rang. "Emily, it's Detective Pritchett. I have good news for you."

Emily sat down in the chair by the phone. "Okay, I'm ready."

"We got the indictment. We went in front of the grand jury this afternoon and they issued it. The official charges are two counts of felony murder, one count of aggravated arson for your fire and one count of arson for the fire in January of 2000."

"Felony murder? I thought you were going for two counts of first degree murder, one count of attempted murder and one count of arson."

Pritchett explained, "We cannot charge him with first degree *and* arson because the fire was the weapon used. If a man walks into a convenient store, shoots and kills the clerk in the process of a robbery, he cannot be charged with possession of an illegal handgun. To prove first-degree murder and attempted murder we would have to prove beyond a reasonable doubt that he was trying to kill you and the kids. We can't prove that. So, we went for felony murder."

"What does that mean?" Emily asked.

"Felony murder falls between first-degree and second-degree. First-degree is when the murder itself is premeditated. In this case, it wasn't. Second-degree murder is when someone is killed without premeditation, like crimes of passion. Felony murder is where the felony that caused the death, in this case the arson, was premeditated, but the murder itself was not. We *can* prove that. Brandon knew that setting a house on fire when there were three people inside could cause one or more of the occupants to die. He didn't necessarily plan on anyone dying, but he knew it was a possibility and he did it anyway. That is felony murder in a nut shell," Pritchett said.

"So, what is the maximum sentence on felony murder? Could he come after us when he gets out?" Emily asked concerned.

"The felony murder charges carry a mandatory life sentence each, but, we have to charge him with the felony he committed that caused the death of your children as well. Aggravated arson carries a minimum sentence of fifteen years. If the judge decides that he should serve the sentences concurrently he will eligible for parole in fifty-one years, but if he decides they should be served consecutively, Brandon won't be eligible in this lifetime."

"So, what happens now?"

"We'll go arrest him. I'll let you know as soon as he is arrested. Then, Tomarano and I will interrogate him. A district attorney will be contacting you shortly after he is arrested to discuss your testimony and let you know what to expect next. Once he is arrested, it's out of my hands and you'll be dealing with the D.A.'s office."

Emily sent emails and called everyone in her family to let them know what was going on.

"When are you going to tell Rachel, Emily?" Terri asked.

"I am going to take her out to dinner tonight and explain it all."

"Do you want me to join you?"

"No, Mom. I think it would be best if I do this alone. I'm sure that Rachel will want to talk to you, so we may be calling you later."

"All right. Well, just let me know."

"I will. I love you, Mom."

"I love you, too."

Chapter 46

Emily took Rachel to her favorite restaurant for dinner. It was a beautiful restaurant with an interesting mix of eclectic cuisine. It was a little pricey but it was nice to have somewhere particular to go on special occasions. The atmosphere was very laid back and comfortable for an upscale restaurant. The décor was very unique. The walls were hand-painted and had glimpses of different parts of the world. There were pyramids, Mona Lisa's face, people dressed like Greeks, all painted on the stucco walls and ceilings.

Emily looked across the table and marveled at the young woman that Rachel had become. At sixteen, Rachel looked a lot like Emily did at that age with long blonde hair and beautiful blue eyes. Pools of tears formed in Emily's eyes knowing that she was about to hurt her daughter beyond words.

"What's wrong, Mom?"

"Rachel, there is something I have to tell you." Emily stopped as she tried to figure out how to break the news to Rachel. She took a sip of her drink.

"What is it, Mom? Is everything all right? Did something bad happen?"

"First, I want to tell you that I love you. That is why I didn't tell you this sooner. I wanted to protect you, but now it is to the point where I can't keep it from you any longer."

Rachel sat waiting patiently as her mother searched for words.

Emily took a deep breath. "Rachel, do you remember Brandon?"

"Brandon? No, who is Brandon?"

"The guy that we lived with after the fire."

"Oh, yeah, him." Rachel didn't attempt to hide the disgust in her voice. "What about him?"

"He set a house on fire in January of 2000."

"Okay. And?"

"And, well, they think he set another one in Georgia a few years before our fire," Emily stammered.

"So? What are you trying to tell me, Mom? Just say it." Rachel was confused and tired of beating around the bush.

Emily decided it was best to just come right out and say it. "He set our house on fire, too."

"What?!" Rachel was completely shocked. Tears began to form in her eyes. "Why? How? What?!"

"Rachel, Michael and Leslie were murdered."

"Why? How long have you known? Why haven't the police done anything about it?" Rachel was beginning to hyperventilate.

266

"Take a deep breath, okay, honey? I'll tell you everything. I'm telling you this now because the police are going to arrest him for it very soon. The detective called me this afternoon and told me that they have a warrant." Emily told Rachel everything from the time of the re-opening of the case until now.

"How long have you known about this?"

"I figured it out four months after the fire. That is why we moved to Chicago so suddenly. I was afraid of him."

Rachel held up her hand, "Whoa, hold up! You have known all along!? Why are you just now telling me? Didn't I have a right to know? They are my brother and sister!"

Emily took a big sip of her soda and pressed on ignoring Rachel's questions. "I called the police from Chicago and tried to get them to work on it. I came back to Nashville and left you with Grandma so that I could be here to help the police investigate it. They didn't have enough evidence back then, so the case was ruled an accident and closed."

"Why are you just now telling me? Why didn't you tell me back then? I asked you why they died when it happened. Why didn't you answer me?"

Deciding that honesty was best, Emily replied, "Well, when you were asking those questions, I didn't know myself. When I figured it out, I didn't tell you because I was trying to protect you. I didn't want you to lose faith in the justice system. I wanted you to feel safe. I didn't want to hurt you."

"Why did he do it?" Rachel demanded.

"He lived in the other half of the duplex, remember?" Rachel nodded. "The landlord was trying to evict him for not paying the rent. He told one of his friends that if he couldn't live there, no one would."

"So, he had to kill Michael and Leslie to get back at the land- lord? You weren't the landlord!" Rachel was furious.

"I know. I don't understand it, but that is what he had said. That is the only motive they've been able to find. I guess some people are just that selfish."

"So, what happens now?"

Emily filled Rachel in on all that Detective Pritchett had told her. Instead of responding, Rachel said, "Can I spend the night at Grandma's?"

"Yeah, why?"

"I just need to get away. I need to process all of this. My brother and sister were murdered ten years ago and my mother didn't think I needed to know that. To be honest, Mom, I am very mad at you right now."

"I'm sorry. I did what I thought was best," Emily said with tears welling up in her eyes.

"Just take me to Grandma's, please. I don't want to talk about it anymore." They ate the rest of their meal in silence.

Emily called her mother as they were leaving the restaurant. "Can Rachel spend the night?"

"You know she can, but what about school tomorrow?"

"I am not going to make her go to school unless she wants to." Emily looked over at Rachel.

"I don't want to," Rachel huffed and crossed her arms.

"She said she doesn't want to go to school tomorrow. She needs time to let all of this sink in."

"What did she say?" Terri asked.

"I'll let her tell you. We'll be there shortly."

~ ~ ~ ~ ~ ~ ~

As Emily drove to her mother's house, Rachel sat in the passenger seat, silently crying and thinking about Michael and Leslie.

She remembered the day she started Kindergarten. Michael did not want her to leave him. She had kissed ten-month-old Leslie goodbye while Emily was changing her diaper. Leslie said, "Buh, buh, Ray-tul."

Michael was standing blocking the door, "My Rachew can't weave me."

Rachel had hugged him, moving him in the process, "Michael, I have to go school. I'll be home later."

"No, you can't weave me," he had demanded.

Rachel had looked at Emily with a help-me look on her face. "Michael, honey, you have to let Rachel go school. She will be back before we eat lunch, okay?"

"She'w be home before wunch?"

"Yes, honey. It's just like when she goes to Meagan's house. She'll be back." Two-year-old Michael slowly and reluctantly moved away from the door.

Rachel was balling by the time Emily pulled into her mother's driveway. Emily started to get out of the car, but Rachel snapped at her, "I'm a big girl, Mom. I think I can handle walking into Grandma's house from the driveway without an escort!" Rachel slammed the door. Emily gently closed her door and sat behind the wheel crying.

Chapter 47

A few nights later, Emily was sitting on the couch in her living room flipping channels enjoying her night off. She stopped when she saw pictures of Michael and Leslie on the TV screen. "Tonight, we have a breaking news story out of South Nashville. A ten-year-old fire that authorities originally thought was an accident has been determined as arson. In that fire, these two small children, Michael and Leslie Carter, lost their lives. Police have just arrested Brandon Charles Brooks. He is being charged with two counts of felony murder, one count of aggravated arson, and one count of arson." The next image that appeared on the screen was of Brandon in the back seat of a police cruiser.

Emily screamed, "They got him. Oh, my god, they got him." She dialed her mother's phone number as Rachel came running down the stairs. Her mother groggily answered on the third ring. "It's on TV. It's on TV," Emily screamed into the phone before Terri could even say hello. Terri bolted up out of bed.

Rachel sat on the arm of the couch watching the news, unable to hear what was being said.

"What, Emily? I can't understand you. Calm down," Terri pleaded.

Emily took a breath. "It's on the news! They got him and it's on the news!"

Terri ran down the stairs with the cordless phone glued to her ear and turned on the TV. "Oh, wow!"

"I can't believe Detective Pritchett didn't call me!" Emily yelled.

"Stop talking so we can hear," Terri said.

They watched the rest of the story and then flipped to the other major networks to see the story they were reporting.

"Wow! That is awesome. They finally got him!" Emily said beginning to calm down.

"Yes, they did." Terri was fully awake now.

Rachel hadn't said a word, but silently slipped back up the stairs.

"Detective Pritchett will probably call you tomorrow," Terri said.

"He said he would call me before they arrest him so I wouldn't hear about it on the news." Emily sounded crushed.

"Well, I'm sure there is a reason he didn't," Terri said trying to comfort her daughter.

Emily's phone beeped in her ear to let her know she had another call. "Hang on a sec." She pushed the button on the phone. "Hello?"

"Emily! Did you see the news? I just saw it. They finally got him!"

"They sure did, Jessica. Hey, I'm talking to my mom right now. Can I call you back?"

"Yeah, sure."

Emily clicked back to her mother.

"Sorry about that. It was Jessica. I haven't seen her in three years and now she calls me. I guess my phone is going to start ringing off the hook."

"I'm sure it is. Turn the ringer off," Terri suggested.

"Oh, I plan on it. Did you see that he hid in the attic and they had to use tear gas to get him out of the house?!" Emily laughed.

"Yeah, I saw that."

"He is so stupid. If the police came to my house with a SWAT team in tow, I don't think I would run and hide!" Emily's phone beeped again, but she ignored it.

"That's good though because it makes him look guilty," Terri reasoned.

"I know. He might as well of said, 'yup, I did it, so I ain't going down without a fight'. And did you see all the drugs they confiscated? He must have been dealing," Emily was recounting everything she had seen on the news, although she hadn't heard any of it.

"Probably was. That one neighbor looked scared to death when he said he had no idea that he had a murderer living next door," accepting the fact that she was going to be up for awhile and deciding not to cut Emily off.

"Well, wouldn't you be if you just found that out?"

"Yeah, I guess I would. Emily, how is Rachel?" Terri asked concerned.

"I don't know. She came down when I screamed, but now she has gone back upstairs without a word. She's still pretty mad at me for not telling her sooner." Rachel hadn't spoken to her mother since they went out to dinner.

"Why don't you go talk to her? I'll watch the news in the morning and see if there is anymore about it."

"Okay, well, call me if there is."

"You want me to wake you up? Why don't I just record it and you call me when you get up?" Terri suggested.

"I don't think I'll sleep much, but all right. That's a good idea." Emily decided that would be best just in case she did fall asleep.

Emily hung up the phone and went upstairs.

Chapter 48

Rachel's bedroom door was closed. Emily rapped on it lightly. "Can I come in?"

"I'm fine," Rachel said through the door as the phone rang again. Emily ignored it.

"Can I come in, please?" she asked through the door.

Emily heard Rachel getting off the bed and the lock on the door turning. She opened the door as Rachel was climbing under the covers. "This is good news." She sat on the side of the bed looking at her daughter's tear streaked face.

"Yeah, I suppose," Rachel grunted.

"You don't think it is?" Emily said, concerned about her daughter.

"It *is* good news. I'm glad they got him, but this should have happened ten years ago," Rachel explained.

"Well, I can't argue with that," Emily agreed.

"He has been free, running around, having a good old time all these years while we have been suffering. How is that fair?"

"Well, Honey, it isn't fair, but they got him now," Emily said trying to focus on the positive.

"Yee haw. He'll spend time in jail. Even if he spends the rest of his life in jail, that still doesn't bring Michael and Leslie back. No, all this has done was ripped open all the wounds that I thought had healed. It feels like they just died."

"I know." Emily reached out to touch her daughter as Rachel pulled away.

"I just want to be alone. Okay?" Rachel asked.

"Okay. If you want to talk about it, I'll be downstairs," Emily said.

"I'm going to bed." Rachel turned her back to her mother.

"Well, goodnight. I love you," Emily said as she stood up looking at her daughter's back. She was fighting tears herself.

"Whatever."

The phone rang again as Emily headed back down stairs. She stood next to it waiting for it to stop ringing. She didn't feel like talking to anyone else she hadn't seen in years. After the phone stopped ringing, she picked it up, switched the ringer to silent, and called Abby at work.

"Well, they got him," Emily announced.

"They did? Wow, that's great, Emily!"

"Yup, it is. So, why am I shaking like a leaf?" Emily asked.

"Probably because the reality of it all is sinking in. Good stress is still stress. Just take a deep breath and try to relax. Do you want me to come over?"

"No, I think I am going to go soak in the tub for awhile and try to relax."

"That's a good idea. Call me if you need anything."

"I will."

Emily hung up the phone and checked her voicemail. Detective Pritchett had called. "Emily, it's Detective Pritchett. I don't know if you heard or not, but we have Brandon in custody. If you get this message before eleven call me on my cell. After eleven, I'll be interrogating Brandon, so I'll call you sometime tomorrow if I don't hear from you tonight."

Emily looked at the clock. 10:35… She dialed Detective Pritchett's number. "Hello, Detective," Emily said when he answered.

"Emily! I'm so glad you called."

Emily cut him off. "I saw it on the news and I got your message. Sorry, I didn't answer when you called. My phone has been ringing off the hook, so I turned the ringer off. Why didn't you call me before the news came on?"

"I'm really sorry about that. We went to his house to arrest him at seven. I thought we would have him in custody and I could call you before the ten o'clock news, but he gave us such a hard time that we didn't have him in the police car until about five minutes to ten."

"Oh, okay," Emily said understanding now why he hadn't called.

"They're booking him right now. Tomarano and I will question him in a few minutes. I'll call you when we're done. What time are you going to bed?"

"Probably about three."

"Okay. I'll call you back."

"I'll turn my ringer back on at about one. I don't think anyone will call that late."

Emily drew a steaming hot bath and soaked for a while. Then she made herself comfortable on the couch. She fell asleep waiting for Pritchett to call her back.

Chapter 49

When Emily woke up the sun was shining brightly. She rubbed her eyes and looked at the clock – 10:23. *Why hasn't Detective Pritchett called?* She forced herself up off of the couch and into the kitchen. Once she had coffee going she realized that she had forgotten to turn the ringer back on. She checked her messages. There were seventeen! Most were from well-meaning friends and family members, as well as more people from her past that she hadn't seen in years. As she was listening to them she fixed herself a cup of coffee.

"Hello, Emily. This is Detective Pritchett. It is 8:15. I hope that since you didn't answer the phone that means you got some sleep. Sorry, I didn't call you earlier, but we just finished questioning Brandon. It has been a long night and I am heading home. I'll call you sometime tomorrow. Don't worry. Everything's fine."

She was glad to hear that everything's fine, but she wasn't sure exactly what that meant. *Maybe he confessed! That would be cool. I don't see it happening, but it would be cool.*

She was surprised there were no calls from the media. Then she remembered the phone is in Jason's name so that Brandon couldn't find her all these years.

The last message was from Terri. "Emily, call me as soon as you get this. I recorded the news for you like I said I would, but you are not going to believe the audacity… I don't want to tell you in a message. Call me!"

Emily dialed her mother's work number. Terri answered on the first ring. "What's up, Mom?"

"Have you seen the news today?" Terri asked.

"No, I just got up a little while ago. I got your message. What was that all about?" Emily asked anxious to know.

"Emily, they showed on the news that he is trying to say you did it!"

"That I did what? Set the house on fire?" Emily was appalled!

"Yeah. They showed him in night court right after they arrested him. He said, 'You want to know who did it? The momma!' I couldn't believe he said it, but what shocks me even more is that they aired it.

Emily was silent; totally speechless.

"Are you there?"

"Yeah. I'm here. I don't know what to say, or how to feel." She felt a lump growing inside her throat. "I just hope people don't believe him."

"I don't think anyone will—at least not anyone significant. I mean the D.A. and the police are pretty convinced he did it."

Emily wasn't convinced that it was no big deal. "Yeah, now we just have to convince a jury. Anyone and everyone who watches the news now thinks that it's at least possible that I did it."

"Well, the jury will hear the whole entire story, not just the bits and pieces of half-truths that the media choose to air. Speaking of a jury, have they set a date for the trial yet?" Terri asked.

"I don't know. I'm not sure how it all works. They just arrested him last night. I talked to Detective Pritchett for about twenty seconds last night. Other than that I haven't talked to anyone who would know the answer to that. I'll let you know as soon as I know."

"All right, Em. Well, hang in there."

"I will. Oh, and will you call me on my cell for now. I am going to leave the ringer off on this phone. I had seventeen messages this morning! No one has my cell phone number except close friends and family. I'm going to call Detective Pritchett right now and leave him a voicemail with my cell phone number."

"Okay. That's a good idea," Terri agreed.

~ ~ ~ ~ ~ ~ ~

Emily was just getting out of the shower when her cell phone began to ring. "Hello?"

"Hello, Emily Payne?"

"This is?" Emily was curious about how anyone got her cell number.

"My name is Shelley Turner. I work for the District Attorney's office. Detective Pritchett gave me your cell phone number. Do you have a few minutes?" *Well, that answers that question.*

"Yeah, I am really anxious to know what happens next," Emily said sitting down on the edge of her bed.

"Well, we will be going to court this afternoon for a bunch of preliminary technical stuff like setting the bail, appointing a public defender, and setting a trial date. You do not have to be there, unless you want to." Shelley was always very matter-of-fact during the first phone call. She had discovered that right after the arrest the victims and victims' families don't want comfort or a friend, they simply want answers.

"I don't really want to go to court until I absolutely have to," Emily stated.

"That's fine. In the case of homicide, the next of kin is considered the victim. I want to inform you of some of your rights as the victim. You have the right to be present whenever Mr. Brooks, or his attorney, have the right to be present—court appearances, depositions, etc. We are required by law to keep you informed of everything—every time we set foot in the courtroom, every time he is moved from one jail or prison to another, every time new charges are filed against him, and so on. Those are just a few of the rights you were given when the crime victims' rights laws were passed back in 1980. I have a written list of your rights if you would like me to mail it to you."

"Yes, please do. I'm sorry if I sound a little distracted. I am just feeling very overwhelmed with all the information I am being bombarded with."

"I understand that. I will be contacting you later this afternoon to schedule a time to meet you, so if you would be thinking of a time within the next few weeks that would be convenient for you to come in that would be helpful. We will talk more about what evidence we have and what to expect at that time. I will also let you know the date of the trial. It will be about nine months from now."

"Nine months! That seems like an awfully long time," Emily felt crushed.

"I know it does, but his attorney will need time to prepare his case. This is a capital murder case in which Mr. Brooks is looking at spending the rest of his life in prison. His attorney will need time to prepare a defense."

"That makes sense, I guess. I just thought it would be sooner than that," Emily felt totally discouraged. *Nine more months!*

"If you would, please write down my name and phone number. I will be your contact person here at the District Attorney's office. If you ever receive a phone call from someone other than me and they say they are with the DA, do *not* speak to them about this case. Some defense attorneys are not the most law abiding citizens and may try to corner you into saying something by making you think you are talking to the DA. If something happens to me—I quit my job, am hospitalized or, God forbid, killed in a car wreck, either I will inform you or you will receive a letter on State of Tennessee letterhead. My name again is Shelley Turner..."

Emily cut her off. "Hang on. I have to get a pen."

Emily took down the information and hung up the phone.

2004

Chapter 50

Emily was sound asleep, when all of a sudden the phone was ringing. Who could that be at this hour of the morning on a Saturday? She looked at the caller ID. She knew that prefix well; it was only associated with Metro Nashville Government.

"Hello?" she said, as she was shaking the cobwebs from her brain. She glanced at the clock. It read 8:04 am.

"Hi, Emily. This is Detective Pritchett. I have some bad news. Brandon and two other inmates have escaped." It was obvious by his tone that Pritchett was not thrilled about having to call Emily and tell her about this.

"Oh!" was all Emily could say. She was awake now! After a second of gathering her thoughts, she asked, "When? How?"

"It was sometime between four and seven this morning. At the four o'clock bed-check they were there and at the seven o'clock bed-check they were gone. They climbed up into the ceiling and out an air vent on the side of the building. They had strung bed sheets together and used them as a ladder. We have every officer on the force looking for them. We have the helicopter in the air and boats on the river. We are doing everything we can to find them quickly."

"Oh, wow," were the only words Emily could find.

"Emily, I am sending an officer over to your house, now. He should be there in about five minutes. He is going to stay with you until further notice."

"Why?" she asked beginning to get nervous.

"Just to be on the safe side. I don't know that Brandon will try to come after you, but we would rather be safe than sorry," Pritchett said.

"Okay. Well, keep me informed," Emily said suddenly in a rush.

"You know I will. And Emily?"

Emily paused, "Yeah?"

"I'm sorry."

Emily hung up the phone. She scrambled out of bed looking for some clothes to throw on before the police officer got to her house. She grabbed some shorts and a t-shirt. She looked out the window at the beautiful June morning. The trial had been scheduled for August and Emily had moved on with her life. Going to church with Abby had become a weekly thing. She and Rachel had been getting along better although Rachel's grades weren't as high as they had been before hearing the truth about the murder. Brandon had been safely behind bars for the last eight and a half months. Until now, that is.

Emily found herself praying while waiting for the officer to arrive. "Dear Heavenly Father, Oh Lord, help me through this. Your

Word says that I can do all things through You, because You give me strength. Lord Jesus, I need Your strength right now. Your Word also says that I can endure all things. Lord, carry me through this. Help me to endure. Father God, You know what I want to say but can't. You know what I am thinking and feeling even though I can't find the words to pray." Emily opened the Bible and read what had become her favorite passage of the Bible, Psalm 37:1-11 out loud. " 'Do not fret because of evildoers, nor be envious of the workers of iniquity, for they shall soon be cut down like the grass, and wither as the green herb. Trust in the Lord and do good; dwell in the land and feed on his faithfulness. Delight yourself in the Lord and He will give you the desires of your heart. Commit your way to the Lord. Trust also in Him and He shall bring it to pass. He shall bring forth your righteousness as the light, and your justice as the noonday. Rest in the Lord, and wait patiently for Him; do not fret because of him who prospers in his way, because of the man who brings wicked schemes to pass. Cease from anger and forsake wrath; do not fret – it only causes harm. For evildoers shall be cut off; but those who wait on the Lord, they shall inherit the earth. For yet a little while and the wicked shall be no more; indeed, you will look carefully for his place but it shall be no more. But the meek shall inherit the earth, and shall delight themselves in the abundance of peace.' Oh, yes, Lord Jesus, please give me peace. I need the peace that passes all understanding. Help me to not be afraid, Father God. Help me to rest in Your ever-loving arms. Give me the words to say as I call my family and warn them. In Jesus name I pray, Amen."

Just then, there was a knock at the door. She looked out the window on the way to the door. There were two police cars in front of the house. She unlocked the door and stepped out onto the porch.

"Ms. Payne, I am Officer Hamblin and this is Officer Ridgewood." Just then another police car pulled up. Officer Hamblin waited for the latest arrival to approach. "This is Sergeant Mobley. I have been assigned to protect you. I will sit in my car in front of your house. I will not leave unless you leave, in which case I will follow you. What did you have planned for today?"

"Not much. I have to go to work from seven tonight until seven in the morning, but that is all." Emily had planned on sleeping all day after having worked all night the night before. She knew sleep was out of the question.

"Well, when you go to work, an officer will follow you and sit in front of your work," Officer Hamblin said.

"Okay, but I am concerned about my mother and my daughter. Mom's address is listed in the phone book; mine isn't, so he can easily find her house. My daughter, Rachel, will come home while I am at work." Emily took a deep breath and tried not to be afraid for her family.

"How old is Rachel and where is she now?" Officer Hamblin pulled out a small notebook and a pen.

"She is seventeen. She spent the night at a friend's last night, but is due home tonight."

"You let me know what time she will be here and we will make sure there's an officer here when she gets home, if Brandon hasn't been apprehended by then. I'll check and see if we can get a unit over to your mother's house as well."

Emily gave him her mother's address and felt much better when she heard the dispatcher say, "We will get one right over there."

Emily went back in the house and tried to get some rest to no avail. She called some friends and talked with them for awhile. She tried to read, watch TV, surf the Internet. She couldn't sit still, couldn't relax, so she started cleaning house. She was a pretty good housekeeper so there wasn't very much she could do.

Emily answered the knock at the door. "Hello, Ms. Payne. I am Officer Drake. I have been assigned to relieve Officer Hamblin. If you need anything, let me know." Emily thanked him for introducing himself and went back in the house.

She decided a hot shower might help. It did, but she still couldn't rest. She didn't know what to do with herself. She had all kinds of time to kill, but couldn't get her mind off of Brandon being loose.

When it was finally time to leave for work, she let Officer Drake know the route she would take to work so that she wouldn't lose him.

When she got to work, she and her co-workers gathered around to watch the news and saw her life on TV for all to see, yet again.

They showed the original footage again. Tears welled up in Emily's eyes as she watched the paramedics wheeling Michael across the yard on the stretcher with an oxygen mask over his little face. Even after almost eleven years, that was one image she would never get used to seeing.

She tried her best to work hard that night, but she was tired and concerned. She felt much better knowing that there was an officer outside in case of an emergency. Her co-workers were so supportive and helpful through the whole ordeal.

When she got off work in the morning, the officer who had replaced Officer Drake followed her home. Rachel had decided to stay at Terri's house, so there wasn't an officer watching the house. When Emily got home with Officer Bresslyn not far behind, she was told not to go in the house yet. Within a few minutes another police car pulled up. "Ms. Payne," Officer Bresslyn said, "we are going to search your house first. We just want to make sure there is no one in there."

Emily stood in the driveway crying as the officers walked around inside her house with their guns drawn and shining flashlights in every corner. She didn't realize that would bother her, but it was just another confirmation of the reality of what was going on.

Chapter 51

When the officers came back out, Officer Bresslyn said, "Ms. Payne, we need to know if you would go into protective custody. We were hoping to catch him by now, but since it has been over twenty-four hours now and we haven't caught him yet, we need to make other arrangements. We just don't have the man power to keep an officer posted here."

"You think protective custody is necessary?" Emily asked.

"We don't want to alarm you or add to your concern, but yes, we do. We would rather be safe than sorry."

"All right, then, I'll go." Emily knew the officers knew what was best.

"Well, get some things packed and then we'll take you."

Emily went in the house. She was so tired. All she wanted to do was sleep, but now she had to pack. She gathered some things together, not knowing where she was going or for how long she would be gone or if she would even have a home to come home to.

She hopped on the Internet and wrote a quick email to her friends and family. "Hello, Everyone; I have some disturbing news this morning. Early yesterday morning, between 4 am and 7 am, Brandon and two other men escaped from the jail where Brandon was being held awaiting trial. Here is a link to the newspaper article covering the story with a picture of him and those who may be with him. Rachel and I are going into protective custody for the time being. Hopefully, they will catch him soon and all will be back to normal. Please keep us in your prayers. I'll try to keep in touch. Love Ya'll, Emily". She logged off and shut down the computer.

She walked outside and told the officer she was ready. Officer Bresslyn took her to her mother's house to get Rachel and then headed off to a safe place.

~ ~ ~ ~ ~ ~ ~

"Here you are," Officer Bresslyn said as he pulled up to the place Emily and Rachel would be staying until Brandon was apprehended. "We ask that you not use the phone provided since you have a cell phone. You are welcome to use your cell phone to call anyone you would like because it won't show your location on a caller ID. We ask that you stay here as much as possible, but we want you to be comfortable. You are not a prisoner and we don't want you to feel like one. The more time you spend away from here, the more danger you put yourself in."

"I can't leave. I don't have a vehicle," Emily stated.

"You may use Yellow Cab. They are really good about keeping information confidential – destinations, passengers, origination points, and all that. There is no need to reveal your name to them or anyone else. If you want to order a pizza, pay cash and use a fake name."

"All right. We'll be okay," Emily said trying to convince herself.

"Here is my cell phone number if you need anything, and you have Detective Pritchett's number, right?" Bresslyn said handing Emily a card.

"Yeah, I have Pritchett's memorized."

"If you need anything at all, call one of us and we will take care of it."

After Officer Bresslyn left, Emily tried to get some rest, while Rachel put her headphones back on. Emily affectionately referred to them as 'her ears' because she saw them more often than her actual ears.

Emily couldn't sleep. She decided to call Abby. She answered on the first ring. "How are you?"

"I'm holding up. I haven't slept in over twenty-four hours now. I have tried, but it just doesn't work." Emily sounded exhausted.

"So, you decided to call me? I feel so special," Abby chuckled.

Emily laughed. "You know, you always make me laugh, no matter what is going on. How do you do that?"

"It is just my overwhelmingly sweet personality oozing through the phone line. You just can't help but love me bunches!"

"Yeah, I love you, ya nut," Emily said smiling.

"I was actually just praying for you when you called," Abby said.

"Well, I need that," Emily sighed deeply. "I just want this whole thing to end."

"That is what I was praying for. I was actually singing God a TAIT song on your behalf. It really fits this situation. Here, let me read you the lyrics. The song is called Fallen and it goes 'She's a wreck, fragile and scarred. Life is work and living is hard. She's tired of the pain, tired of the fix. She's tired of the games and the politics. She's running on empty. She wants an alternate ending. She can feel the weight of the past. It drags her down but she's fighting back. She wants to fly far away from here. She wants a God that won't disappear. She's all out of chances. She is looking for answers and she's falling. She's falling in love with You. She's so hopeless... she's hopelessly drawn to You. The sun is on the rise. New day's coming. You see it in her eyes. She's running head long into the light. Let the new day come.' "

"Yeah, that about sums it up. It amazes me how this whole thing has brought me closer to God. When it first happened this was the thing that pushed me away from Him." Emily said.

"Em. They are going to catch him, and put him away for the rest of his life. The new day really is coming if you'll just hang on a little bit longer."

They talked and prayed together before Abby said, "you need to try to get some rest. If you don't sleep, at least close your eyes for a bit."

"All right. I'll call you later. Thanks, Abby."

Emily laid down and began to pray. "Lord, this has been going on for over ten years. Is it ever going to end? How many times do I have to fight this war?" Emily began crying a river of tears. She just laid there hugging the pillow until she finally cried herself to sleep.

Chapter 52

"Mom! Mom! Wake up! They got him!" Emily hadn't even realized she had fallen asleep. She rolled over. "What?" she asked groggily.

"They got him. Look!" Rachel turned up the volume on the TV.

"We have a late breaking story. The mastermind behind the escape from the Metro Jail was caught less than forty-five minutes ago. We'll go to Hamilton Park where Jonathon Suffolk joins us live. Jonathon." The scene cut to the park. The camera man was showing a dog on a leash held by a police officer. "Thank You, Darla. This is Officer Viper. He is the one credited with the apprehension of escapee Brandon Charles Brooks. It took Viper about twelve minutes to find Brooks in the woods hiding under a bush. Brooks tried to fight the dog off causing severe injuries to his left leg and right arm. They are transporting him to the hospital now, where he will be treated for the dog bites." The camera man cut to show Brandon limping with an officer on each side of him. "A tip led police to the woodsy hideout, where police say they also found camping gear. They are not sure if Brooks planned on camping here for awhile or if he planned on moving again under the cover of night. That is all for now, Darla. We will update you as more information becomes available."

Emily turned the TV off. As the story ended, the phone on the bedside table rang. Emily was a little nervous about answering it. Her friends would be calling her cell phone. No one was supposed to know where she was.

Emily answered apprehensively, "Hello?"

"Did you see the news?" It was Detective Pritchett.

Emily sighed a sigh of relief. "Yes, I did. Good news."

"Yes, very. I wanted to call you before the news aired, but I just didn't have a chance. He's at the hospital right now. We have him chained to the bed and sedated. He will probably be hospitalized for a few days before being taken back to jail."

"So, what happens now?" Emily asked.

"Well, you are welcome to go home if you'd like, but I would rather you stay where you are, at least for tonight."

"Okay." Emily's forehead furrowed. "Why?"

"Well, so far Brandon is the only one of the three that we have apprehended. I just don't want to find out that this was a case of you-scratch-my-back-I'll-scratch-yours. I mean, what if Brandon was supposed to eliminate one of the other escapees' victims or witnesses and one of them was supposed to eliminate you? We just don't know and needless to say, Brandon isn't cooperating."

"All right. I'll stay here tonight. I didn't really feel like moving right now anyway. I haven't slept much in the past thirty-six hours."

"I will call you in the morning. You get some rest."

"All right," Emily hung up the phone. "What time is it?"

"It's a little after five," Rachel answered.

"What do you want for dinner?" Emily asked realizing that sleep was out of the question again.

"I don't care. Pizza is fine," Rachel said.

"Well, I would rather go somewhere to celebrate. Let's take a cab and go out and have some fun. I feel like a night out. What do you say?" Emily said trying to encourage Rachel.

"Did you get enough sleep?" Rachel asked her mother.

"No, but now I'm too excited to sleep," Emily replied.

"It's up to you. You're the mother around here," Rachel said chuckling.

Emily got up and pulled her suitcase out from under the bed. She had only packed one dressy outfit and now she was glad she did. She took it into the bathroom and hopped in the shower.

Rachel got dressed up as well and put make up on, which she very rarely did. She was very down-to-earth and thought make up used to make someone look good was stupid.

When Emily came out of the bathroom and saw her daughter standing there all dressed up with make up on, tears came to her eyes.

She loved Rachel so much and she couldn't stand the thought of ever losing her. She had turned into such a beautiful young woman.

They decided to go to a local restaurant that was off the beaten path. Emily's face had not appeared on the news, so although, the escape was the talk of the town, no one knew who she was.

Overnight that night, the police apprehended the other two escapees. The next morning, Emily and Rachel gladly went back home.

2005

Chapter 53

Emily awoke an hour earlier than necessary. She took out her Bible and read Psalm thirty-seven again. Then she prayed, "Lord God, I just ask that Your will be done in the courtroom this week. I pray that whoever You want on the jury is selected. Lord, You are the only One who knows for sure what happened that day. If Brandon did set the house on fire and kill Michael and Leslie, I pray that he is convicted. But, Lord, if he didn't do it, I pray that he's acquitted. I do not want to send an innocent man to prison for the rest of his life, but if he's guilty I want him off the streets so that society is safe. Lord, I ask for Your will – nothing more and nothing less. In Jesus' name, Amen."

As Emily drove into the parking lot, she and Terri saw two network news vans parked in the front row. She found a parking spot in the second row. She looked up at the beautiful six-story stone building. There were six tall columns standing five stories high. The top of the courthouse was peaked and had a large seal of the State of Tennessee carved in the stone where the sixth-story windows should have been. They walked quickly through the cold winter air into the courthouse. Due to the escape, the trial had been reset for the second week in January.

After entering the courthouse and going through the metal detectors, Emily looked around. She was perplexed at how amazing this building was. It had ivory-colored marble floors with dark cherry wood pillars. There were cherry wood borders framing the windows and doorways. The walls were painted an olive green and had some classic paintings adorning them.

She and Terri entered the elevator which would take them to the fourth floor. The hallway looked the same here as it did downstairs. The courtroom doors had white textured glass. Emily saw Shelley to her left talking with a man in a uniform whom Emily had never seen before. She would later discover the man was Mr. Allison, the fire investigator who worked for the city. Shelley lifted her fingers in a cordial wait-a-minute gesture.

"That is Shelley over there in the red suit," Emily whispered to her mother. Terri looked over and saw a beautiful woman in her late twenties standing about five feet six inches tall with light brown hair and brown eyes.

Looking around some more, Emily saw cameramen down the hall the to her right. The cameras were sitting on the floor next to computer monitors. There were wires littering the floor. The reporters were all standing around talking to each other. Emily recognized a few of them. "Don't look now, Mom," Emily said as she gestured down the hall.

"I see that," Terri said with disgust in her voice.

"Well, at this point they have no idea what I look like, but that is about to change," Emily stated.

"Yeah, as soon as they see you talk to Shelley..." Terri let her words trail as Shelley approached.

"Good morning," Shelley said.

"Good morning. Shelley, this is my mother, Terri Payne." Terri and Shelley shook hands.

"Nice to meet you, Shelley," Terri said.

"Nice to meet you, too. Let's go into the victim witness room." Shelley continued to talk as she led the way down the hall toward the news crews. She turned down a small hallway to their left just before reaching the media. She punched in a code on a door and opened it. "This is your safe haven throughout the trial. No one is allowed in here except victims, witnesses for the prosecution, and district attorneys. The defense attorney and the defense's witnesses have a separate room on the other side of the courtroom. The media is not allowed in either room. There is coffee, a refrigerator, and a microwave over there." Shelley pointed to her immediate right and then pointed into the corner. "That door there is a restroom. We will be here for a few days to a week. You may bring a lunch with you or go out for lunch, whichever you prefer. Make sure you mark you stuff though and don't leave anything valuable in this room because we are not the only ones using this room. Make yourself at home and Candice will be right with you." The room was very comfortable looking. It had three cubicles with computers lined up along the wall to the left of the door. Along the back wall there was a conference table with eight chairs. Along the right wall, there was a couch. There were two chairs facing the couch with a coffee table between them.

Candice Moore was the district attorney that would be trying the case. Candice was a little woman standing no taller than five feet two inches and weighing no more than a hundred and ten pounds. She had blond hair and beautiful green eyes. Emily had met Candice shortly after the arrest and they had seen each other a few times since. Emily quickly learned that despite her size, Candice was a woman to be feared, if you were a homicide suspect, that is. Candice was a specialist in homicide cases who, in her twenty-two years in the district attorneys office, had won more homicide trials than any other DA in the state.

Candice came in the room about five minutes later talking to a man. He was about six feet tall and built like a football player. He looked to be in his mid-thirties and was very attractive with his jet black hair and deep-set crystal blue eyes. Candice smiled when she saw Emily and approached immediately. "Emily, I'd like you to meet Brent Smythe. He is another district attorney and he will be sitting in on this trial. Mr. Smythe is a child abuse and neglect specialist. He travels the country teaching district attorneys nationwide tactics in trying cases in which the victims are children."

"Nice to meet you, Ms. Payne," he said in a deep voice matching his physique.

"Nice to meet you, Mr. Smythe. Please, call me Emily."

"Okay, but only if you call me Brent," he said, smiling.

Emily liked him immediately and introduced Terri to Brent and Candice.

"Let's have a seat for just a minute, okay?" Candice said ushering Emily and Terri to the couch. Once they were seated, Candice said, "Jury selection is set to begin in fifteen minutes. As you make your way around the courthouse before jury selection is complete, do not look at anyone. You never know who may be on the jury. You are welcome to sit in the courtroom during the jury selection, but you are not allowed to look at any juror or potential juror. Once the trial actually starts, you may not make eye contact with a juror, so to be safe, just don't even look that direction. You cannot show any emotion while in the gallery during jury selection or during the trial itself. Keep a straight face as much as possible." Emily had heard all of these instructions before, but her mother hadn't and she thought it would be good to hear them again anyway. When Candice was finished, Emily took a deep breath and they all headed toward the courtroom.

Emily and Terri took seats in the back row for jury selection. It was a large room with twelve foot ceilings. It has the same cherry wood trim as the rest of the courthouse and the walls were painted yellowish beige. The gallery seats were like old church pews with comfortable tan padding. The floor was the same off-white marble. *So, this is where I am going to spend the next week. This is where my life is going to change forever. This is where I will find out once and for all if Brandon really did kill Michael and Leslie.*

Jury selection began with the judge telling the potential jurors what would be asked of them, what to expect and where to go if stricken. The defense and the prosecution each had the opportunity to ask each juror questions and then to decide if they wanted to strike that juror or not. The doors were locked during jury selection so that there would be no disturbances of people coming in and going out of the courtroom.

"It is just too boring in there," Emily told her mother when it was time to go back in after the first break. "I don't want to sit through any more jury selection."

"I was hoping you would say that," Terri said, relieved.

"You are more than welcome to go home. You don't have to be here for this. The actual trial will begin in the morning. You do have to be here for that," Shelley informed them.

A few hours later, Shelley called Emily to let her know the jury had been selected. She told Emily what time to be there in the morning and that Candice had decided that after opening statements, Emily would be the first witness to testify.

Chapter 54

"Please state your full name for the court." Candice began the trial.

"Emily Lynn Payne." Emily was nervous and her voice was shaking. She was dressed in a black pantsuit. The only makeup she wore was waterproof mascara and a touch of lipstick because she was sure she would cry at some point.

"Ms. Payne, are you related in any way to a Henry Michael Carter?"

"Yes, I am his mother."

"Are you related in anyway to a Leslie Lynette Carter?"

"Yes, I am her mother."

"And, Ms. Payne, do you know a Brandon Charles Brooks?"

"Yes ma'am." Emily had been instructed to answer only the question asked. If more detail would be required it would be asked as a separate question.

"Do you see Mr. Brooks in this courtroom?"

"Yes ma'am. He is right there." Emily pointed toward Brandon. She refused to make eye contact with him and tried her best not to even look that direction.

"Can you please tell the court how you know Mr. Brooks?"

Emily took a deep breath and prayed her voice would stop quivering. She didn't want to give Brandon the satisfaction of knowing that she was a nervous wreck. As it was he was staring her down trying to intimidate her. She refused to look his direction. She decided to keep her eyes on Candice and pretend that they were in her office just chatting about all that had happened. "I was looking for a place to live. I had found an ad in the paper about a two-bedroom duplex for rent. I had called the number and scheduled an appointment to meet the landlord, Mr. Lloyd, at the duplex. I arrived before Mr. Lloyd did so I sat in the car waiting. Mr. Brooks came out of the house and asked if he could help me. I told him what I was doing there. We talked for a few minutes before Mr. Lloyd arrived. Then, Mr. Lloyd and I went into one half of the duplex, while Mr. Brooks went back into the other side."

"What happened next?"

Emily had regained her composer and pressed on confidently. "Well, I talked to Mr. Lloyd and decided to rent the property. I signed the lease and began moving in the next day."

"So, Mr. Brooks was your neighbor?"

"Yes ma'am. He lived in the other half of the duplex that I lived in."

"And did you two become friends?"

"Um… not right away. I worked a lot of hours and I was only awake at home for about two hours a day. The rest of the time I was there, I was sleeping."

"When did you become friends?"

"We had gotten to know each other some living next door to each other, but we didn't really get to be friends until after the fire."

"Did Mr. Brooks have a key to your house on Bailey Street?"

"No, again we didn't really get to be friends until *after* the fire."

"Okay. We'll come back to that later." Candice pulled out a large poster and put it up on an easel facing the jury. "Ms. Payne, do you recognize this picture?"

"Yes ma'am. That is the sketch I drew of the apartment that burned down." Emily proceeded to describe the floor plan and the placement of the furniture to the jury.

"Thank you, Ms. Payne. Can you please tell me about the morning of September 30, 1993?"

"I woke up at my usual time and woke my children up. Rachel, my oldest, had school that day. I went into the kitchen and fixed breakfast for everyone. Rachel was dressed when she came into the kitchen, Michael and Leslie were not. After breakfast, Rachel left to go to school. Michael, Leslie and I went into the kids' bedroom to get their clothes out. I gave them their clothes and told them to get dressed. Then, I went in my room to get dressed. I pulled my clothes out of the dresser, sat down on the bed and started getting dressed. The next thing I knew the house was filled with smoke and the living room was full of flames." Emily sniffled and the bailiff handed her a box of Kleenex. "I got up and went towards the kids' room. I bumped into something in the hallway and discovered it was Leslie. I took her back into their bedroom where I found Michael sitting on his bed crying. I knelt on the floor and took both of the children in my arms. I told them to lay down on the floor and that I would be right back. They were crying, but they did as they were told. I took a deep breath and climbed up onto the dresser and tried to open the window. I couldn't get the screen open. I tried to push it out with my shoulder, but it wasn't working. Then I thought I heard someone calling my name, so I yelled 'We're in the kids' room'. I needed air and tried to get below the smoke, but I breathed in too soon and passed out."

"Okay. Let's back up for just a minute. When Rachel left for school, where did she go? Did she walk to school or to a bus stop?"

"No, she walked next door to Robert's and he took Rachel and his kids to school. Then I would pick them up after school."

"And when Rachel left, did she lock the door behind herself?"

"No, she didn't. The door remained unlocked after she left."

"Was that typical?"

"Yes ma'am, it was."

"Do you know where Mr. Brooks was during the whole episode you have just described for us?"

"No ma'am, I don't."

"Was it his voice you heard?"

"I believe it was Robert's voice."

"You believe?"

"Yes ma'am. I can't be certain."

"So, you passed out getting off the dresser. What happened next?"

"Well, the next thing I remember, I was in the emergency room at Vanderbilt..." Emily went into as much detail as she could about the following thirty-six hours between the time she arrived at the hospital until they all left and went to Marvin and Terri's house. As she finished telling the court about when the life support machines were turned off, the judge called a recess. Emily was relieved to get out of there for a few minutes.

Abby and Terri met Emily in the hallway. They brushed past the reporters and the cameras. Surprisingly, the media people were not bothering them. "Are you all right?" Abby whispered.

Emily sighed, "Yeah, but I'll be better when it's over."

"Your testimony or the whole trial?"

"Both."

"I'm proud of you, Em," Terri said. "You're doing a great job."

"Thanks. At least the hardest part is over. I'm done talking about how they died and what that was like. Now I just have to testify to what happened over the next few months and how I figured it all out. Then, cross-examination. Now, that should be fun!" Emily said very sarcastically.

"You'll do fine. Just tell Candice the story and pretend like there is no one else there, like she told you. When Mr. Cordova is cross-examining you, just pretend he is your friend and he's just wondering what happened. Picture yourself sitting across the table from him at a coffee shop if that will help."

"Thanks, Mom." Emily hugged her mother.

"No problem. Well, it looks like we had better get ready to go back in."

Chapter 55

"Ms. Payne, do you understand that you are still under oath?" Candice asked as Emily sat on the witness stand.

"Yes ma'am."

"Just before the recess you told us about the day that your kid's died. Can you tell us what happened next?"

"I stayed with my parents for a few weeks after the fire. Mom moved to Chicago during that time. She had to get away. I decided it was time to get a place of my own. I had talked to Brandon a few times after the fire and we decided to be roommates since neither of us had a place to live."

"When did you move in together?"

"November first."

"How did Brandon treat you?"

"At first he was very attentive and compassionate, but before long he began telling me to just 'get over it already'. Then on Christmas he told me that I was wrong for sending Rachel to Chicago with my dad for a week. Not long after that, he became downright rude and cold towards me. I began saving money so I could move out."

"Can you tell us what happened near the end of January?"

"I came home from work one night and he was drunk and high…"

Mr. Cordova jumped to his feet. "Objection, your Honor. Ms. Payne has no way of knowing my client's state of mind."

"Sustained."

"What led you to believe that Mr. Brooks was drunk and high?" Candice asked.

"There were empty beer bottles all over the coffee table and a tray that he always used for rolling joints with pot on it was sitting on the couch next to him."

"What happened next?"

"He said he was going to discipline Rachel for leaving toys out and I told him that I would take care of it. I also told him that I was going to be looking for another place to live. He got mad and said that I wasn't going to leave him stuck like that. I told him that I was telling him now so that he could start looking for another roommate. He said, 'This is the same crap that Suzie pulled before I set her house on fire. No one burns Brandon!'"

"What did you think about that?"

"At first I was shocked. I tried to stay calm and get him to talk. He eventually told me the whole story and ended it with, 'so I figured if I couldn't live there, no one else would either.' I excused myself and went to my room. I began thinking about the possibility of him setting my house on fire. Little things that hadn't make sense before were beginning to fall into place. The next night when I went to work, I called my parents and told them what I suspected. We decided it would be best for Rachel and I to move in with my mother in Chicago. That night, I left Rachel with a friend of mine and I spent the night packing. My dad was going to get a rental van for me and bring it to the house first thing in the morning."

"What happened next?"

"I finished packing and went to bed. I was only going to get a few hours of sleep, but I needed it. I didn't sleep well. When my alarm went off, Brandon was sitting on the arm of the loveseat I had in my room looking at me. I freaked out. He asked me where I thought I was going. The phone wasn't on my nightstand. It had been removed. Then I noticed that he had locked the bedroom door. I was petrified. He proceeded to tell me that he thought I started the fire because it was so hard being a single mother. He said that I spared Rachel because she was my favorite. He said that I was trying to kill myself, Michael and Leslie. He said that I thought they would be better off dead since growing up half-black would be so hard on them. I was too shocked and too scared to speak. Then he said he was going to help me finish what I had started. He handed me a piece of paper with a suicide note written on it, a blank sheet of paper and a pen and told me to copy the note in my hand-writing. I was really scared.

"He proceeded to tell me how no one needed a loser like me in their lives listing my family and friends one by one and telling me what a burden I am to them. I couldn't write it. I just sat there killing time and hoping my dad would hurry up and get there." Emily couldn't stop shaking as she remembered the fear that had taken control of her that morning eleven years prior. It was almost as if she was back on that bed.

Candice noticed that Emily needed a breather and took her time before prompting her to go on. "What happened next, Ms. Payne?"

"My dad got there. He was pounding on the front door. Brandon was standing between me and the bedroom door, so I couldn't have answered it. Brandon was acting as if he didn't hear it. He said, 'Write the note.' After a few minutes he got mad and told me I had better not leave that room and he went to answer the door. As soon as I heard him talking to my dad, I went across the hall and grabbed a baseball bat from Rachel's room. I stood at the top of the stairs and when Brandon got to the top I swung that bat and sent him flying back down the stairs. It knocked him out and gave me and my dad time to get the van loaded. Brandon started coming back around right before I left. He didn't try to stop me. I went and got Rachel and got out of Nashville as quickly as possible."

"Did Mr. Brooks try to follow you?"

"I don't know. I don't think so."

"When did you contact the police about your suspicions?"

"I called them the next day – the day after I arrived in Chicago."

"What did they say?"

"Objection, your Honor. That calls for hearsay."

"Sustained. Rephrase the question, Ms. Moore."

"What happened next?"

"I was transferred about twenty times and finally talked to someone in homicide. He took down all of the information and said he would call me back. A few weeks later, he still hadn't called, so I called him again and left a message. Within the next two months time he had only called me three times and that was always when I wasn't home, so he would leave a message. After two months, I was no longer afraid, I was mad. I left Rachel in Chicago and I came back down here to see if I could get some answers. After a few more months I decided I wasn't being the mother I had set out to be, so I had to let it go. It was consuming my life and no one was cooperating with me anyway. I went back to Chicago and got Rachel and moved her back to Tennessee. I decided to get my life back and do some things I wasn't able to do before Michael and Leslie died, so I registered for classes the University. In a last ditch effort to get someone to look into it, I wrote a letter to the district attorney telling him why I suspected what I suspected and that the police wouldn't cooperate with me. I received a letter from him not long after that telling me that there was not enough evidence to warrant reopening this case and if I came up with anything else to let him know. I filed the letter and put it behind me. That was November of 1994. In January of 2000, Detective Tomarano called me out of the blue and told me that they had decided to reopen the case." Candice had told her that she cannot say why they decided to reopen the case because that other fire cannot be brought into this trial. "I cooperated with him the best that I could. I answered all of his questions, helped him find a potential witness, took him to the grave, and even went to the house with him to point out how it all happened while looking at the layout of the house. I met with Mr. Rutherford once to answer all of his questions. Then I met with Detective Pritchett and answered all of his questions."

"So you jumped in full force?"

"I wanted to do whatever I could to help, yes, but I didn't do any research on my own as I had before."

"No further questions, Your Honor."

"Okay, we will have a lunch break until one o'clock. Then Mr. Cordova can begin cross-examinations."

Chapter 56

"**M**s. Payne, you said that Rachel didn't lock the door behind herself. How do you know that?" Mr. Cordova jumped right in.

"Rachel never locked the door behind herself," Emily stated.

"So, you are not positive that on that particular morning she didn't. You can only positively say that it was normal routine for her to leave the door unlocked."

"Yes, I suppose, but why would she…"

Cordova cut her off. "I'm asking the questions, Ms. Payne. You are answering them."

"Yes sir."

"So, again, you cannot say for certain that Rachel left the door unlocked?"

"No sir."

"Ms. Payne, did anything unusual happen the night of September 29, 1993?"

Emily had to think for a minute. "Not that I recall."

"Isn't it true that you had received a phone call from someone in Chicago telling you that your best friend from high school had been found murdered?"

"Oh, yeah. I forgot about that!" Emily said without thinking.

"You forgot? How convenient! How did that news affect you?"

"Naturally, I was upset."

"Upset? Were you depressed?"

"Yeah, I would say I probably was depressed. I know the news was a total shock to me. I had just talked to her a month or so before that. Her mother called me and told me that she had been missing for a few weeks before they found her body in a dumpster."

"You just gave us quite a bit of detail for something you forgot."

"I meant I forgot that news came in the night before the fire."

"No further questions." Emily looked at the judge.

"Ms. Payne, you may step down. Ms. Moore, please call your next witness." Cordova took his seat as Emily made her way back to her seat in the gallery.

Candice rose from her seat. "The State calls Robert Tibbs." A door behind the witness stand opened and Robert was brought in. The court clerk read the oath and Robert was sworn in.

"Would you please state your full name for the record?" Candice inquired.

"Robert John Tibbs," he stated.

"Mr. Tibbs, you used to live on Bailey Street, correct?"

"Yes."

"What was your address?"

Robert leaned closer to the microphone to answer each question. "Oh, boy. I don't remember. 257 maybe."

"Do you remember a woman named Emily Payne?"

"Yes ma'am. She lived in the building next to mine."

"And did you know her well?" Candice leaned on the table.

"Um. She and my wife were really good friends. And I would give her oldest daughter a ride to school in the morning, then Emily or Emily's mother would pick Rachel and my kids up after school and give them a ride home."

"You said Ms. Payne was good friends with your wife?"

"Yes, my wife called Emily her best friend."

"Mr. Tibbs, was your wife black as well?"

"Yes, she was," Robert answered obviously confused by this line of questioning.

Changing gears, Candice asked, "Did you see Ms. Payne interacting with her children?"

"Oh, yes, almost daily! All three of her kids played with my kids while Emily and my wife sat around talking."

"Would you say Ms. Payne loved her children?"

"Yes, she adored them. She was a very good mother." Tears began forming in Emily's eyes as memories of her children came flooding back.

"Did you ever see Ms. Payne discipline her children?"

"Yes, I did."

"Can you tell us when?"

"Whenever they did something they shouldn't do. I saw it more than once. I mean they were really good kids, but all kids get into trouble sometimes."

"Would you say Ms. Payne was abusive?"

"No, I wouldn't. She would swat one of the kids on the bottom if necessary, but she never overdid it. She put the kids in time out more than anything else. She loved her kids – all of them – and it was obvious!"

"Did you know Brandon Charles Brooks?"

"Yes, he lived in the other half of the building that Emily lived in."

"Would you say you were friends with him?"

"No, I didn't know him that well. I just knew him because he was my neighbor, but we didn't hang out together or anything."

"Were Mr. Brooks and Ms. Payne close friends?"

"I think so. He had a key to her house, so I assume they were pretty close." Shock registered on Emily's face though she tried to hide it. *Brandon had a key? How did he get a key?*

"How do you know he had a key to her house?"

"I saw him going into her house one day when she wasn't home. I asked him what he was doing and he said that Emily gave him a key."

"Did that seem strange to you?"

"Yeah, a little, but I just thought maybe there was more there than meets the eye. Emily never said anything about him, but I decided to just mind my own business."

"Did you ever ask Ms. Payne about it?"

"No. I figured if she wanted me to know she would tell me."

"Did you ever ask her why she had given Brandon a key?"

"No, it was none of my business."

"Did you see Ms. Payne the night of September 29, 1993?"

"Yeah, she came over to our house when she got home from work."

"Was this common?"

"Yeah. I mean she didn't do it every night, but sometimes she did."

"Do you remember what you all talked about?"

"No, I don't."

"Did she tell you anything about a friend of hers who was murdered?"

"No, she didn't," Robert stated clearly not knowing what Candice was talking about. Candice decided it was time to move on to the fire itself.

Chapter 57

Candice continued to question Robert Tibbs, Emily's neighbor. "Do you recall what happened on the morning of September 30, 1993?"

"Yes, I do."

"Could you tell us in your own words what you remember about that morning?"

"Well, Rachel came over to the house and we left. I took the kids to school and dropped them off. When I turned on my street, I saw smoke. I remember thinking 'I wonder where the fire is.' As I got closer I realized it was Emily's house on fire. I pulled in my driveway, threw the car in park, and began running toward her house screaming 'someone call 911. EMILY!' As I got close to her house Brandon came out of his house rubbing his eyes asking me what was going on. I said, 'there's a fire! Quick! Help me.' I kicked the door in and flames rushed out practically pushing me off the steps. I ran around the side of the house just as Mr. Greenwood came from the back. He helped me push the air conditioner out of the window of the kids' room. The smoke rushed out as I pushed the window up the rest of the way. Then we heard the fire trucks and ran around the front. The fireman asked me if there were people inside. I told him that there was a mother and two small children in there. He asked me to step back. I watched him pass Leslie out the window and hand her to another fireman who started doing CPR on her. Then he passed Michael out the window to another fireman, who started doing CPR on him. A few minutes later, my wife put her arm around me and guided me over to our front porch where we watched. They put the fire out and then brought Emily out through the front door. They laid her on the ground and worked on her before putting her in the ambulance. They had already taken the kids in another ambulance."

"Let's talk about Brandon's actions for a minute. You said he came out of the house rubbing his eyes as if he just woke up?"

"Yes, that is correct."

"And then he asked you what was going on?"

"Yeah. That really surprised me because his house was on fire at that point also. How could he not know what was going on?"

Mr. Cordova jumped to his feet. "Objection, Your Honor. The witness is speculating."

"Sustained. The witness will only answer the question asked."

"What were you thinking when he asked what was going on?"

"I was thinking 'how can he not see that the house is on fire?'"

"You said you kicked the door in. Where was Mr. Brooks then?"

"I thought he was right behind me, but when I jumped back when the flames came rushing out, he wasn't there. He was putting his cats' cage in his car."

"Where was Brandon when you were asked to step aside so the firemen could rescue the children?"

"Moving his car."

"Moving his car?"

"Yes ma'am. After he put the cats' cage in the backseat of the car, he moved the car out of the driveway and onto the street."

"What did he do next?"

"Well, I looked back at the firemen because they were passing the kids out the window. I watched them for awhile. When I looked back Brandon was gone."

"Gone?"

"Yeah, I mean, his car was still there, but I didn't see him anywhere. In fact, I didn't see him again it was all over. It was probably one or two that afternoon. He was in the front yard arguing with Mr. Lloyd."

"Do you know what they were arguing about?"

"No ma'am. I didn't pay attention."

"No further questions, Your Honor," Candice said taking her seat.

"Mr. Cordova?" The defense attorney stood and approached the witness stand.

"Mr. Tibbs, you testified that Mr. Brooks had gone into Ms. Payne's apartment when she wasn't home. How often did that occur?"

"I only saw it once, but I didn't make a habit of watching Brandon's every move."

"And you said he had a key?"

"That is what he told me when I asked him what he was doing in her house when she wasn't home."

"So, you never saw the key?"

"No, but..."

"Just answer the question. No, you didn't see his key. So, you never saw him open the door with a key?"

"No, I didn't."

"How would you say Ms. Payne treated her children overall?"

"Like their mother." Everyone chuckled.

"Would you say Ms. Payne chose favorites?"

"No sir, she didn't. She treated all three of her children the same." Tears flooded Emily's eyes again as Robert talked about how much she loved her children. Judge Hafford had been watching her throughout the testimony and he could tell she needed a break.

"No more questions."

Before Mr. Cordova was back in his seat Emily got up and rushed out of the room. Abby followed her. "Hey," Abby called catching up to her in the hallway. "What's wrong?"

"I just had to get out of there." Emily walked straight toward the victim/witness room. She didn't want to talk about it in the hallway where all the reporters could hear her. As soon as the door shut behind her she said, "I don't know why that bothered me so much. All he said were good things, but it ripped my heart out listening to him talk about my relationship with my kids. The memories his testimony brought back made me miss them really bad."

Emily looked up as the door opened and her mother came in the room followed by Shelley, Brent, and Candice. "The judge called a fifteen minute recess," Terri stated.

"Guess he could tell I needed a break?" Emily said sarcastically.

"I think you walking out of the courtroom was a good indication of that," Shelley said. Everyone laughed.

After the recess, Candice called one of the firefighters to the stand. He testified to what he remembered from that day. His testimony supported what Emily and Robert had already said.

After the firefighter's testimony Judge Hafford recessed for the day.

Chapter 58

The first witness Candice called on Wednesday morning was Officer Summers. He was one of the officers at the scene of the fire, the one who called Terri, and the one who drove her to Vanderbilt Hospital. Emily thought that was a good move on Candice's part since his testimony refreshed everyone's memories about what was said the day before.

She then called one of the paramedics who were at the scene of the fire. He was the one who attended to Michael at the scene. He talked about Michael's condition and summarized what the reports said regarding Leslie and Emily.

Mr. Greenwood took the stand next. He was the one who maintained all of Mr. Lloyd's properties including the unit at 255 Bailey Dr.

"Mr. Greenwood, where did you live in September of 1993?"

"I lived at 254 Bailey Dr. which is where I still live today."

"Do you recall what happened on September 30, 1993?"

"Yes ma'am, I do. I had looked out the window of my home and noticed that the house across the street was on fire. I wasn't sure which house it was at that point. I was a little panicky. I grabbed the phone and called 9-1-1. As I was hanging up the phone, I saw Robert Tibbs going up the steps of the house. I ran outside and told him not to go in. I told him that I called the fire department and they were on the way. He yelled back to me that Emily and the kids were in the house. I ran across the street to try to help him get them out. Robert ran up the front steps while I ran around the side of the house. I thought we might be able to get in through one of the back windows. I was trying to get the back bedroom window open when Robert came running around the side of the house. He said he had heard Emily yelling and she sounded like she was in the front bedroom. I lifted him up to the window and he pushed the window-box air conditioner into the room. Then, he pushed the window up all the way. The smoke was billowing out and we were not able to get in. We heard the fire engines, so I lowered Robert back down. He ran over to the fire truck and told them that there were people in there and he showed him the window we had tried to go in. Then, Robert and I both stepped back and watched as they went in with gas masks on their faces."

"Would you say that this is an accurate sketch of the floor plan at 255 Bailey Street?" Candice put the drawing back up on the easel.

"Yes, it is. I am not positive about the placement of the furniture, but the floor plan itself is right."

"Which window did you and Mr. Tibbs try to enter?"

Mr. Greenwood pointed to the kids' bedroom window that was on the side of the house. Emily had tried to open the window in the same room, but on the front of the house.

"Do you recall where Brandon Brooks was during all of this?"

"Um, I didn't see him at first, but when they were putting one of the kids into the ambulance I noticed him walking down the street."

"Down the street? Coming or going?"

"He was going somewhere. I don't know where he went. There was too much going on right then. I was thinking about what could have caused the fire. I was reviewing in my head all the repairs we had done to the place right before Emily moved in."

"What repairs were done?"

"We replaced the refrigerator and the stove. We put in new carpeting and painted the place. I did some plumbing work in the bathroom."

"No electrical work?"

"No ma'am."

"Had you had problems with the base board heaters in the past?"

"No, we hadn't."

Mr. Cordova chose not to cross examine Mr. Greenwood and he stepped down.

Then Candice called Mr. Lloyd, the landlord of the property. Everyone in the courtroom listened intently as he testified about the day he had shown Emily the property.

"Mr. Lloyd, how was Ms. Payne as a tenant?"

"Oh, she was a good tenant. She always paid her rent on time, she never complained about anything and I never received any complaints against her."

"Was Mr. Brooks also your tenant?"

"No ma'am. Mr. Brooks was a friend of the man that I had leased the apartment to. Mr. Brooks was living there without permission."

"When did your tenant, Mr. Brook's friend, move out of that apartment?"

"Sometime in August. I don't recall exactly when, but his lease was up at the end of August and when I went to inspect the property at the end of the month, he had moved out, but Mr. Brooks refused to leave."

"What did you do next?"

"I called my attorney and told him the situation. We filed the necessary papers against Mr. Brooks to have him evacuated from the property. Mr. Brooks was given a final notice by personal service from the sheriff a week before the actual evacuation date."

"And when was the eviction scheduled to take place?"

"If Mr. Brooks had not vacated the property by September thirtieth, the sheriff would be accompanying me over to the duplex to remove him by force."

Mr. Lloyd testified to how he was informed of the fire, that he had arrived about four hours after the fire, what state the home was in when he got there, and the confrontation he had with Brandon.

Brandon had accused Mr. Lloyd of being a murderer. This surprised Mr. Lloyd because it was his understanding that everyone was alive. Upon calling the hospital after the confrontation, Mr. Lloyd was informed that Emily, Michael and Leslie were still alive. Mr. Cordova asked a few questions that did nothing but solidify the fact that his client was squatting at that home.

Chapter 59

"The State calls Mr. Rutherford to the stand," Candice said rising to her feet.

Mr. Rutherford made his way to the stand. After he was sworn in and seated, Ms. Moore said, "Please state your name and occupation for the court."

"My name is Mark Rutherford and I am a fire investigator." Candice asked a number of questions establishing the fact that Mr. Rutherford was a fire expert, then she asked the judge to recognize him as such. He did.

"Who do you work for?"

"I'm self-employed. I own a fire and bomb investigation company," Mr. Rutherford answered.

"Were you self-employed in September of 1993?"

"Yes ma'am, I was."

"Do you recall a fire in September of 1993 on Bailey Street?"

"Yes, I do."

"Did you investigate it?"

"Yes, I did."

"Who employed your services?"

"The owner of the property's insurance company."

After laying the groundwork, Candice went into more specific questions about Emily's fire. "And what did you find when you investigated this particular fire?"

"I found that the fire had to start right inside the front door, not across the room as was originally believed."

Candice feigned surprise. "Why do you say that?"

"The roof beams were laying the wrong way," Mr. Rutherford stated matter-of-factly.

Candice addressed the judge. "Your Honor, I would like to enter a series of pictures into evidence."

"Granted."

Candice presented a poster-sized picture of a burnt out living room with blackened two by fours leaning at an angle. "Look at this picture and tell the jury how the beams would have been laying had the fire started where it was originally believed the fire began."

"These are the roof beams here." Mr. Rutherford reached to point at the picture with the pointer that Candice had provided. Moving the pointer as he spoke, he said, "This is the south wall, where the heater was. If the heater had started the fire, the beams would be lying the exact opposite way than they are in this picture. As you can clearly see the most intense heat had to be at this end of the beam which is what severed it, therefore causing it to fall this way indicating that the fire had to start on the north side of the room."

"You said the fire had to have started right inside the front door. How do you know that?"

"Can I see the picture of the living room window from inside the house?"

Candice placed the requested picture on the easel.

Mr. Rutherford again pointed with the pointer. "This is the living room window. The front door was over here. As you can see the roof beams and the wall supports are much more charred in this corner than in the corner furthest from the door. That is how I know it started right inside the front door in the northeast corner of the living room."

"Ms. Payne testified that, and I quote, 'I pulled my clothes out of the dresser, sat down on the bed and started getting dressed. The next thing I knew the house was filled with smoke and the living room was full of flames.' Is it possible that the living room would be full of flames that quickly?"

"Yes ma'am, it is. It is called flash point. That occurs when all the oxygen in the room as been consumed by the fire and for the fire to continue burning it must find more oxygen. The fire would go from being a small fire in the corner of the room to the whole entire room being engulfed in a matter of seconds. This is also the point at which the windows will shatter as the fire begs for more oxygen."

"So, Ms. Payne didn't necessarily 'lose time'?" Candice asked with a tone of curiosity.

"Not necessarily. I cannot say for certain at which moment the fire began or exactly what Ms. Payne was doing at that moment, but it *is* possible that she didn't notice the house was on fire until the whole living room was in flames and the house was full of smoke."

"Let's go back to the drawing already entered into evidence." Candice put Emily's sketch back up on the easel. "Is this an accurate account of the home?"

"Yes, it is."

"Do you see anything in the pictures or in this drawing that could possibly have started the fire right inside the front door?"

"The only thing that was there was the light switch controlling the porch light and the living room lamp."

"Could that have been the culprit?" Candice asked.

"No ma'am. We know that it isn't for a few reasons. First of all, when you look closely at the picture, you'll see that the switch is burnt evenly with its surroundings, but the wires in the wall are not burned at all. Second of all, if it was the light switch that started the fire, the fire would have spread through the walls of the home along the wiring. It could have actually flamed there at the site as well, but the wires throughout would have been destroyed as well, and as you can see, that is not the case."

"So, in your expert opinion what started this fire?"

"I cannot say what did start it, but I can say what didn't. It was not electrical in nature, nor was it the heater. And I can say with all certainty that the fire started in the chair right here." He pointed to the chair in the sketch which was sitting in front of the living room window.

"How do you know that?"

"If I could see the picture of the chair." Candice put the picture of the remains of the chair on the easel. "You see this damage here? This is the most intense damage of all, more than we saw to the wall where the heater was, more than we saw to the front wall, more than we saw in the corner where the door was. Due to the intense heat and the extreme damage to this chair, it is safe to say that the fire started here."

"Do you think that this fire could have started at the hands of a human?"

"I would say, yes, it *had* to be set by a human."

"Do you think it could have been arson?"

"Yes, it could have been, although there was no residue of an accelerant used. I suppose someone could have come in and set the chair on fire and then left out the front door without Ms. Payne even knowing they were there."

"Could it have been set unintentionally by someone else like one of Ms. Payne's children?"

"Yes, that is also possible."

"No more questions, Your Honor," Candice took her seat.

Chapter 60

The media had been hanging around and had a camera rolling in the courtroom at all times throughout the trial, but they hadn't been bothering anyone. Emily was so glad that she didn't have to fight that fight.

"Mr. Cordova, your witness," Judge Hafford said when the clock was approaching four o'clock on day two of the murder trial.

Cordova began speaking before he stood. "When you did your investigation, did you ever note whether or not the door was locked?"

"No sir," Mr. Rutherford answered.

"Why not?" Cordova asked, rising to his feet.

"I didn't realize that the door being locked or unlocked was an issue." Emily was wondering what Cordova was getting at. *The door being locked or unlocked proves nothing about who started the fire or how.*

"Can you tell now, looking at the pictures whether or not the door was unlocked?" Mr. Cordova handed Mr. Rutherford a picture of the door frame after the fire.

"No sir. I see no damage done to this door frame proving that the door was locked. However, I cannot say for certain that it wasn't locked either."

"Your Honor, I would like to enter into evidence this report filed by Mr. Rutherford on October 15, 1993," Cordova handed Judge Hafford a piece of paper. He also handed Ms. Moore and Mr. Rutherford a copy.

After examining the paper the judge said, "Granted"

"Mr. Rutherford, do you recognize this report?" Cordova asked standing about halfway between the stand and the gallery.

"Yes, sir, I do," Mr. Rutherford said after skimming the report over quickly.

"Could you read the highlighted portion aloud for the jury, please?" Cordova asked forcefully as if just reading it would exonerate his client.

"It says, 'Source of ignition: unknown' and the next highlight says 'location of initial ignition: northeast corner of the living room, just inside the front door'."

"You just testified that the fire began in the chair with all certainty. Is that correct?" Cordova said approaching the stand.

"Yes, I did." Mr. Rutherford was not sure where Mr. Cordova was going with this.

Mr. Cordova leaned on the partition in front of the stand. "But your report contradicts that testimony. So which is it? Did the fire begin in the chair or just inside the front door?"

"It began in the chair which was…"

"It began in the chair!" Cordova yelled. "So, then, why did you write in your report that it began just inside the front door?" Cordova asked in an accusatory tone.

"The chair was right inside the front door." Mr. Rutherford was getting frustrated but trying not to let it show.

"But if you could be so certain now, eleven and a half years later, why couldn't you be so certain on October 15, 1993, two weeks later?"

"I was certain then, I just didn't get specific on the report." Mr. Rutherford knew what Mr. Cordova was trying to get him to say. He didn't like it, but couldn't avoid it any longer.

"And why not?"

"Because I was afraid that the fact that it started on the chair meant for certain one of the children did it. Since the two younger ones were in their bedroom, it had to be the little girl, the older child. She had been through enough… six years old and her brother and sister were dead and they had lost everything they owned in that fire. I couldn't pin that on a six-year-old to live with for the rest of her life. I just couldn't do it. So, I wrote the report vaguely, but I *didn't lie* in it," Mr. Rutherford added firmly.

"Do you still think that it is possible that Rachel Payne, the older child, did do it?" Cordova asked in a softer tone.

"Yes, but I also…"

Cordova cut him off. "No more questions, Your Honor."

Judge Hafford declared that court would recess for the day and reconvene the next morning at nine o'clock.

Emily collapsed into the chair in the victim/witness room. "Is it really only Wednesday? It seems like this trial has been going on for two weeks."

"Nope, just two days," Terri said sinking onto the couch. "Let's go out for dinner tonight."

As soon as they entered the restaurant, they knew that was a bad choice to make. No one said anything, but all the patrons in the restaurant began to stare. As they were seated, Emily whispered, "I forgot my face has been all over the news the last two days."

"I forgot about that, too. Can you imagine how celebrities feel? This is what they get every day of their lives!" Terri whispered back.

"First person that asks for my autograph will get one alright, right in the face," Emily laughed and felt the tension release.

Chapter 61

Abby, Terri and Emily took their seats in the front row and waited patiently for day three of the trial to begin.

"All rise." Once the judge was seated behind the bench the bailiff said, "you may be seated."

"Now before I bring in the jury, Ms. Moore, we need to talk about your next witness," Judge Hafford announced.

"Yes, Your Honor. The State will be calling Ms. Patricia Hampton to the stand," Candice said rising to her feet.

"I understand that there is some controversy regarding her testimony, Mr. Cordova?"

Cordova rose as well. "That is correct, Your Honor. Ms. Hampton is my client's ex-girlfriend and the State would like her to testify to extensive abuse inflicted by my client. I feel that this is irrelevant to the case at hand."

Ms. Moore jumped in. "Your Honor, it is very relevant to the case at hand because during these abusive situations, Mr. Brooks would threaten to kill her child the way that he killed Michael and

Leslie Carter. He also admitted the details of the fire that killed them to her."

"I don't understand why she can't just testify to what he said to her without bringing the abuse to the jury's attention," Cordova argued.

"Your Honor," Candice said as calmly as possible. "We want to show the jury the intensity of these threats. If Ms. Hampton simply says, 'He said he would kill my child the way he killed Emily's' there is not much of a threat there. The jury has to understand the reality of it."

Judge Hafford spoke next. "Ms. Hampton, would you please come to the stand? I am going to swear you in and then I am going to tell you what you are allowed to say and what and you are not allowed to say. Then I will ask you if you understand and you will answer under oath."

Once Patricia Hampton was sworn in, the judge said, "Ms. Hampton, you will be allowed to testify to the fact that Mr. Brooks physically abused you, but you will not be allowed to describe any specific acts or incidences. Do you understand that?"

"Yes sir." Patricia was looking straight at the judge and refusing to look in the direction of the defense table where Brandon sat staring holes into her.

"You will be allowed to tell the court what Mr. Brooks said to you regarding Michael and Leslie Carter or Emily Payne, but you will not be allowed to say what he said to you regarding any other threats or other abusive relationships. Do you understand that?" Judge Hafford asked.

"Yes sir."

"Do you also understand that if you violate any of the rules we just talked about you will be held in contempt of court and you will prosecuted to the fullest extent of the law?"

"Yes sir."

"You may step down." Judge Hafford addressed the whole courtroom, "I want to remind all who are present that the purpose of this trial is to hear the case of the murder of Michael and Leslie Carter. It is not about Mr. Brook's past treatment of the females in his life. I will hold anyone who oversteps the bounds in contempt of court. Is that understood?"

"Yes sir." Candice said, half-rising from her chair.

"Yes sir." Mr. Cordova rose from his chair.

"Bailiff, you may bring in the jury." Once the jury was all in place Judge Hafford said, "The State may call its next witness."

Ms. Moore rose to her feet. "The State calls Patricia Hampton to the stand." A short, stocky woman with dark brown hair made her way to the stand. After being sworn in Ms. Moore said, "Would you please state your full name for the court, please?"

"Patricia Ann Hampton," she stated, getting the box of Kleenex handy.

"Ms. Hampton, do you know Brandon Charles Brooks?"

"Yes ma'am, I do."

"Do you see Mr. Brooks in the court room?"

"Yes ma'am. That's him right there." Without taking her eyes off of Ms. Moore, Patricia pointed in the direction of the defense table.

"How do you know Mr. Brooks?"

The disgust in her voice was apparent as she said, "I dated him and lived with him for a few years."

"When was that?" Candice asked.

"I met him during the summer of 1994. We began dating immediately and we moved in together in December of 1994."

"Who all lived in the house with you?"

"It was me, my then-seven-year-old daughter, and Brandon."

"When did you and Mr. Brooks break up?"

"Um, it was around October 1997."

"So you dated for a little over three years?"

"Yes, that is correct."

"Ms. Hampton, have you ever heard of Emily Payne?"

"Yes ma'am. Brandon said he lived next door to her for a while and then they moved in together."

"Did he tell you why they moved in together?"

"He said the building they lived in when they lived next door to each other burned down and they were both homeless. He said Michael and Leslie died in the fire. I asked him who Michael and Leslie were and he said they were Emily's kids."

"Why do you think he told you about that?"

"At first he told me because we were talking about things we had been through in life..." Candice cut her off before she could go any further.

"Okay. We'll come back to this. How would you describe your relationship with Mr. Brooks?"

"At first it was good, but shortly after we moved in together he began being abusive."

"What do you mean by abusive?"

Patricia looked at the judge. "Answer generally," Judge Hafford said.

"He started saying really nasty things to me and then he started hitting me. Eventually, he abused me much worse than just hitting me."

"Why did you stay with him for so long?"

"I didn't have anywhere to go that he didn't know about and I was scared for my life and for the safety of my child."

"Why?"

"Brandon used to tell me that if I didn't do what he wanted or if I tried to leave him he would kill my daughter like he killed Michael and Leslie." Patricia's voice began to quiver as she answered.

"Did he say how he killed them?"

"He said he set the house on fire and killed Michael and Leslie."

"Did he threaten you just once?"

"No, he used to say it all the time. Not worded exactly the same way each time, but he said it often." Patricia began to shake as she recalled the threats on her life and her daughter's life.

"Can you tell the jury other ways he said it?"

"He said, 'Would you like your daughter to die the way those half-breeds did?' or 'If you don't watch it, your daughter can die, too.' Stuff like that." Patricia pulled a Kleenex out of the box.

"Did he ever tell you why he killed Michael and Leslie?"

"No, he just said he did it and he always referred to Emily as 'that witch'."

"Did you ever ask why he killed them?"

"I was pretty scared of him, but I did ask one time. He said, 'Don't worry about what I have done or why I have done it. Just know that I have done it and I will do it again if you burn me. Anyone who burns Brandon gets burned'."

"Did he ever tell you how Emily supposedly burned him?"

"No. I never did figure that out," Patricia said, taking a deep breath.

"I have no further questions for this witness."

"Mr. Cordova?"

Half rising, Cordova said, "I have no questions, your Honor."

Chapter 62

After a short break, Candice called Detective Tomarano to the stand next. He told the jury about his investigation from beginning to end. He talked about the interrogation quite a bit and said that Brandon denied everything, but contradicted himself a number of times. "If you were to put all that Mr. Brooks said in chronological order, you would see that it is humanly impossible for his story to be the truth," Tomarano stated when concluding the testimony about the interrogation.

Judge Hafford decided to take a break at the end of Tomarano's testimony.

Due to the media coverage of the case, Emily and Terri decided it best to stay in the safety of the victim/witness room during the breaks. When they entered the room, Detective Tomarano approached Emily. "Hello, Emily. How are you holding up?"

"I'll be better when the trial is over, but I'm doing good," Emily answered.

"I'm glad to hear that."

Emily introduced Tomarano to Terri. They chatted for a few minutes before Shelley announced it was time to get back in the courtroom.

"Well, I have to run anyway," Tomarano said. He put his arm around Emily's shoulders. "I told you we'd get this guy. It took much longer than I had hoped it would, but we finally got him," Tomarano spoke confidently.

"Well, I'm not counting my chickens before they hatch. You can say that again when he is convicted."

"He'll be convicted. Don't worry." Tomarano always had a way of making Emily feel better.

Detective Pritchett took the stand next. He told the jury that he was a cold case homicide detective with twenty-five years of cold case experience. He explained when he was brought in on the case and why. Then he summarized his investigation. His testimony about the interrogation lined up perfectly with what Detective Tomarano had already said. He also said that during the interrogation Brandon made comments about Emily's family being racist and that they had never accepted Michael and Leslie.

All week, Brandon had been trying to intimidate Emily with a contemptuous glare. Emily finally had enough and just looked Brandon straight in the eye. The look on her face was one of threat and challenge combined. He knew immediately that intimidation wasn't going to work and pulled his gaze away. He didn't so much as glance in Emily's direction for the remainder of the trial. Emily wondered and hoped that the jury saw this exchange.

After Pritchett's testimony, Candice played clips of the inter-rogation video for the jury. The jury heard the contradictions in his statement for themselves. They also saw the look of hatred in his eyes whenever race was mentioned.

After lunch, Candice called the one of the SWAT officers who testified about the arrest. He went into detail about how Brandon evaded arrest but was finally captured.

She questioned the guard at the jail who had found the bunks of three inmates empty when she did her seven a.m. bed check in June of 2004 and found the makeshift ladder of bed sheets.

Candice also called one of the officers who were present when Brandon was recaptured after the escape. He testified about how Officer Viper found Brandon camping in the woods as well as what they found at the site.

Emily thought they were done hearing all of the testimony and then Candice said, "The State calls John Bayer to the stand." Terri looked at Emily who just shrugged her shoulders with an I-don't-know look on her face.

A tall, slender, Caucasian man in his early twenties was brought in. He had dark hair and brown eyes. He was dressed in a bright orange jail suit.

Once he was seated and sworn in, Candice said, "Please state your full name for the record."

"My name is John Marshall Bayer."

"Mr. Bayer, do you know a Brandon Charles Brooks?"

"Yes, he is right there," John said pointing at the defense table.

"Let the record indicate that the witness identified the defendant. Mr. Bayer, how do you know Mr. Brooks?"

"We were cellmates at the County Jail."

"When?"

"Um, I was already there when he was brought in. I think it was October 2003, but I am not sure. I was transferred out in April of 2004."

"So you shared a cell for about seven months?"

"Yes ma'am."

Emily was curious about the testimony, but was also a little upset that Candice hadn't mentioned it to her. Shelley had said that she would be informed about everything. *I would think a witness in my children's murder trial would be part of everything.*

"Could you describe the cell for me?"

"It was more like a pod. There were eight bunks per cell. They were bolted to the floor about six inches apart, lining the wall opposite the bars. The toilet was in the back corners about three feet from the last bed."

"Were the beds head to toe or side by side?"

"They were side by side."

"So you could easily sit on your beds and talk to each other?" Candice said painting a mental picture for the jury.

"Yes ma'am."

"Where were yours and Brandon's beds located?"

"From the toilet I was in the fifth bed and he was in the sixth. We were both in bottom bunks."

"Did you and Mr. Brooks ever discuss your crimes?"

"Yeah, of course."

"What did he tell you about why he was there?"

"At first he said that he was there because this witch killed her kids and was trying to blame it on him."

"Did he say why she was blaming it on him?"

"He said that she didn't want anyone to figure out that she did it, so she was blaming him."

"Did he say how she did it?"

"Yeah, he said she set her house on fire. That she was trying to kill herself and her kids, but she survived."

"Did he say when this happened?"

"Not right away, but the more he talked about it I could tell that it had been a long time ago."

"Did you ask him about that?"

"Yeah, I just said, 'when did she do it?' He said 'September 30, 1993.'"

"What did you say to that?"

"Nothing that time. I had to think about that. It didn't make sense to me."

"What didn't make sense about it?"

"I wondered why she would wait ten years to report it. Eventually I asked him about it."

"What did he say?"

"He said, 'I don't know. I have never understood that witch.' I kind of let him talk to build the trust so that he would tell me more. By then, I was suspecting that he had done it, but I didn't want him to know that I suspected him. I had to sleep six inches away from him, you know?"

Now Emily understood why Candice had called John Bayer to the stand. She also knew the confession was just around the corner.

Chapter 63

Candice leaned on the prosecution table as she asked her next question of John Bayer, Brandon's cellmate. "Did he ever tell you that he did do it?"

"Yeah. I think it kind of slipped one time when we were talking about kids. We had been talking about my niece and nephew when he asked me a strange question." John paused as if he wasn't sure if he should go on.

"What did he ask you?" Candice prompted.

"He asked me if they were all white or if my sister had married a black man. I told him that they were all white and asked him why he asked that," John answered. He was clearly getting nervous.

"What did he say?" Candice asked, hoping that John wouldn't crack on the stand. That would not be good. This was the closest they had ever gotten to a motive in this case.

"He said, 'That witch married a black man and had two half-breed kids.' I asked him who he was talking about and he said, 'that nigger-loving witch that lived next door to me.' I said, 'the one who's kids died?' He said, 'the world don't need trash like that, so I took them out. I tried to kill that nigger-loving witch too, but she didn't die! I let the oldest kid live, though, because she was white and I kind of liked her.'" Emily did her best to control her emotions as Candice had instructed her to do, but she was sure the shock and anger showed on her face. She wanted to scream. *I knew he had referred to them as half-breeds, but I had no idea that he hated them, or me, enough to kill us! And he waited until Rachel left on purpose because she is WHITE?!* Emily thought she was going to vomit, but she didn't want to leave the courtroom, so she fought the bile she felt rising up in her esophagus.

Candice pressed on. "What did you say?"

"I said, 'you killed them?' He said 'yeah, I did! If you tell anyone I said that I'll kill your niece and nephew, too.'"

"Did you tell anyone?"

"Not while we were incarcerated together. I told someone after I was transferred."

"Was that the only time he said it?"

"No, he said it a number of times after that. It was always very quietly and to remind me that he would do the same thing to my niece and nephew if I ever told anyone."

"Did he ever tell you what happened that day?"

"Yes ma'am. He told me that he waited until the oldest kid left for school because he didn't want to hurt her. He said that he stood at the door outside her apartment listening for a minute. Then he heard the mother and kids talking but their voices were far away, so he knew that they were in the bedrooms. Then he quietly opened the door, lit a piece of paper and put it on the chair. He slipped back out the door but peeked in after a few seconds to make sure the chair was on fire. It was, so he snuck back over to his house and laid down on the couch to wait for someone to wake him up. Before long the house was filling up with smoke. Then he heard his other neighbor yelling so he went to the door like he didn't know what was going on. He said he was acting like he just woke up. Once he found out what was going on, he let the neighbors worry about saving the family, and he went and got his cats. I asked him where the cats were and he said that he had put them in a cage before he started the fire so that they would be all right. He got the cage out of his bedroom and brought it out to the car and put it in the backseat. Then he moved the car onto the street because the fire was so hot."

"Did he tell you anything else?" Candice prompted again.

"Yeah, he said that he told a reporter that he thought it was probably the heater that started it because they had had problems with that heater before," John stated.

"Is that all he told you?"

"Yes, ma'am, that's all."

"I have no more questions for this witness," Candice said returning to her seat. She looked at Emily to see how she was doing. She was pleasantly surprised that Emily was toughing it out.

"Mr. Cordova?" Judge Hafford asked.

Mr. Cordova rose and said, "No questions, Your Honor."

Brandon looked at his attorney as Cordova sat back down.

Judge Hafford addressed Candice again, "Next witness, Ms. Moore?"

"The State rests, Your Honor."

"Mr. Cordova, you may call your first witness," the judge said.

"The defense rests, Your Honor," Mr. Cordova half-rose.

Emily and Terri were surprised that Brandon wasn't even going to try to put on a defense. *Wow, that's it? No more testimony, huh? Brandon isn't going to call one witness? He isn't even going to testify himself?*

The judge explained Brandon's right to testify on his own behalf and Brandon said under oath that he chose not to testify.

Judge Hafford looked at the clock. "Ladies and gentlemen, it is now three fifteen and I don't want to get into the closing statements this late in the day. So, I am going to recess for the day. We will reconvene at nine o'clock tomorrow morning." Looking at the jury, he said, "I expect all of you to be here no later than eight thirty. Have a good night." He dismissed the jury and called a recess.

Chapter 64

Emily rose early Friday morning. *This is it. Hopefully, this is the last day that we will have to spend in that courthouse, but today will probably be the longest and most boring.* Emily dressed in one of her most professional looking outfits – a brown wool jumper with a black wool blazer worn over it. She woke Rachel who was going with her to court today. Rachel had not wanted to hear the whole trial. She wanted to be in school with her friends; however, she and Emily thought it would be best for her to hear the closing arguments and the verdict if one was returned today. Rachel wore her black jeans with solid purple blouse. She had bracelets adorning her arms. Her fingernails were painted lilac. She wore her long hair down so she could hide her face from Brandon and the cameras that were sure to be there.

When they arrived at the courthouse, Abby was already there waiting. "Hey, girl," she said hugging Rachel. "How have you been?"

"Fine," Rachel said hugging her mother's best friend.

"You ready for this?" Abby asked them both in a soothing tone.

"Yeah," Rachel said, shortly.

Emily said, "I think so. I know I am ready for it to be over, but I don't know if I am ready for what we have to do to get to that point".

"Hi, Rachel," Terri said to her granddaughter with Larry right beside her. Larry had been very close to Michael and Leslie and he needed to hear the verdict from the horse's mouth. They, also, thought it would be good for Emily's black brother to be in the courtroom to show the jury that they didn't have any issues with black people.

"Hi, Grandma. Hi, Uncle Larry." Rachel hugged her grand-mother tightly.

"Sorry, I'm late. Traffic was a big pain today. Lucky for you, you didn't have to come that way."

Shelley, Brent, and Candice walked up to them. "Good morning."

"Good morning." Everyone said.

After Emily introduced everyone Candice said, "Well, we'd probably better get in there."

They filed into the first row to the left of the aisle. Rachel went in first and sat by the wall. Abby went next. Emily sat in the middle with Terri on her right. Larry sat on the end. Shelley passed a couple of boxes of Kleenex down the row.

The gallery filled up quickly with people who had testified, media people, and curious onlookers. When they brought Brandon in, he looked straight ahead. Rachel was sitting with her head down and her hair covering her face, so Brandon didn't see her. The podium was blocking Brandon's view of Larry.

Judge Hafford came in and then the jury took their seats in the jury box. Once everyone was in place and the stage was set, Candice rose to begin her closing statement.

"Emily Payne, a single mother of three children, got up one morning and started her day as usual." Ms. Moore addressed the jury who were listening and watching her intently. "She woke her children up and fed them breakfast. After Rachel left for school, Emily, Michael and Leslie went into the bedroom to get dressed for the day – a typical morning, just four innocent people going about their lives, minding their own business, not bothering anyone. All of a sudden this family is thrust into terrorizing chaos as their home begins to burn around them. Ms. Payne, whose main concern is Michael and Leslie, leaves her room and finds her crying and scared children. She tries her best to sound calm and comforting as she instructs her children to lie on the floor giving them the impression that Mommy has it all under control. She then stands up into the smoke, climbs up onto the dresser and, using all of her upper body strength, tries to open the window. She fails and tries again. She soon finds that if she doesn't get oxygen, she will be of no help to her children, so she climbs down to get air. As she is coming off the dresser she hears someone calling her name. Using up the last of her oxygen she screams to her potential rescuer. In desperate need of air, she takes a breath too soon and passes out. Mr. Tibbs, also going about his day as usual, comes home from driving the children to school to find his wife's best friend's house on fire. His natural instinct to save the people in the house kicks in and he puts his life on the line to try to save this family." Candice pointed to Emily and Rachel. "He runs up the front steps and kicks the door in! The flames are so powerful and so hot that they send him reeling backwards and off the porch. After he discovers he cannot get in through the front door, Mr. Tibbs goes to the side of the house and tries to get in through the window. Only after realizing there is nothing else he can do, he steps back and watches in horror as the firemen do their jobs. Mr. Brooks, on the other hand, comes out of *his* burning house rubbing his eyes as if he has just awoken peacefully from a good night's sleep and innocently asks what is going on. Let's be serious, people. If Mr. Brooks had awoken to his house on fire I doubt he would have been so noncha-lant about it. Actually, he probably would have jumped up in panic mode – unless of course, he knew about the fire before this point in time." Candice paused for effect. "Next, Mr. Brooks, knowing there was a woman and two small children in the house, gets his cats, who were already in a cage, as Mr. Bayer told us. And where was Mr. Brooks while the firemen are saving his neighbors' lives? Moving the car and then walking away from the scene. If my house was on fire, I can't imagine where on earth I would go! I would be watching in horror and praying that all my things were not destroyed. Add to that, the neighbor and her innocent children who are trapped in the fire. How could any rational, caring human being walk away and disappear – unless, of course, he has something to hide.

"No, ladies and gentlemen, we don't have a smoking gun, so to speak. No one saw Mr. Brooks in Ms. Payne's apartment that morning. But we do know, based on Mr. Tibbs testimony, that Mr. Brooks had a key to Ms. Payne's apartment. We don't know how or why he had it, but the fact remains he had it. So, he had the opportunity to commit this crime. Based on Mr. Bayer's testimony, we know that Mr. Brooks despised those children simply because of the color of their skin and he detested Ms. Payne because she exercised her right to marry the man she loved, who just happened to have a different color skin than she had. It was a legal marriage in the State of Tennessee, the children were born within the bounds of the marriage, but because Mr. Brooks disagreed with the State, he decided he would eliminate 'trash like that'. So, you see, we have motive and we have opportunity. The defense would like you to believe that Ms. Payne, who was distraught over her friend's murder tried to kill herself and her children, but yet, they offered no proof to substantiate that. Yes, Ms. Payne admitted to being depressed the night before the fire, but she had just discovered her best friend from high school had been murdered. If she wasn't a little upset about that, *then* we would have cause for concern, but because she did respond with negative emotions, we see that Ms. Payne is normal – not suicidal. The defense didn't produce any witnesses to testify that she was handling this worse than expected. In fact, the one witness that Mr. Cordova did question about it, Mr. Tibbs, testified that Ms. Payne hadn't even mentioned it. If you were suicidal don't you think you would at least talk to your best friend about what is bothering you? You may not mention that you are contemplating killing yourself, but you would mention that something is wrong! Instead of doing that, Ms. Payne waves at Mr. Tibbs and hollers 'good morning, Robert' as she sends Rachel out the door. Does this sound like someone who is about to kill herself and her children? The defense is trying to convince you Ms. Payne has a dual motive for her supposed suicide attempt. Not only is she depressed about her friend's murder, she is the racist even though her current best friend is a black woman, her brother is black her children are half-black and she has never done anything in her entire life to indicate that she is racist. The defense would have you believe that she murdered her own children because of the color of their skin, although that didn't prevent her from marrying a black man, conceiving his children, and giving birth to them as opposed to aborting the pregnancies. No, she would rather wait until they are toddlers before killing them to, quote, protect them from this world, end quote. You heard Mr. Brooks on the video tape say that her family had problems with the fact that Michael and Leslie were black, but yet when Ms. Payne was a teenager, her parents adopted and have since raised a black child, who is sitting in this courtroom today." Candice looked over at Larry. She paused as the jury looked at Emily and her family sitting in the front row.

Chapter 65

Candice continued with her closing. She recanted the testimony of Mr. Rutherford, using the pictures to refresh their memories. She reviewed Mr. Tibbs' and Mr. Greenwood's accounts of what happened that fateful day, as well. She had painted a clear visual picture for the jury before moving on to accuse Mr. Brooks.

"The only logical explanation is that Mr. Brooks did it. If he didn't why would he confess to two people that he did? Two people who didn't know each other. Two people who would have no reason to lie. He told Mr. Bayer point blank that he did it and he told Ms. Hampton in no uncertain terms that he would kill her child the same way he had killed Michael and Leslie. No, he may not have given Ms. Hampton a step-by-step detailed account, as he did Mr. Bayer, but there was no doubt in her mind that he had killed two children and therefore would kill hers as well.

"When the investigation was complete and the grand jury returned an indictment, the police went to Mr. Brooks' home to make an arrest. They knocked on his door. There was no answer, but they knew he was in there. They used intercoms to call him out. He didn't respond. They shot tear gas into the house. He still didn't respond. They shot more tear gas. No response. They shot a total of nine cans of tear gas into the house. He still didn't come out. Then they sent in the S.W.A.T. team to remove Mr. Brooks from the premises. They found him up in the attic hiding between the rafters with a piece of insulation covering him from head to toe. Unfortunately, for Mr. Brooks the floor of the attic wasn't very strong and he fell through the bathroom ceiling and landed in the tub." Candice had to pause while waiting for the chuckles to stop.

"Eight months later, Mr. Brooks concocts a well-thought-out escape from the county jail where he was being held awaiting trial. He and two others string bed sheets together and stuff jumpsuits with towels and clothes. They put the jumpsuits on their beds and cover them. They tie the end of the bed sheets to the bunk bed. Then they climb up through the ceiling and into the air vent where they slither along until they reach the vent on the outside of the building. There they use the bed sheets as a ladder to climb down the side of the jail three stories to the ground. At that point, they go their separate ways. Mr. Brooks walks to a restaurant about a mile from the jail in nothing but his boxers and a tee shirt where he meets an old girlfriend who drives him away. He was missing for almost thirty-six hours when someone called the police and said they suspected Mr. Brooks was camping in the woods. The police went to the scene with a K-9 officer named Viper and found Mr. Brooks hiding under bushes with loose brush pulled over him. He fought Officer Viper sustaining deep lacerations in his right leg and left arm. Upon investigation of the site, the police found camping gear – sleeping bag, flashlight, five packages of batteries, and so on.

"So, Mr. Brooks, who is in the process of being evicted, puts his cats in a cage before the fire. He is more concerned about getting his cats to safety than a woman and her two small children. While his house is burning, he tells the media that the heater started the fire and then he leaves the scene. Later that day, he argues with Mr. Lloyd accusing the landlord of being a murderer twenty-one hours *before* anyone dies. A few months later, he moves in with Ms. Payne to make sure she doesn't figure it out, tries to kill her again when she does figure it out, and eventually uses this fire to control Ms. Hampton. He doesn't answer the door when the police come knocking, doesn't come out when the police shoot nine cans of tear gas into his house, runs up to the attic, and hides between the rafters using insulation as a cover. While awaiting trial, he tells his fellow inmate details about this fire that no one could possibly know, plans and executes an elaborate escape from the county jail, prepares to camp in the woods and move by the cover of night, and then resists arrest again receiving multiple lacerations in the process. These are clearly not the actions of an innocent man. Ladies and gentlemen of the jury, it is your duty to find Mr. Brooks guilty of the murder of Michael and Leslie Carter, two innocent toddlers who did nothing more than be born to a white wife and a black husband. It is your duty to protect society from this kind of racial cleansing. It is your duty to protect the United States of America from Mr. Brandon Charles Brooks." Candice sat down as the whole courtroom sat in silence.

Chapter 66

Mr. Cordova addressed the jury next. "Ladies and gentleman of the jury, there is such a thing in this country called reasonable doubt. You are required by law to assume that my client is innocent until the State proves beyond a reasonable doubt that he is guilty. The State has failed to do that. Ms. Moore has offered a lot of confusing, circumstantial evidence that makes my client appear guilty, but she has not exhausted all possibilities.

"It is possible that Ms. Payne tried to kill herself and her children. The state has told you that Ms. Payne grieving her friend's death is normal and is no cause for an attempt at suicide, when in reality; there are a numerous cases in which someone kills themselves following a death of a close friend or loved one.

"It's also possible that Ms. Payne didn't realize the magnitude of problems she would have raising bi-racial children in this country until after she and Mr. Carter were divorced. She and Mr. Carter were married and thought they would be forever. That is probably why she didn't abort the pregnancies.

"And what about the possibility of Rachel starting the fire? You heard Mr. Rutherford say that even *he* believed Rachel had done it and that is why he falsified his report. You see, there are many possible scenarios other than just that Mr. Brooks is the culprit.

"Ms. Hampton does have a reason to lie. She was jaded by Mr. Brooks when he left her after a long term relationship. What better way to get back at your ex-lover who ripped your heart out than to say he told you that he murdered someone? She couldn't give any details of the crime to convince us that he did in fact start this fire. All she could give were statements that he had threatened her.

"Mr. Bayer is a convicted felon. He was convicted of fraud. Need I remind you that fraud is lying? Why should we believe anything he says? The State did not offer any kind of evidence to substantiate the claim that my client is a racist. He has no prior convictions of race related crimes. On what grounds are they accusing him? The testimony of a convicted felon is all they have offered you.

"Ladies and gentlemen, I believe I have presented you with enough possible scenarios to raise reasonable doubt. Now, it is your responsibility to find my client, Mr. Brandon Charles Brooks, not guilty of the crime in question."

Candice rose again and walked straight to the jury box. "Ms. Payne testified that Mr. Brooks mentioned the children's race the day that she was moving to Chicago eleven years ago. Ms. Hampton testified that Mr. Brooks referred to Michael and Leslie as half-breeds. That was the foundation that was built long before Mr. Bayer told you that he heard Mr. Brooks say with his own ears that he had deliberately killed those children because of their race and tried to kill Ms. Payne as well for giving birth to them. Those are not things we just made up and threw out to you. They are supported contrary to Mr. Cordova's claim that they are not.

"As Judge Hafford will tell you, it was my job to prove to you that Mr. Brooks committed the arson which resulted in the death of Michael and Leslie Carter. There is no question regarding the cause of death. It was this fire that killed those children. Even if Mr. Brooks hadn't meant for anyone to die, he did mean to set the house on fire and I believe I have sufficiently proven that. Felony murder is, by definition, the murder that occurs during the commission of a felony as a direct result of that felony even if the death itself was not intended. Felony murder is first-degree murder and carries a mandatory life sentence.

"Mr. Cordova would like you to believe that the State did not meet its burden of proof because there is no *direct* evidence pointing at Mr. Brooks. No one saw Mr. Brooks start the fire. There was no accelerant found when the ashes were tested that could be tied directly to Mr. Brooks. Please keep in mind, however, that circumstantial evidence can sufficiently prove guilt by proving that other events and circumstances reasonably infer the guilt of the suspect. I showed you that he had the opportunity. I showed you that he had a motive. Earlier I showed you how all of the fingers in this case point to Mr. Brooks. Yes, one of them points at Rachel as well as Mr.

Brooks, and one may point at Emily as well as Mr. Brooks, but he is the only person that *all* of the evidence points to.

"What does the phrase 'beyond a reasonable doubt' mean? It does *not* mean beyond a shadow of a doubt. 'Beyond a reasonable doubt' means that you can say with certainty that Mr. Brooks is guilty. Have I shown you that our suspicions are more than just imaginary? Have I presented enough evidence to convince you that Mr. Brooks did in fact set that house on fire? Can you say, 'Yes, Mr. Brooks set Ms. Payne's house on fire' without hesitation? If you answered yes to any of these questions then I have sufficiently proven that Mr. Brooks is guilty of the aggravated arson and, therefore, the felony murder of both Henry Michael Carter and Leslie Lynette Carter.

"This fire has been smoldering for eleven and a half years. Are you going to put it out? Or are you going to let this man," Candice pointed accusingly at Brandon sitting behind the defense table, "watch the embers burn forever?" The courtroom fell silent except for the click, click of Candice's shoes on the marble floor as she made her way back to her seat.

Judge Hafford shook his head as if he was snapping himself out of the deep thought that he was in. He read the jury all of the applicable laws and explained what each one meant. He reminded them of the rules of deliberation and told them that if necessary they could have any part of the testimony read again or review any evidence that had been entered. He then dismissed them to the jury room to begin deliberations. Once the judge left the courtroom and Brandon was taken out, Emily, Abby, and Terri made their way out of the courtroom. They brushed past the media pushing cameras and microphones out of their faces and went back into the victim/witness room to wait. Emily started a fresh pot of coffee for the long wait ahead.

Chapter 67

An hour and thirty-five minutes later, the phone rang and Candice answered it. "Already! Wow! Okay, we are headed that way." She hung up the phone and looked over at Emily. "We have a verdict."

Emily started shaking and fighting the tears. For eleven and a half years she had waited for this moment and in now it was here. *Now I will find out for sure if Brandon really killed my kids,* she thought remembering the prayer she had prayed on Monday morning. Her stomach was in knots as they walked back to the courtroom, the cameras focusing on her the whole way. Shelley was walking with them. "I believe this is a record. I don't think I have ever seen a jury come back this fast especially in a murder case!"

"Is that good or bad?" Emily asked.

"Let's hope it's good. What it does tell me is that all twelve of them agreed immediately. They didn't have time to review any evidence or testimony. All they had time to do was elect a foreperson, vote, and read the votes."

Emily took a deep breath and stepped into the courtroom. The bailiff ushered Brandon in and once he was seated, the bailiff said, "All rise." Emily's knees were weak as she stood up. "You may be seated." Abby handed her a handful of tissues.

The jury filed into the jury box. Emily tried not to look at them, but she couldn't help it. She needed to see their faces. She needed to see if the answer was written there. There were no clues. The jury took their seats.

"Would the foreperson please rise?" the judge asked.

A woman in the front row of the jury box rose.

"Ms. Foreperson, raise your right hand. Do you swear that the verdict you are about to read is the consensus of all the jurors in this case?"

"I do."

"Bailiff, please…"

The bailiff took three papers from the woman and handed them to the judge. You could hear a pin drop in the courtroom as the judge looked at the first piece of paper, then the second, then the third. He handed them back to the bailiff who returned them to the foreperson.

"Will the defendant please rise?" After Brandon and Mr. Cordova were on their feet, Judge Hafford continued, "Madam Foreperson, would you please read the verdicts?"

"Count one, felony murder of Henry Michael Carter we, the jury, find the defendant, Brandon Charles Brooks, guilty."

Emily buried her head in her hands and began to sob. Brandon just dropped his head.

"Count two, felony murder of Leslie Lynette Carter we, the jury, find the defendant, Brandon Charles Brooks, guilty. Count three, aggravated arson of a multi-family dwelling located at 255 Bailey Street, we, the jury, find the defendant, Brandon Charles Brooks, guilty."

The judge thanked the jury for their service and dismissed them. "Mr. Brooks you will be held in the Meadow Grove Maximum Security Prison until the sentencing hearing which will be on February tenth, at nine am. Until then, this court is adjourned."

Emily stayed in her seat sobbing for a long time after the courtroom had cleared. Abby was on her right, with Rachel by the wall, and Terri was on her left with Larry sitting on the aisle. Shelley had taken a seat in the row behind her. Candice went out in the hallway to talk to the media.

"Can I sit here until the media leaves?" Emily asked.

"Unfortunately, that probably won't happen. They'll wait forever. Just say 'no comment' if you don't want to say anything," Shelley advised.

"Well, then let's go now while Candice has them occupied. Maybe they won't notice we left."

Everyone laughed as they rose. They formed a circle around Emily the best that they could as they made their way to the door.

Before they even got to the door the cameramen saw them coming and were ready and waiting as the group walked out into the hallway.

Emily was assaulted with questions, "Ms. Payne, how do you feel about the verdict?"

"Ms. Payne, I'm sure you're relieved that this is finally over after all these years. How does it feel to be able to finally put this behind you?"

"Ms. Payne, what are your plans for your future now that this is behind you?"

With microphones in her face, Emily said "No comment. No comment. No comment." She walked as quickly as she could toward the victim/witness room.

Once in the victim/witness room Emily fell into a chair, laid her head on the desk and wept. She surprised herself by her reaction, but eleven and a half years worth of tears were finally being released. The verdict broke the dam as she remembered what she had prayed Monday morning. *Lord, You are the only One who knows for sure what happened that day. If Brandon did set the house on fire and kill Michael and Leslie, I pray that he is convicted. But, Lord, if he didn't do it, I pray that he is acquitted.* Well, she got her answer. There would be no more wondering. Emily continued to cry for about fifteen minutes. The only time she had ever cried like that was on October 1, 1993, when the doctors told her the kids would not survive off of the life support machines.

Rachel walked up to her mother and put her hand on her shoulder. "I love you, Mom," she whispered. Rachel hadn't said those words to her mother in years. Emily stood up and they held each other for a long time as the verdict mended their relationship. All the years of blaming her mother slipped off of Rachel's shoulders like an over-stuffed back pack as she realized that her mother wasn't to blame after all and that Emily really had done all that she could to try to save her brother and sister. She, also, finally let go of the guilt that she had been carrying her whole life that she could have done something if only she was there. She now realized that there was nothing she could possibly have done.

Emily made a few phone calls to inform people of the verdict before it hit the news. Candice, Detective Tomarano, Detective Pritchett and Shelley took turns hugging her. Shelley said, "We'll get together next week and talk about your impact statement."

"Impact statement? What is that?" Emily and Terri asked in unison.

"You have the right to make a final statement to the court before the judge announces the sentence. It should state how this has impacted your life and what sentence you feel Brandon should get. Felony murder carries a mandatory life sentence, but the judge will decide if the sentences should be served concurrently or consecutively."

"I can't think about that right now." Emily felt overwhelmed.

"I know. That's why we'll get together next week."

"I'm ready to go home. Is the media still out there?" Emily asked.

Shelley peeked out the door. "Yeah, they are. Just make a run for it like you did coming in here."

"If I hadn't left my coat in here, I would have headed straight for the elevator and not had to worry about it again."

"I'll go get the van and pull it up to the front door," Larry offered.

"Thanks, Larry."

"I'll stand by the window and let you know when Larry pulls up with the van. Then I'll get the elevator," Abby said handing Emily her coat.

"Thanks, Abby. What would I do without you guys?"

"You'd be chewed up and spit out by the media frenzy." Everyone laughed.

When Abby gave the signal, Emily, Terri and Rachel made a run for it pushing past cameras and microphones all the way to the elevator. The elevator doors opened just as they got to them. "Wow! How perfect was that?" Rachel said as the doors closed between them and the news crews still shouting questions.

Emily spent the next few days on the phone and watching her face all over the news. Then she started working on the impact statement. When she had the first draft done, she emailed it to Shelley Shelley emailed her back with a few minor suggested changes and informed her that it was good and there would be no reason for them to meet.

Chapter 68

On February tenth, Emily walked into the courtroom with Abby and took a seat in the front row. Terri decided she wanted to skip it and go to work. Rachel said she just wanted to go on with her life, so she went to school as usual. Emily fully understood that. She just wanted to go on with her life, too, but she had one more thing to do before she could put this behind her once and for all.

When they brought Brandon in, Emily looked away.

"All rise," the bailiff said.

The judge took his seat on the bench and said, "You may be seated. Ms. Moore?"

"Yes, Your Honor. Ms. Payne would like to exercise her right to make a statement. Ms. Payne?"

Emily rose and made her way up to the witness stand. She looked beautiful in a sapphire blue pantsuit. She had her hair up and minimal makeup on. She had a new glow about her that wasn't apparent before. Confidence has a way of adding stunning beauty to an average woman. She took a seat and the bailiff handed her tissues, as the cameraman positioned the camera on her so closely that her face dominated the screen.

"You may begin when you are ready," Judge Hafford said.

"Thank you, your Honor." Emily unfolded the paper she had written and read a million times. "When Brandon set my house on fire, Michael and Leslie lost their lives. They lost the opportunity to experience friends, school, summer camp, church, playing sports, boyfriends/girlfriends, dances, prom, graduations, marriage, children, grandchildren... Michael was three when he was murdered and Leslie was two when she was murdered. Most people can remember back as far as age four or five. If you think back to your very first childhood memory, they lost that. Everything, every single thing, you remember about your life was taken from them. They will never get to experience any of that. Michael and Leslie didn't ask to born to a black father and a white mother. They didn't have any say in the color of their skin. They also didn't have a problem with the color of their skin, Brandon did. It is appalling that he thought he had the right to terminate these two lives and many people's futures because he disagreed with the decision that I made to marry a black man.

"When Brandon set my house on fire, I lost everything – Michael and Leslie, all of the belongings I had worked so hard to acquire, my pictures, my wedding rings, my high school yearbooks, and the list goes on.

"Because Brandon set my house on fire and killed Michael and Leslie, my surviving, happy and content daughter was shoved into adulthood at the age of six as she tried to console her grieving mother. She was, and still is, bitter, angry and full of resentment. I was very protective of her for the remainder of her upbringing, constantly afraid of losing her too. I did lose her, but in a different way because we have never been close like we were before the fire.

"As a result of Brandon setting my house on fire and killing Michael and Leslie, my parents got divorced after thirty-three years of marriage as Mom cried daily and Dad immersed himself in his work. My brothers were devastated and still are to this day, affecting each of them in their own ways. I have lost years of my life as I slipped into my own little world, building walls that to this day no one has been able to penetrate. This man," Emily looked right at Brandon, "betrayed me in the worst possible way. He murdered my two innocent children, stole my security, my faith in God, and my trust in people. Fear and pain have become my daily companions. I found comfort in my pain because I knew that no matter what *it* would never leave me.

"In the summer of 1994, I decided to go on with my life and I went back to college. A year later, I was barely scraping by – failing some classes and passing others by the skin of my teeth – when I decided I couldn't go on like that. I came to the conclusion that I had to let go of the hatred and resentment toward Brandon. I realized that forgiving him wasn't condoning what he had done, letting him off the hook for it, or forgetting it. So, on that day in July of 1995, I forgave Brandon for setting my house on fire and killing my kids. It wasn't immediate but soon I began feeling better. I began to live. I began making better grades and creating new dreams.

"I graduated in December of 1998 with my degree in accounting and I gave my life to Christ in December of 2001. God is using my story to share His love and His forgiveness with others. The death of a child is different from any other death because it is not just the loss of the past, but of the future as well.

"I still mourn for Michael and Leslie. I still miss them. I still cry and I still visit the grave occasionally. I have come to accept the fact that I always will. Michael would be fourteen now and Leslie would be thirteen if they were allowed to live. I try not to think about what life might be like now if they were still alive because it's too painful. It just reminds me of all that Brandon destroyed and stole.

"Since the conclusion of the trial and Brandon's conviction, I have finally been able to put my past in my past and begin actively working on my future. Murder is devastating, but I have learned that it doesn't have to be the end of your life. I decided that I hold the future in my hands and my life, or lack thereof, is whatever I choose to make it. Brandon has taken enough from me and I have decided not to let him take anymore.

"I would like to see Brandon receive the maximum sentence allowed by law. I would like to see those sentences served consecutively because while the children were close to each other, died the same way and on the same day, they were two separate individuals and their lives should be recognized individually. Brandon should spend the rest of his life in prison as I have to spend the rest of my life without my children, my daughter without her brother and sister, my parents without their grandchildren and my brothers without their niece and nephew. Brandon has had ten years of freedom which is ten years more than we got. The biggest difference is that we didn't deserve the life sentence we got. He does deserve to spend the rest of his life in prison!

"I would like to close by reading a poem I wrote entitled *I Had Dreams.*

Leslie, My little angel, that's what I called her.

So cute and energetic is the only way to describe her.

But, I'll never see her ride a bike, or her two front teeth fall out.

I'll never teach her how to drive, or tell her what life is all about.

I won't ever answer the phone and hear, "I need to talk to Les."

And I won't ever get the chance to help her find the perfect wedding dress.

I will never help her through labor while she is having my grandchild.

I had dreams about these times, now broken by a fire.

I comfort myself by thinking, 'she's in heaven. She's happy there.

She's with Michael and they're together forever, in God's loving are.'

Michael, a little Aladdin; he had a magic touch.

To everyone he was around, he brought love and happiness, so much.

But, I'll never send him off to school, or ask him what he learned that day.

I'll never see his report card, filled with compliments and A's.

I won't see him try on a uniform to see if it fits,

Or hear him tell his friends, 'Hey, man, my sister is off limits!'

He won't graduate from high school or learn to change a tire.

I had dreams about these times, now broken by a fire.

I comfort myself by thinking, 'He's in Heaven. He's happy there.

He's with Leslie and they're together forever, in God's loving care.'"

Without another word, Emily rose and walked back to the gallery. All was silent as she walked through the courtroom. Looking around she noticed that the only dry eyes in the room belonged to Brandon and his attorney. Judge Hafford was doing his best to hide his tears. Even the reporters were crying.

Judge Hafford broke the silence. "Thank you, Ms. Payne. Does the State have anything else to say before I make my determination?"

"No, Your Honor," Candice said.

"Does the defense have anything else to say before I make my determination?"

"No, Your Honor," Mr. Cordova said.

"Will the defendant please rise?" Brandon and Mr. Cordova stood behind the defense table. "Mr. Brooks, as you know, felony murder carries a mandatory life sentence so we are not here to determine the length of time I will sentence you to in that sense. However, I do need to decide how long you will serve for the aggravated arson and whether these sentences should be served concurrently or consecutively. The maximum sentence for aggravated arson is twenty years before being eligible for parole. If I sentence you to serve them concurrently you will be eligible for parole in fifty-one years. You are currently forty-one years of age, and while it is a slim chance that you will still be alive at the age of ninety-two, that is a chance society is not willing to take. Therefore, I hereby sentence you to two life sentences plus twenty years for the aggravated arson to be served consecutively. You will be eligible for parole in the year 2127, one hundred and twenty-two years from now. Mr. Brooks, the remainder of your life will be spent at Meadow Grove Maximum Security Prison. This court is now adjourned."

Epilogue

While this book is written as a novel, it is based on a true story—my story. I believe that God wants to use my story to raise awareness about racism, an issue that we must continue to address. "For he raised us from the dead along with Christ, and we are seated with him in the heavenly realms—all because we are *one* with Jesus Christ. Together as *one* body, Christ reconciled *both groups* to God by means of his death, and our *hostility* towards each other was *put to death*. We who believe are carefully *joined together*, becoming a holy temple for the Lord. This was his plan from all eternity, and it has now been carried out through Christ Jesus our Lord. May you experience the love of Christ, though it is so great you will never fully understand it. Then you will be filled with the fullness of life and power that comes from God." Ephesians 2:6, 16, 21; 3:11, 19 NLT (emphasis mine)

We, as a country, have come a long way but we are not completely diverse yet. So many people think we have "made it" and that racism is no longer an issue. I want to help people see that it *is* still an issue that people need to be aware of. We need to continue to work on it. I want to fire people up about it and get them emotionally involved again. It's like we have gone to the doctor and gotten an antibiotic. The doctor says, "Don't stop taking this when you start feeling better. You must take it until it is gone or your illness will come back." We have begun feeling better and we have stopped taking the steps to necessary eliminate racism from our society. If we stop now, racism is just going to rear its ugly head again.

For more information on how you can help prevent further racism in our society, please contact the ERACE Foundation (Eliminating Racism and Creating Equality) at www.erace.com.

I believe God also wants to use my story to show people that He *is* love. That he *does* turn ashes into beauty. That all things do work together for good when you give your life to Him. I didn't believe it when I was going through it, but eventually, God broke through the pain, and used that pain to speak to me. It is my prayer that if you don't know Jesus as your personal Savior, that you will at least research it. If you have questions about Jesus Christ or are interested in accepting Him as your personal Savior, please call 1-888-NEEDHIM (1-888-633-3446) or visit www.notreligion.com.

Thank you for taking the time to read this book. You are in my prayers. God bless you, Tracey L. Perger

CPSIA information can be obtained at www.ICGtesting.com
Printed in the USA
LVOW080548180512

282210LV00001B/5/A